Entropy's End

Chris Reher

Chris Reher

Quantum Tangle

Terminus Shift

Entropy's End

Also by Chris Reher

Sky Hunter

The Catalyst

Only Human

Rebel Alliances

Delphi Promised

ACKNOWLEDGMENTS

To Jim Kolter
my science guy

Many thanks to Dee Solberg, Andy Brokaw
and the S3G

ONE

"Can you drown in this stuff?"

"Only if you're short. Think of it as snow. Poisonous snow."

Ciela leaned forward into the concave windscreen of the sled to peer through thick fog over the trackless blanket of white stretching before them. On either side of the valley, jagged peaks rose too steeply for the powder to cling and presented only a vague wall of darkness in the murk. "You don't die from breathing too much snow," she said.

"Well, you don't freeze in this, so there's that." Sethran Kada looked up from the navigator on the dash and pointed past her nose to the west. "Should start to see something over that way."

It had taken little time to descend into the valley from where they had left his ship atop one of the mountains, the only place out here to land a cruiser of that class without churning up toxic clouds of the powder that covered much of this continent. The dust of Tor Ag did not settle quickly in the planet's light gravity and, once disturbed, hovered in the air to clog lungs, respirators and machinery for hours. The sled they had borrowed left little more than a gentle wake which closed quickly as they passed, leaving no track. Despite these precautions a fine mist hung in the air, hiding any other vehicles traveling through the valley.

"You think she's still alive?" Ciela turned in the narrow

cockpit and put her knees onto the seat to fish for the protective gear they had brought with them.

"She's useful to them." Seth took a respirator and goggles from her. Although oxygen existed here, it was laced with things neither of their species tolerated for long. "Stupid place to keep a Human, though."

Ciela dropped back into her seat and used her fingers to comb her thick blue hair back from her face. "Typical Shri-Lan rebel logic: this place will probably kill the doctor they stole but it's the last place Air Command would come looking for her."

"This *is* about the last place," Seth said. "They've been looking for her for over a year now. If that Centauri back on Pelion wasn't such a blathering drunk, they'd be looking for ten more years."

"If you hadn't started him blathering, we never would have gotten stuck with this rotten assignment. You Centauri can't handle alcohol. Everyone knows that."

"So says the Delphian."

"If we ever decide to pollute our heads I'm sure we'll handle it just fine." She fastened her respirator over her mouth and nose and then wrapped a burnoose around her head. Although her people, rarely found off-planet, were a constant target for abduction by rebels and pirates, she no longer colored her naturally blue-black hair or bothered to change the brilliant blue of her eyes. When necessary, it took little to fool most people into assuming her to be Centauri or perhaps Human.

Seth grinned when she checked the long blade tucked into her sleeve, ready for deployment. Her marksmanship had improved in the year since she had joined him aboard the *Dutchman*. Her genetically enhanced spatial acuity allowed her to aim as precisely as any targeting tool. But still, she found comfort in knowing a deadly weapon was available even at close range. "Try not to poke anyone with that," he said. "I don't expect any trouble here."

"I expect trouble every time you say that."

Seth turned the sled toward a broken line of rocks, following the beacon recognized by its navigational system. "Well, I don't want any trouble while we have only this piece of tin to get back to the *Dutchman*. I'm surprised it's gotten us this far. So behave."

"What's that supposed to mean," she said, a slight edge in her voice audible even through the respirator.

He didn't bother to remind her of her tendency to treat Shri-Lan rebels with the sort of contempt that was common among their rival faction, the Arawaj. She had long ago cut her ties to the Arawaj who had raised her far removed from the gentle, intellectually advanced influence of her people. Growing up in that world had made her a fierce opponent of the Commonwealth that ruled these worlds although, since joining Seth, she had softened her stance. But her opinion of their common enemy, the Shri-Lan faction, had not changed. He reached out to give her mask a gentle tug. "Just watch your step in this place. It's a rough bunch."

"Have you looked in a mirror lately?" she replied. "You're lucky I have a thing for ruffians."

Seth ran his hand over the thick stubble along his jaw. Like Humans and some Feydans, his people were blessed with hair growing in places other species found peculiar. He was probably due to do something about the current crop as well as the thick shock of black hair in dire need of cutting. To round out his appearance as an utter vagrant, he wore faded black combat trousers and a scuffed flight jacket over a rumpled shirt. In contrast, Ciela, typical of Delphians, looked tidy and oddly elegant no matter what she wore. "It helps to look like a rough bunch," he said. "Comes with the job."

"Hmm, sure," she replied and turned her attention to the scattering of massive boulders that marked the edge of the powder layer and the beginning of higher ground. The sled scraped painfully along some of the bare rock before it remembered that it was not a multi-terrain vehicle and came to a crunching halt. Long scratches on the ground showed where other drivers had come to the same conclusion. More of the customized skimmers lined the bank of the silt flat, left there by the occupants of Piara, erstwhile village of indigenous herd ranchers and now a hiding place for Shi-Lan operations.

Seth adjusted his own respirator and goggles and then raised the sled's canopy to step onto solid ground. The reek of ammonia crept into his mask despite the high-quality filter and he felt his eyes watering.

A tumble of pre-fab buildings clustered at the base of the gray cliff rising up into thinner, dust-free air. Threads of native stone dwellings followed ledges to where small herds of goats of some sort still roamed. Many of the locals these days simply subsisted by supplying the rebels with foodstuffs and water and were paid extra to include their silence.

Ciela stood by the shore and gingerly poked her booted foot into the powder. A puff of silt swirled around her feet, slow to settle in the light gravity. They had added extra weight to their footwear like most off-worlders here did.

"You coming?" Seth said.

"Feels weird here," she said. "Like sound gets absorbed, too. It's so… still, I guess."

He looked out over the expanse of white which did not sparkle like snow in the waning sunlight, but simply seemed to blank out the valley floor like an unfinished painting. "Peaceful?"

"Creepy." She turned to walk with him toward the modular buildings. "Lifeless."

"Lots of things live in that stuff," he said. "Just very tiny things. Which way?"

She nodded toward a domed shed. They had seen some images of Piara and, from their drunken informant's description, she had fleshed out a general idea of the town's layout. Her enhanced memory made maps and coordinates here unnecessary. The individual building modules, some augmented with ramshackle additions, huddled close enough together to suggest that many of them connected to form a rambling complex. A few people moved among them but none seemed curious about the newcomers. Neither windows nor visible cameras suggested that anyone watched their approach. "Depot there, legit goods. Those barracks are private. Machine shop over there. This is the one we want."

The door to the building squealed in its warped frame when Seth pushed it aside. His scanner had revealed four individuals to the left of the door and he looked that way at once, his hand not far from his gun. Ciela slipped in behind him to cover the other side.

"Cazun bless," Seth said in greeting when he realized that three of the men here were, like him, Centauri. Nearly indistinguishable from their Human cousins except for their long-limbed height, their most startling feature were eyes that, like Seth's, reflected the dim light in violet iridescence. The fourth, a woman, was a Feydan whose traditional tattoos were nearly invisible on her reddish-brown skin. They lounged on what appeared to be stuffed animal skins, arranged around a crate serving as table for their drinks. A brazier puffed feeble trails of fragrant smoke to combat the bite of the ammonia in the air.

This rebel hideout looked no different from any Seth had seen in dozens of places where Air Command didn't visit too often. That usually meant crude conditions in the least hospitable of climates. Eventually someone tipped somebody off, either to the lair's location or to the approaching military patrol, and the place was blown to bits, before or after the rebels had managed to bug out. It took a vast network of informants, spies, agents, and of course currency in the right places to keep up to date on where the more interesting outposts were to be found.

Ciela, rarely given to chatting with strangers, shifted closer to the Feydan, able to interpret the complex tattoos far more easily than most off-worlders.

All four Shri-Lan rebels stared at the visitors with a mixture of suspicion and curiosity but no surprise. Although no outlooks had greeted them, their approach would not have been missed by even a simple hand scanner. Seth removed his respirator to show them his friendliest smile.

"Heard this was the place to get a new pet," he said when none of them returned his greeting.

There was some exchange of glances. The elder among them returned his attention to his drink. The man beside him was busy ogling Ciela but the other two kept wary eyes on Seth. "Is that what you heard?" the Feydan woman said.

"Trevor Geory says I can get my moonfish replaced here," Seth said, dropping the name like a password.

She appraised him silently, then looked over to Ciela. "He mentioned a couple of Arawaj smugglers looking for some caps."

"That'd be us," Seth said. "Are we in the right place? Looking for quality."

"You don't look like you can afford quality."

Seth reached into a pocket and withdrew a short chain of small, joined spheres. He dangled it over the table until the Centauri elder held out his hand. Everyone watched when the man stood up to move to the dusty counter where he pulled the cover from a scanner. Some small animal was napping there and he shooed it aside. After adjusting the controls he held the spheres into the brilliant blue pool of light, squinting.

"Pure," he rasped after a moment and coughed. He snapped the spectrometer off. "No leaks, either."

"We'll take five *tawn* sets for that," Seth said.

The Feydan turned her suspicious eyes back to him. It was a fair price. "Four."

"Five. Ten embryos each. Properly capped for transport."

She seemed to consider this. Finally, with a silent look to the elder, she nodded and tapped her com band. "Doc, we need fifty tawns ready to go. Get busy."

A moment or two later they heard a woman's voice, barely a mumble. "Mirk went to bed. Could use a hand."

"We'll go," Seth said, sounding put-upon. "Don't get up."

The elder had already stuffed the payment into a pocket of his ragged overcoat and returned to his drink. "That door.

To the left and you'll get to an evac shuttle. You'll find the doc there." He coughed a dry laugh. "Come back for a draft of the good stuff, when you're loaded up. News from outside would be nice for a change."

Seth nudged Ciela to move to the door. Like him, she had removed her facemask and goggles and her eyes looked raw and teary.

"I have to get off this rock," she said to him, sniffling. "My eyes are on fire. If that wind picks up we'll be stuck here."

Seth looked back at the rebels and waved a hand at Ciela as if to silently complain about her burdensome fragility. "Thanks, but I think we'll head back."

Ciela pressed her respirator to her face as soon as they had entered the corridor. "Can we come up with something to do on a pretty planet some day? They say Bellac is nice on the north end."

"Bellac is boring these days," he said but frowned when she coughed. It sounded painful. "Take some deep breaths."

She gave him a look that reminded him of the last time she accused him of coddling her and so he moved ahead through the walkway which seemed to be a conduit between some of the modules. As the elder had directed, they found the sloped door to the type of armored shuttle often used by Air Command to transport evacuees or prisoners through hostile territory. It was unlocked.

"Hello?" Ciela called when they ducked inside.

Much of the interior had been cleared out and they stared in wonder at two racks of shelving from which tangles of conduits led to unidentifiable equipment at the far end of the vehicle. Even the cockpit had been removed to make room for the contraband. Seth engaged the lock from the inside.

"Back here," a woman called out from behind one of the racks.

Seth and Ciela followed the voice to find its owner stooped over five capsules she had already pulled from their storage space. She did not look up from setting the controls for each of these pods to ensure the survival of the embryos without the lab's support system.

"You need to keep these frozen. They've got enough backup to get to the airfield and after that you'll need to supplement with your own coolant. These adapters should connect." She finally straightened, wincing as if she spent too much time bent over her work and standing erect was more effort than her slump. "These are the best we've got here. With luck, you'll end up with a fifty percent survival rate."

"Doctor Hedvig?" Seth said, taken aback by the tired expression on the woman's face. The images they had studied of her showed a smiling, well-groomed Human who exuded energy even via the holographic interpretation. But this undernourished individual, enslaved on this hostile planet by the dregs of the Shri-Lan's membership, regarded them with lifeless eyes in a pale face surrounded by a halo of graying blonde hair.

Ciela spun slowly, her eyes on her data sleeve. "No recorders of any kind in here." She moved closer to the Human and, after a few moments, nodded. "It's her."

The doctor recovered from her surprise. "Yes, I'm Lara Hedvig. Why… How…?" Her words faded away as if she didn't have the strength to complete her question.

"Doctor Hedvig," Seth said. "My name is Sethran Kada. Colonel Carras on Targon sent us to get you out of here." He watched Ciela switch to a medical program. "This is Ciela, my navigator."

The woman's brows drew together as if she had not quite followed his words. Her red-rimmed eyes shifted to Ciela and then back to him. She occupied a prominent position at the enormous exobiology research complex on Targon, an otherwise unpopulated planet that also housed Trans-Targon's primary military headquarters. Her work was most often in service to Air Command and its off-world operations, but if she still hoped for rescue she probably would have expected uniforms aboard a battlecruiser. "Targon? They sent mercs? Or are you Vanguard?"

"Malnutrition, dehydration, some bone loss, inflamed joints," Ciela murmured. She looked up from her scanner. "Imminent kidney failure."

"Let's hurry," Seth said. "I'd like to cross the valley before dawn and the nights are a little on the short side here."

Ciela inspected the five large capsules, now ready for transport. "Why would anyone do this to some poor embryos?"

Hedvig blinked and shook her head as if to clear it. "They are quite unaware, I'm sure. And worth a fortune in the right private zoo."

"How do they get born, then?" Ciela touched a finger to a container to see if I was as cold as it looked.

"They don't. They more or less hatch. Once a certain temperature—"

"Doctor, please!" Seth said. "Ciela, we're not here for a biology lesson. We need to leave."

Hedvig looked up at him and then ran a nervous hand through her hair. "I'm afraid that won't be possible, but I do appreciate your colonel's efforts. And yours, of course." She turned her head to show a small metal implant behind her ear, looking like some poorly-made version of the far more useful neural interface they all carried.

Seth nodded to Ciela. They had expected Hedvig to be confined in this way. The crude device was used to control animals when other methods of domestication failed. The Shri-Lan had no scruples about also using it to control more sentient species. This one would ensure that the doctor experienced a great deal of pain when stepping outside a designated radius but left her free to work in her lab. That its overuse caused brain damage was likely not of much concern to the rebels.

Ciela took the woman's arm. "Sit over there." She led her to a stool facing the counter.

The doctor resisted briefly, but then sat to watch Ciela open the protective seal of her overcoat to withdraw a flexible datasheet. She laid it out on the table and peeled back a piece of adhesive cloth fused to it.

"What is it?" Hedvig asked.

"Countermeasure," Seth said. "It has a program that'll fool the receiver that the ticker is still connected to your brain."

"What? No!" Hedvig drew back and covered the implant with her hand. "That's not possible."

Seth reached over to Ciela and tugged her scarf from her head, revealing the deep blue hair. Not exactly a proof of identity but the meaning was clear. If anyone could remove a ticker without the matching hardware that controlled it, it would be a Delphian.

The doctor peered more closely at Ciela, nodding when she saw other indications that this was not a Human about to attempt brain surgery under these conditions. The deep blue eyes could also be simply cosmetic but the slight blue cast of her lips, the angular features of her thin face and, now that she removed her gloves, the blue fingernails offered more clues. "What are you going to do?"

"She is well prepared for this," Seth assured her, sounding as confident as he could. Since learning that the doctor was enslaved in this miserable lab on this miserable planet, Ciela had consulted and studied with several Delphian experts, badgering them for information that they generally not shared with the commoners among them. Eventually, they devised a way to counter and extract the mechanism, using the sort of noninvasive techniques practiced by their healers and *Shantirs*.

A useful skill, Seth thought, although the Shantirs had bemoaned the fact that, ever since Ciela had rejected her life as Arawaj rebel and came to live and work with Seth, she had avoided their more traditional teachings. Delphians grew up to look inward, to study the mind and its possibilities, to attain serenity and move beyond the common cravings afflicting the off-worlders they regarded as inferior. Ciela, however, had no interest in returning to the planet of her birth to make up the training she would have received there. She saw far greater value in taking advantage of her heritage to discover more practical skills. Of course, he thought, the genetic modifications she had suffered and that led to her life among the rebels also served her quite well. Those were a secret not even shared with the military that now employed them.

Ciela closed her stinging eyes for a moment, heedless of a few tears trickling over her pale cheeks. Seth resisted an urge to wipe them away, understanding her need to concentrate and achieve the necessary state of mind, a *khamal*, to interact with the Human.

"She's going to take a look," he said, keeping his voice low. This was probably not the moment to explain that Ciela's experience with the shared khamal, the mind link, was a fairly recent addition to her skill set. Her mentors praised her abilities for this khamal, used for communication, meditation, healing and even sex, but a few months under their tutelage could not replace lifelong learning. She had occasionally joined her mind with his, something that would no doubt horrify her tutors, making it an irresistible taboo for both of them. It gave her a headache.

"What's amusing?" the doctor said when she noticed his smirk.

Seth shook his head. "What else do you have on ice here?"

She scowled. "The *tawns* are just some expensive pretty things. That entire bank of caps is for musk moles."

He wandered over to the rack holding rows of cryogenically preserved embryos. The glands of these rodents yielded a substance ranging from dangerously intoxicating for some species to downright deadly. Typical, he thought. The Shri-Lan abscond with one of the most highly regarded exobiologists in all of Trans-Targon and put her to work manufacturing dope. "Got alarms set?"

"No. Big turnover on these."

Seth walked down the row of containers and, one by one,

deactivated the controls that kept the creatures alive.

"I've been wanting to do that," Hedvig said, watching him destroy her work. "Though now I really have to hope you can get me out of this place. That's a lot of profit you're tampering with."

"Speaking of tampering…" Seth came back to where they were sitting and put his hand on Ciela's shoulder. "Sweetness? Could you maybe hurry it up a little?"

Ciela opened her eyes. "I was waiting for you to finish chatting." She turned to Hedvig. "He's like a little old lady sometimes. Centauri like to socialize, I've noticed."

The doctor's tired expression lifted with her smile. "They do, don't they?"

Seth sighed and went to the door. His scanner showed no one nearby except for the signatures of the rebels in the tap room.

Ciela came to her feet and stood close to Doctor Hedvig. She touched the loathsome mechanism holding the woman hostage and closed her eyes again. "Try to relax," she said. "Don't think of me, try not to think of what I'm doing or you'll just end up fighting me."

Seth watched in fascination although the two women remained immobile and silent. A small groove appeared between Ciela's brows as she concentrated on the device, lodged in the prisoner's brain much like their own neural interface modules were. But their military-grade mechanical enhancements allowed them to operate complex machinery as instantly and easily as parts of their own bodies. It made him a better pilot and her a more adept deep-space navigator. Their own devices, if accidentally torn away, simply released from the filaments. Tampering with the doctor's ticker, however, guaranteed a prolonged and painful death.

"I think I have it," Ciela said. She reached for the datasheet without opening her eyes and felt for a fine wire attached to it. "The taps are coming loose. Did you feel that?"

"No."

"Your brain itself cannot feel pain. But the ticker can make you think you feel it." Ciela clipped the wire to the interface.

"Are you doing that?" the doctor asked. A small smile appeared on her face when she felt the Delphian's deep mental state.

"Trying to help you stay calm. This is… delicate," Ciela said in a near-whisper. She fell silent again until, finally, she reached for another tool. "This will hurt a little now, because your skin has grown around the unit. I'll try to mitigate what I can."

Seth reached into a pocket and took out a sterile bandage. The doctor's hands gripped the edge of the counter when Ciela cut the ticker away, leaving a ragged wound behind. He moved between them to stanch the blood while Ciela's hands remained pressed to the woman's head. "I got it," he said, aware that her mental contact with the Human had to end quickly to avoid a debilitating headache. They were a still long way from rest and recovery for both women.

Ciela took a deep breath and slowly released the doctor, turning immediately to the device now lying on the datasheet like a blood-stained beetle turned onto its back. She ignored the doctor's pained gasp when the soothing influence of the Delphian khamal dissipated. Without wasted movement, she connected the ticker to the system, following precise instructions from memory. Seth was reminded that her nearly perfect recall likely made them one of the more valuable team of operatives within Air Command's Intelligence sector. Of enough value, certainly, to choose their assignments and carry them out as they wished. Colonel Carras had learned to avoid questioning their methods and think of them as mere mercenaries.

"No surface damage that can't be fixed," Seth assured the doctor who had lost even more of her formerly robust color. "The taps are still in your head but they will be removed when you get back to the clinic. A transport is standing by to pick you up at the jumpsite near Targon."

Doctor Hedvig took the bandage from Seth and applied it herself while he wrapped a scarf around her head and then carefully fastened her respirator. "Since I'm still alive, I can say I have a fair amount of trust in your ability to actually get me there."

All three looked to the door when the lights on its panel announced someone outside.

"Doc, dammit, why're you locking this thing?" The gruff voice added a curse.

Seth faded soundlessly into the narrow space between the stacks of capsules.

"Oh, sorry," the doctor called and went to the door. Her frightened eyes met Seth's through a gap between the storage modules before she tapped a code into the key plate to allow a male Feydan into the lab. Behind him entered two Humans, wrapped in full body suits to protect against the caustic air. "We were just getting ready to take these caps to the shore," Hedvig said. "Berno gets so nasty if I leave the place unattended."

"More late customers," the rebel said with a jerk of his thumb at the Humans. "It's a good day for doing business. They'll take a full set of moles. Get busy, woman." He took her arm to shove her toward the stacks when he spotted the tools spread out before Ciela. She was still attaching the last of the controls to the ticker and did not look up. "What's that, then?"

He got no further than one more step toward her when the tracer of Seth's gun played over his face. Seth hesitated for only a moment as he considered the doctor's sensibilities, and then lowered the tracer to fire instead into the man's chest, leaving little but a hole there after the Centauri dropped to the floor.

The two customers turned toward the door but Seth leaped from his cover to jab his elbow into one of their masks, shattering the flimsy faceplate and possibly the nose behind it. He had long ago perfected ways of moving his long limbs in small spaces and a flurry of well-placed maneuvers had both of the Humans on the ground and silent within moments. He crouched and applied a palm stunner to make sure they stayed that way.

The doctor had backed away and now just stared at the dreadful scene, shocked by what had taken only a few seconds.

Ciela stood up and helped Seth drag the bodies into the stacks before returning to her task.

"Is someone going to be looking for them?" Seth asked the doctor.

Hedvig's eyes remained glued to a hand protruding from the edge of a shelf. Seth nudged it aside with his foot. "Ah, I mean… depends on how drunk they are," she said finally.

"Done here." Ciela folded the datasheet around the ticker and tucked it into a pocket where it continued to transmit to whomever may be monitoring the doctor. After securing their protective layers, she and Seth each picked up two of the metal cocoons, leaving one for Hedvig to carry. A door at the far end of the lab led directly outside, where now the night was absolute in the absence of visible moons and illuminated only sporadically by overhead lights. Ciela, unable to see well in these conditions, clipped a visor over her eyes.

"Then my sister starts complaining about the bugs invading her greenhouse," Seth said conversationally as they passed the windows of the front building. "I guess I would, too. They were everywhere."

"Watch where you step on those rocks," Ciela said. "Slippery. So how did they get rid of them?"

They continued chatting about nothing all the way to the shore where their sled awaited them. As they had practiced before leaving the airfield, they worked efficiently to store both the capsules as well as the doctor in the rear compartment of the sled.

"The ticker," Seth reminded Ciela.

Ciela nodded and slipped into the mist along the shore to hide the package, hopefully delaying the time before someone suspected the doctor's disappearance.

Seth bent over the sled. "It might get a little bumpy, Doc, but it's not far to the airfield."

"I've made it this far," she said. A coughing fit shook her body and Seth helped her to sit up again until it passed. "Thank you. It's getting—" Her eyes snapped to something behind him just as he felt the too familiar sensation of a gun pressed to his neck.

He raised his arms and straightened slowly, turning away from the sled to see a Feydan woman, the rebel they had met in the shop, at the end of the gun. Seeing that she was alone, he sidled away from the skimmer.

"Where do you think you're going with our lab rat?" she said. "Where is your friend?"

He took another step sideways, his arms well away from his guns. "Funny story, actually. You see, the doctor is actually not a doctor at all. She's an opera singer. Wait, no. That's not it. She's a—"

"Shut up and answer me," she snapped. "Who sent you? Are you Arawaj?"

"Yes," he said. "Well, no. We're starting our own pet shop in the city. That's it. But we have no tech. So we thought we'd borrow yours." He winced when he saw her raise her arm to activate her com band.

But then a dark shape leaped out of the murk and the rebel suddenly convulsed, unable to even call out before crashing stiffly to the ground. Ciela crouched over her and used her gun again, pressed into the woman's clothes to avoid the telltale flash. She looked up at Seth. "Pet shop? Did you think that up all by yourself?"

He shrugged. "Do you still have the ticker?"

"Yeah."

He took it from her and pushed it into the rebel's jacket. "Grab her arm." They dragged the body across the shoreline rocks and as far out into the silt as they could without letting the powder seep into their boots. It closed over the rebel to leave an undisturbed surface.

"Told you this stuff is creepy," Ciela said as they hurried

back to the sled.

The doctor, aghast, was still looking out over the valley. "The sediment will recede when the sun interacts with it. It'll expose the body." She swallowed hard. "But they won't come looking for a while. I often take walks as far as the ticker will let me go. They'll assume I've... I've walked out into this on purpose."

"Don't think about it," Seth said and heaved the sled off the rocks. The woman's words sounded like there might have been times when she had contemplated doing just that. "We'll be long gone before dawn."

They shoved off into the whiteness flowing through the valley and watched the Piara outpost dwindle on the dashboard screen. Soon only the mist drifted through the headlights of the sled, making navigation by sight impossible. Seth kept his eyes on the sensors as he reached out to hook his arm around Ciela's neck to pull her close. "You are amazing," he said and kissed the top of her head.

She grinned. "We're not out yet."

"Technicalities." He shrugged but ramped up to the sled's top speed. "Let's hope they don't notice anyone missing for a while." He glanced over his shoulder. "Still with us, Doc?"

"I am." Hedvig sat up with some effort. "Not feeling my best, but I haven't felt that way in months." She leaned forward to address Ciela. "That was a remarkable operation, young lady. I'm surprised to see someone with your talents so far off-planet."

Seth winked at Ciela. "I think the good doctor is trying to be polite. What are you doing with a felon like me on this piss of a planet is what she meant." He slowed when the sled approached the hills on the other side of the valley. "I often wonder that myself."

Ciela turned to Hedvig. "Now he's expecting me to assure him that my life on his ship is every girl's dream."

The doctor actually laughed although the pleasant sound quickly turned into a cough. "And is it?" she gasped.

Ciela pulled up her medical scanner for another diagnosis

of the woman's condition. "I lived aboard one ship or another most of my life," she said. "It's all I know."

"Thanks," Seth said. "I'm so appreciated."

"You are Air Command, then?" Hedvig asked. "We don't have a lot of Delphians working for the military."

"He is," Ciela said. "Sort of. Used to be. I'm an Arawaj rebel. I was, anyway. They raised me when our ship was pirated. I'd never even been on Delphi until after Seth arrested me."

"Arrested?"

"Yeah," Seth said. "Still looking for a jail that'll hold her. So I figured I'd let her tag along for a while. Don't tell anybody. Good navigators are hard to find."

"Well, I suppose jumping through subspace is what your people are most valued for," Hedvig said. "Far too valuable to put in a jail cell. And, obviously, you have other talents." She let that last sentence hang in the air for a while, perhaps waiting for more explanation. Seth reminded himself that she was a top-level exobiologist and would most certainly be well schooled in Delphian physiology and the apparent limits of even their Shantir sect. But she would also be aware that Delphi guarded secrets that few outsiders were privy to.

"Almost there," he said. "A few more minutes and we'll have you tucked into a clean bed, freshly deconned and suitably medicated. How does that sound, Doc? We even cleaned up the crew cabin for you."

"We?" Ciela pinched his thigh. "He means he stuffed everything in a bin and then paid a crew to clean the ship."

"Well, it all sounds like a beautiful dream. I suppose it'll take a few weeks to get back to Targon. I'll try not to be a burden."

"We're happy to have you," Seth said politely with a glance at Ciela. Truly, the journey home would take them through several jumpsites, each separated from the next by several days' travel in real-space. The first jumpsite, located near the fifth planet of this solar system, would take them to Callas and from there another gate would send them all the way to Bellac. After another ten days in real-space, one more leap would let them rendezvous with the military transport arriving from Targon.

Most pilots like Seth used the well-charted jumpsites that made deep-space travel possible. These mapped coordinates allowed their ships to span great distances to emerge at a designated terminus much like through a two-way tunnel. Rare adepts, mostly Delphian navigators, were the key to turning tiny fissures, or *keyholes*, into these commercial jumpsites. Their mental abilities spanned the Big Nothing to locate a useful terminus, most often a habitable planet, and create charts needed by other, less gifted, pilots. It was this skill that made Delphians the most sought-after talent in this slice of their galaxy.

But the doctor would not expect a shortcut about to reduce their journey to just a few days. She would not know that Ciela was not only one of the Delphian spanners but that her genetic modification also made it possible for her to emerge from subspace at any exit she chose, not just the one determined by the keyhole itself. Few individuals were even aware that it was possible to change direction once in subspace. The sheer value of this skill to anyone, friend or foe alike, made it necessary for her to remain hidden, which, in true Ciela-fashion, she chose to do in plain sight.

Seth took the sled uphill along a rail lifting them back to the rental place near the airfield, only half-listening to whatever the two women were talking about. If not for the urgency of returning the Human to Targon, he would choose to take the long way back. Using Ciela's skill meant revealing her rare talent to the doctor, adding another person to the small group aware of it. Each person who knew meant added danger to Ciela's life as his navigator.

And not just navigator, he reminded himself. She had become so much more in such a short time, apparently content in his company. Likely, he was taking advantage of her loathing for the more structured life waiting for her should she decide to use her fine brain for more worthwhile causes.

Ultimately, he felt guilt, he supposed. Guilt over selfishly corralling her talents for dangerous and often questionable deep-cover missions, and over using her willingness to engage in black ops without scruples. Her skills enabled him to reach otherwise unattainable targets and so had become indispensable to him. He, he knew, was the greatest danger to her.

"What's wrong?" Ciela said, poking him in the ribs and startling him out of his thoughts.

He frowned. "Wrong? Why?"

"You looked awfully dark for a moment."

"It's my crust of face hair. I'll deal with it later. When we pull up to the *Dutchman*, get the doctor inside and through the decon scanner at once. I'll get the caps. I want to be gone as soon as we can get cleared for takeoff."

"We're taking the embryos?"

He shrugged. "I'm not leaving them for these Shri-Lan thugs to sell. They're worth a fortune."

Ciela turned back to the doctor. "He's not only a deliciously handsome pilot and Union agent, he really is a smuggler on his days off."

"I can't blame him," Hedvig said. "I happen to know what Air Command pays."

TWO

"What's going on here?"

Ciela automatically checked her scanner when Seth spoke. They had cleared the valley mists and the rail line had brought them onto the airfield where they had left the *Dutchman*. He slowed the sled as they passed several other cruisers near the launch pad. There was always a bustle of pilots and passengers along with those who made their living on and off airfields no matter where ships came and went. But this was not the usual runway routine. People stood in small groups, talking, or hurried from plane to plane, or from the crafts to the supply and repair buildings. Humans, Centauri, a couple of Caspians and a few Bellac; everyone seemed to have reason to loiter despite the mountain temperature and the stench of ammonia.

Ciela drew her gun but kept it out of sight. "Maybe Piara noticed they're missing a doctor."

"Possible," Seth said but this was not a mob of rebels here to reclaim their captive. He saw no weapons ready and no one paid much attention to their arrival. He stopped the sled as close to his ship as possible. "Let's go."

The doctor winced when Ciela and Seth helped her out of the cramped rear compartment but she found her feet and nodded reassuringly. "I just need a little rest," she said. "Is that your ship? It looks, ah, capable."

Seth smiled up at the snub-nosed cruiser, his only home for a dozen years or more. A little patched here and there, retrofitted a few times, augmented and upgraded until it looked every bit as ill-used as the other ships parked up here today. "It'll get you home, no worry."

"Kada!"

Seth turned at the call and cursed silently when he saw a Human wave to them from across the taxiway. The ground tech wore protective coveralls and a clear full-face mask that looked a whole lot more comfortable than the multi-purpose gear that the short-term visitors were making do with. He hurried toward them, attracting a few curious glances from others nearby.

"Do you know someone everywhere you go?" Ciela asked. "How do you manage to keep your head down at all?"

"It's useful. Most of the time anyway. This one thinks I'm Arawaj, so be careful."

The man reached them, out of breath. "I thought that was you on my flight list. Someone told me you got scragged out on Aikhor."

"Apparently not," Seth said. He tipped his head toward a huddle of pilots and crew. "What's going on?"

"Jumpsite's closed. No one's going anywhere unless you're sightseeing other parts of Tor Ag. I've got six ships here now. Usually we're lucky to see two or three a day to keep things lively. We're rerouting everyone else to the city."

"Closed? What are you talking about?" Seth raised his arm to tap a few commands into the interface on his sleeve, engaging the *Dutchman*'s pre-flight sequences. The city of which this man spoke was firmly in Air Command hands which meant that the folks up here were those who tended to avoid cops. Pirates, rebels, perhaps fugitives whose business on this remote planet was likely of the illicit sort.

"The gate beacons are owned by the Union, not Tor Ag. Air Command shows up and shuts them down."

"Why?" Seth raised an eyebrow when he glanced at Ciela.

No beacons meant that mere chartjumpers like him were marooned here, unable to enter subspace without the guidance of the charted and stable jumpsite. A small twitch of her brows and the barely perceptible tilt of her head was as good as a shrug. She did not need the beacons to get them out of this place.

"No one knows. We're waiting for news. Listen, do me a favor, would you? Get rid of some of these ships for me. Some of these characters are getting awfully peeved. Won't be long before we've got Air Command nosing around here. I don't need that here."

"What does that have to do with me?"

"I've heard you're packing a spanner these days," the man said, looking from Ciela to the doctor as if to guess which one of them might be the navigator. "You can take a convoy through."

"For someone squatting on top of a mountain all day, you're awfully well informed," Seth said, dismayed when a Caspian male approached them. No doubt he was not the only one listening to this conversation.

"Is that right?" His heavily-accented voice rasped through an inadequate respirator. Despite the cold, he wore only a thin kilt to better display the reddish pattern on his chest and shoulders. He had not skimped on the weapons at his belt. "One of your girlfriends is a spanner?"

"What's it to you?" Ciela snapped. Seth winced.

Two hefty Centauri stepped up to flank the Caspian, both of them with a hand casually on the grips of their guns. The doctor gasped and moved closer to Seth. Their leader looked from Ciela to the doctor, his yellow raptor eyes narrow. "That one," he decided, pointing at Ciela. "Looks like a Delphian. She'll get us out of here."

"No, she won't," Ciela said. "Those beacons are down for a reason. Do you have any idea how much it costs to turn a keyhole into a stable site? How long that takes? Months, if they have the right people. They wouldn't do this no matter who's hiding on this rock. I doubt you're special enough for them to go through all this trouble."

"She doesn't sound like a Delphian," the Caspian's companion said.

Seth gripped her wrist. Two Bellacs, both female and heavily armed, openly wearing the black neckwrap of the Shri-Lan, now came to stand behind him. The Human technician had backed off, also sensing that something was about to go very wrong here. "She's right," Seth said. "We're going to lie low in the city. We'll find out soon enough why the site was shut down. You don't want to jump through there without knowing more."

The Caspian raised his gun and his crewmen did the same. "I have a hold full of toys and I'm not about to get caught with them. How about we take your spanner if you're too frightened to make the trip? She looks braver than you."

"And you're going to make me jump how, Furface?" Ciela said. Seth squeezed her arm but she ignored his warning.

For a moment, the pirate looked undecided. Then his eyes lit on the doctor. "We'll take that one with us. You can have her back once we get to Callas."

The Bellac behind Seth shoved the doctor toward the Caspian.

"Don't do this," Seth said, watching her stumble. "She's ill. We need to get her to a clinic."

"All the more reason to get out of this dump. You won't find much help in the city. Unless, of course, you want to try a Union med-station."

Ciela stepped forward to grasp the doctor's arm and found the guns now pointed at her. Seth pulled her back again. "All right, no need for this. If you want out, we'll get out. Just make sure to treat her well. She needs fluids and some food." He gestured to his sled. "I need to unload."

Curious, one of the pirates peered into the vehicles and laughed. "We'll take this, too."

Seth exhaled sharply. The hangar jockey shrugged apologetically and retreated back across the taxiway, not terribly bothered by the hostage taking.

"Let's do this. Now." Seth turned toward the *Dutchman*, tugging Ciela along with him.

He said nothing while the ship's cargo door opened to admit them into the small hold. The overhead display showed the decon process as they were checked for contaminants or disease before being allowed into the main cabin.

"You're just going to let them take her?" Ciela said as she followed him through the cabin and into the *Dutchman*'s cockpit.

"Must you start a brawl?" he said. "Furface? That took some nerve. Those were pirates, not some smugglers hiding out here. You don't argue with them when you're outgunned five to one. Especially not a Caspian."

"Five to two," she reminded him.

"Still not odds worth dying for. Nor are the caps. And neither is the doctor."

"That's heartless."

"Damn right." Seth dropped into his pilot bench and linked the ship's control system to the neural interface at his temple. "That's why I'm still alive."

She started to snap something back at him but then just slumped in her bench with a scowl.

"You saw what the damn Shri-Lan did to the doctor," Seth said. "Do you want to end up like that? Slaving around on a pirate ship with those bastards? You might think they can't make you work for them but I know what they're capable of. Damn straight you'll end up doing what they want." He reached up to signal his intent to lift off. "*Anything* they want. Do you get that?"

"He's a Caspian," she said, not willing to concede. "They don't—"

"His crew isn't!"

She held her hands up. "All right, you don't have to shout."

Seth fumed silently as he launched the *Dutchman* with two

other ships in his wake, soon clear of Tor Ag's atmosphere. The Caspian's Fleetfoot followed closely, and further back came the Bellacs' small transport.

It wasn't his way to shout at anyone but this was not the first time that Ciela's quick temper and lack of training nearly endangered their mission. Her upbringing among rebels had left her undisciplined and reckless – a definite liability in his line of work. He watched her lounge casually in her bench, attempting to snag her headset from its rest with her foot.

"Get ready to jump to Callas," he said after a while. "I'm hoping the patrol won't stop us. They don't really have any jurisdiction here without good cause. Let's not give them any."

"We're not jumping straight to Targon? If we signal Air Command they'll arrest everybody. I'm sure they won't mind taking out a couple of pirates."

Seth shook his head. "This jump only reaches to Callas. The last thing I want is for our pirate friends to see you shift exits in there. That'll start rumors we don't need. So Callas it is."

"Easy jump, then. I'm feeling a bit scratchy with all that Tor Ag crud in my system so it's probably for the best." She stood up to pull an oxygen mask from an overhead compartment.

He watched her tuck her long legs under herself and settle back with the air supply. "Safer for the doctor, too. If we jump to Targon and Air Command comes down heavy who knows what that pirate will do to her. She's not up to any hostage situation."

"You think they'll hurt her?"

"Yah, I do. You don't cross a Caspian. But I think he'll give her back if we get them through. She knows enough not to tell them who she is. They can keep the damn embryos."

"Not so heartless, are you, Kada?"

He smiled when she reached across the small space between the cockpit benches to ruffle his hair, forgiving her lapse of restraint, as always. It was his job to train her for this, to help her blend into the dark fringes he used to move covertly among the enemy. If she slipped, it was his lack, not hers.

The *Dutchman*'s scanners alerted them to a single Air Command patrol near the inactive beacons.

"That's it? One cruiser? They're not here to catch anyone," Ciela said, voicing his own thoughts. "We've got them outgunned just with the *Dutchman*, never mind those other two."

"We'll see what they have to say. They'll be on edge with us coming up so fast. Let me do the talking."

She glared at him with narrowed eyes but he saw her lips twitch in a smile she tried to hide.

It wasn't long before the patrol ship knocked on their door. The *Dutchman*'s sensors reported their scans as they tried to get through its defenses, and then the com console emitted a squawk.

"Hello, officer," Seth said genially. "We could have sworn there used to be a jumpsite in these parts."

Ciela amused herself by running the exchange through a program designed to analyze and record vocalizations. Seth had only recently wheedled the expensive upgrade from Intelligence and she had not tired of testing it at every opportunity.

"I'm sorry, Pilot," the com officer on the Air Command ship replied, masking her irritation over Seth's failure to identify himself with bland politeness. "It is a temporary measure. Please return to Tor Ag. We will notify the governors when access has been restored."

"Temporary? How do you temporarily shut a jumpsite? We'll be stuck here for months."

"We apologize for the inconvenience."

Seth pondered, for a moment, over releasing his security code, guaranteed to make this officer a little more forthcoming. He decided against it. None of this was important enough to reveal his identity to a mere patrol and, more significantly, he had no idea what sort of listening equipment the Caspian behind him carried.

"I have a spanner aboard," he said. "We'll take our chances with the keyhole."

"We advise against that," she said. "The Callas sector is currently not safe for travelers." She cleared her throat. "A rebel incursion has destabilized the region and the jumpsite there is in Shri-Lan control. All traffic is being rerouted."

Ciela snickered and pointed at the speech analysis. "She's a really bad liar."

Seth nodded and closed the com channel. "Half of Tor Ag is crawling with Shri-Lan. And you're not the only spanner around here. They're just halting regular commercial traffic for some reason." A glance at his scanners showed the pirate's ship moving up beside him now, taking a rather aggressive stance. An armed showdown with Air Command ranked fairly low on Seth's list of how to deal with this today.

"Also possible that there is something going on in the city right here," Ciela said. "Maybe they're cutting off Tor Ag, not Callas. They did that a few years ago when they cleared the rebels out of Pelion. Like shutting the door to a trap."

"Seems likely. There's nothing going on near Callas worth an incursion. It's just a stop on the way to the other gate to Bellac. And that gate is heavily guarded by Air Command."

Ciela leaned back into her bench and pulled her headset over her neural interface in preparation of the jump. She closed her eyes to slip into the type of khamal necessary for the task ahead. While a simple chartjump through a stable jumpsite required little more than a powerful processor and good shields, opening a keyhole long enough to jump through subspace taxed even the most talented of Delphians. Once through, Seth would be on his own to get the doctor back from the pirates while Ciela recuperated during several hours in a deep sleep state.

He opened the com channel again. "We'll take our chances, Officer. But thank you for the warning. As you've probably noticed during your scan of my arsenal, we're prepared to deal with those Shri-Lan scofflaws."

Ciela smiled at that but did not open her eyes.

"You're on your own then," the officer said, clearly not pleased. But the patrol ship moved aside, giving the approaching ships enough room to safely open the keyhole.

"Ready?" Seth said to Ciela.

"Let's crack this thing and get going."

Seth signaled the other ships and maneuvered the *Dutchman* into position. Using the coordinates of the original keyhole, he fed the ship's energy into the fissure, enlarging it to the point that all three vessels were able to pass through. Only the sensor's visual interpretation showed anything out there at all, but soon the gate was about as stable as it would ever be without the beacons.

He watched Ciela's immobile face when she ramped up the ship's processors, working with them to reach into the opening, feeling her way into the unknown nothing beyond to find the exit to Callas. Only she, among thousands of spanners of her caliber, also saw the means to reach out to other exits in a complex network of tangled equations, waiting only to be grasped. An accident of her birth, perhaps. Or some complex design by those who had modified her genes before she was even born. Whatever it was, it was a gift better kept secret from those who would exploit it. And so today she simply reached for the keyhole's obvious exit, the gate to Callas.

At her signal, he launched the *Dutchman* into the void, steeling himself against the absolute nothing beyond the threshold she had created. His world disappeared, taking along with it every sensation, every photon, every hint of gravity as the ship careened through something no one had ever seen or even fully understood. His mind, untethered, rebelled at the unnatural state and as always he felt panic threaten to overwhelm him even as he reassured himself that all of this would be over in mere seconds.

Except that it wasn't. It didn't end. Something held them, something threatening and even darker than the absence of light before his wide-open eyes. He cast his thoughts around for some hint that Ciela was nearby, firmly in control of the traverse, but he felt nothing but terror. Whether that was her fear or his was less certain.

* * *

Something beeped somewhere. And then a squawk that might have been the com console. Or the food processor talking to itself in the main cabin. Then that beep again. Annoying.

Seth opened his eyes, wondering why he had fallen asleep here in the cockpit. He rarely did that, since the bed he used was the comfortable lounger in the main cabin only a few steps away. No, this didn't feel like he had passed out, but he felt oddly lethargic. He stared at a blinking light on the console for a while before recognizing it as a warning.

He sat up but when he groped for his headset he found it no longer attached to his neural node. He looked around for it and saw Ciela still on her bench, eyes closed as always after a jump.

"What the..." He reached for the ship's controls when he realized that the *Dutchman* was drifting through space, slowly tumbling end over end, not having been told otherwise since emerging from subspace. Seth stabilized the spin and scanned the region. Where were the other ships?

"Ciela, sweetness. I could use your help right now. You can sleep it off later." He frowned when the ship returned the results of his scans to inform him that they had emerged not far off Pelion Gate, a long way and several jumps from Callas. "Damn. What happened? We lost the other ships." He set course for the large station guarding the jumpsite near Pelion and turned to his navigator. "Ciela?"

She lay limply in her couch, her Delphian-pale face nearly completely bloodless. No matter how exhausted, she finished every jump with at least some gesture that she was all right. He felt something huge and dark crawl up his spine when he reached out to touch her shoulder. "Babe?"

Her head drooped to the side and he saw blood on her lip

where she had bitten it.

"No!" he said, his mouth almost too dry to get the word out. "Ciela!" He shook her shoulder harder. Maybe she had fallen asleep already. Delphians didn't really sleep. It was just another state of mind for them, one from which they were not easily roused. Surely, that was it. "Wake up!"

But he knew better, didn't he? He had seen it for himself. Even simple chartjumpers like him ran a risk with every leap through subspace. Something gone wrong with the processors, some feedback loop through the delicate neural interface that linked navigator to machine, some minor aberration in subspace itself, any of this had kept other navigators from returning from their journey. Some died. Some remained in a worse state than that.

He dropped to his knees beside her bench and activated his scanner. "Ciela? Wake up, baby. Please!" He saw that she still breathed, perhaps a little too deeply. The scanner told him nothing. Why didn't he know more about Delphians? And what little he knew seemed to have deserted him. He lifted her eyelid which told him nothing, either. Desperate, he slapped her face as gently as he could, hoping to startle her out of her trance.

After a moment, she twitched her brow in a frown and moved her hand in a weak gesture.

"Ciela? Talk to me!"

A small groan escaped her lips.

"Gods, you're back! Ciela? Can you hear me?"

"Yes," she whispered.

He dropped his forehead onto her arm for a moment, contemplating how close he had come to losing his mind just now. "Don't do this!" he gasped. He heaved himself up and bent to lift her from her bench, not sure if his suddenly very rubbery knees would support them both. He carried her through the narrow cockpit door and out into the main cabin, the ship's largest living and working space. After placing her onto the wide lounger he hurried to the cabinet containing medical supplies.

He returned to the lounger and shifted her to cradle securely in his arms. Carefully, he dabbed at her bleeding lip, glad when she winced. "Are you with me?" he whispered. "What can I do?"

She turned her head to rest her cheek against him. "I'm so tired," she whispered. "I was so frightened. I almost didn't make it out."

He pressed his lips to her forehead. "Are you all right?"

"Shh," she said. "Head hurts."

Seth shifted her until she rested on his chest, her face buried in the curve of his neck. "Just sleep," he said. "Don't worry about anything." He tipped his head back against the wall beside the lounger, feeling her soft breath on his skin, terribly aware of how close he had come to losing her. Why had he snapped at her earlier? Completely unnecessary. That vexing rebellious streak made her a fearless fighter who never gave up her ground. Dangerous at times, perhaps, but useful and necessary for their way of life.

But when had he last treated her as anything but a comrade in arms? The magnificent nights they spent on this very lounger meant much to both of them but had he ever told her that? Was she his lover or his navigator? Did she know? "I'm sorry," he said, mostly to himself. "I shouldn't have shouted at you. I shouldn't expect you to know how to handle Caspians." He stroked the deep blue hair from her face. Her skin felt warm and soft and wonderfully alive. "Just tell me to shut up when I'm being a jerk."

"Shut up," she whispered. "And listen."

He tilted his head to hear her words.

"Something went weird with that jump," she said, speaking with effort. "The Callas end just slipped away from me. I've never seen that before. So I changed course. Something... Uh, something was there. Like a big wave or something. I felt it. I felt it grab for you."

"For me?"

"Yes," she said. "I cut off your interface. I thought I was seeing some sort of loop heading for your link. Then it came for me. I didn't recognize it. I almost just grabbed another terminus, that's how scared I was." She paused for a few breaths. "I can't think of anything more dangerous than taking an exit when you don't know where it ends up. Not without a lot of study. Not without probes going through, first."

He nodded. Although some spanners took risks in rushing through an unexplored exit in search of fortunes to be found on the other side, a good number of those same spanners never returned to tell about it. Most newfound keyholes were carefully explored before anyone dared to send a ship along its span.

"I fought that… whatever it was. It was so strong! I finally got the *Dutchman* away from it and found the exit to Pelion. Then I don't know any more."

"We lost the other ships," he said. "They didn't make it out."

"Gods, Seth…"

"Shh, don't worry about them. They may have emerged just fine."

She rested for a while, perhaps drifting off to find the sleep she needed so badly right now. But then she spoke again. "Do you think maybe Air Command knew there's something going on in that span? And that's why they took the beacons down?"

Seth thought about this. That layer of nothingness they called subspace, that other universe none of them would ever truly experience or measure, was not as void of matter as assumed. He himself had seen beyond the Big Nothing and found life there, even if it was life as none had ever encountered. The thought that something lurked in this place, that something might actually interact with their feeble real-space existence, seemed not as farfetched to him as it was to most people. And certainly, it would not seem that way to the vast collaboration of highly trained minds that drove the Union's scientific complex. They knew what he knew and, like him, kept it secret.

He reached up to grope around a shelf beside the lounger, moving carefully to avoid jarring Ciela. When he found the interface tablet to the *Dutchman*'s internal systems he accessed the com console to create a message packet.

"What are you doing?"

"Getting some intel and some help for you. I think you can use a break."

She closed her eyes and smiled.

Seth coded the packet for Caelyn, a Delphian working with an astrophysics team out of Magra Alaric, a Union-controlled continent on Magra. Seth wanted to avoid Delphi for now. They had offered to shelter Ciela, in part because they felt just a bit responsible for losing her to begin with, but they frowned upon Seth and his questionable influence on her. He already blamed himself for her current state - adding a helping of Delphian disdain wasn't necessary right now. Caelyn was not only Seth's closest friend but was also aware of Ciela's true nature and far less judgmental. Like her, he worked as a deep-space navigator although the missions he chose were for exploration. Unlike her, and more typical of Delphians, he had little interest in the rebel wars or who happened to be gaining ground in them.

"Hello, my friend," Seth began, recording without video. "I'm calling to let you know we're heading to Magra. Should be there in about twenty hours. Listen, Ciela's got a bad case of the bends after a nasty jump just now. Out of Tor Ag. Could you see if there's a Shantir on Magra that has a little time for her?" He winked at Ciela who smiled tiredly. The Shantir sect was directly responsible for her genetic abnormalities and any Shantir would fly to Magra on a broomstick for the chance to join in even just a healing khamal with her.

"Send him the logs," Ciela said, reminding him of the expensive subspace scanner he had appropriated some time ago in his ongoing quest to learn more about that great unknown. Until today, none of their jumps had revealed anything at all in there – no signal, no particles, not even some random electrons on their way to nowhere. But she had felt *something* in there, and so perhaps had the mechanical sensors.

"Good idea," he said and turned back to his recording. "I'm sending you some scans we ran during the jump. Something happened in there to give Ciela such a turn. Can you run that by your people? Whatever is going on, it's also possible that Air Command's aware of it, so send a copy to Targon if you find anything useful. I'll see you soon."

"It'll be nice to see him," Ciela murmured after he completed the message to Caelyn and dispatched it to the jumpsite at Pelion from which it would be forwarded to Magra to arrive many hours before they did.

"Sure will be." Seth rearranged her gently and rose from the lounger. After setting the ship's system to nighttime routines, he helped Ciela remove her clothes and took them, along with most of his own, into the cargo hold where their whiff of ammonia would not bother them. Lastly, he set up a scanner to monitor Ciela's health while they slept, sure to wake him at the slightest downturn.

"Seth?" she said when he slipped into their bed and pulled her close.

"Hmm?"

"Who's Khoe?"

THREE

As Seth expected, one of Delphi's sect of Shantirs, generally assumed to be mystics and healers, stood ready to meet them on Magra. But instead of joining them on the surface, where a Delphian astrophysics team operated a sophisticated lab, he awaited them aboard an orbiting antenna array. On approach, Seth scanned the vicinity for Air Command cruisers and found only a distant squadron patrolling the western coastline. From up here, it was easy to forget that the two main continents had been at war for over one hundred years.

Ciela still hovered in some sort of fog, slipping again and again into her sleep state during the time it took for him to make the jump from Pelion to the Aikhor-Magra sector. Seth barely left her side although he was painfully aware that, beyond making sure she ate enough and whipping up cups of her favorite tea, there was nothing he could do to help her. He felt a weight lifted from him when the *Dutchman* settled into the station's ports and the umbilical between them pressurized. They had just cleared the brief decon scan when he saw Caelyn and a blue-robed elder Delphian rush toward them.

Seth threw a puzzled look to Caelyn when he recognized the Shantir. This was not one of the healers he had expected but one of the astrophysicists working out of Targon. "I'm pleased to see you, Shan Quine," he said, using Delphian mainvoice. "It's been years since I saw you last."

"Two, as they are measured on Targon," Quine agreed. He put his arm around Ciela's shoulders to lead her out of the landing ring and into the station.

They stepped onto an open lift to the main lab circle, a vast, dimly lit space lined floor to ceiling with display screens. Images and cyphers scrolled by without end, delivering information from the station's own telescopes as well as those aboard various research and Air Command ships in other parts of Trans-Targon. More workstations clustered in the center of this space, where a number of specialists, mostly Delphians, huddled over their work. Only the Shantir wore the traditional blue vest and pantaloons; his kinsmen had chosen whatever off-world fashion appealed to them. Not given to depart too far from convention, all of the Delphian men here observed their custom of growing their hair as long as they could, kept in a thick blue braid while working.

Seth and Caelyn followed the Shantir when he took Ciela into another lift rising to the upper floors. These held residential spaces and other amenities for the staff, including a lounge where Shan Quine wasted no time to engage Ciela in a khamal, no doubt far more extensive than the mind link achieved by most Delphians. The merest touch of his hand on her shoulder was all it took for him to begin to explore her neocortex for what damage her trip through subspace may have caused.

Seth and Caelyn sat silently by a curved window. A few moons hovered above the planet's broad curve but Seth had no eyes for that today. He watched nervously while Ciela reclined on a tilted chaise, Shan Quine seated beside her, although there was nothing to see. Whatever deep healing the Shantir dispensed, it involved neither word nor touch. Still, he fidgeted as nervously as if she was undergoing some major operation. In a way, she was.

"She'll be fine," Caelyn said, barely above a whisper. "Just a rough trip. I've had a few of those myself."

Seth just nodded, not bothering to remind his friend that Ciela wasn't exactly like any other Delphian.

Indeed, Caelyn was well aware of that. "It's a lucky thing she was able to grab another exit. Most spanners would have been lost."

"Don't remind me."

"So how did my transfer sheet work? You've said nothing about that."

Seth smiled, glad for the distraction. "Worked exactly the way you designed it. Ciela got the ticker out pretty quick and it lived just fine on the sheet. That was some damn fine engineering. The doctor barely felt a thing."

"We don't just sit around staring at stars, you know," Caelyn said, sounding mildly pleased although his expression remained Delphi-straight. While he felt close enough to Seth to allow his moods to show now and again, the presence of the prominent Shantir here today seemed to compel him to stick to decorum. "We'll send the specs for the design to Targon. They might find it useful."

Useful, for certain, Seth thought. Innovations such as the ticker foil were exactly the reason that Targon favored and protected Delphi more than any other world in the Commonwealth. The high-level spanners were another reason, of course. The arrangement served Delphi well; they accepted Targon's tribute of protection without having to even formally join the Commonwealth Union. Safely tucked in Air Command's military defense net, they were able to maintain their secluded ways, interacting only when they chose to. Which they didn't. Few outsiders were even allowed to visit the planet without good reason.

"Would have been even better if we hadn't lost the doctor in subspace, after all that," Seth said and added a mumbled curse.

"Yes, I don't suppose that was the goal of the mission."

"Targon won't be pleased. I guess I should make my

report to Colonel Carras."

Caelyn shrugged. "It can wait. Take a few days. You know you're welcome to stay at the lab on Magra."

"Shan Caelyn," the Shantir interrupted them. "Your assistance, please."

Seth watched his friend cross the room, gathering up his hair into a loose braid, to sit on the edge of the lounger. A light tap on his wrist allowed Quine to include him in his khamal with Ciela and now all three sunk into a silence from which Seth felt pointedly excluded. Their world seemed so very remote and unreachable for short-lived creatures like himself, serene and detached from all the tedious drama that beset other species. Seth realized how much the two men looked alike and reminded himself that Caelyn, whom he considered a peer and friend, was far more advanced in years than he seemed. Like him, they were part of the Prime species of Trans-Targon, inexplicably related but separated, at some recent moment of their evolution, by the vast space between planets that was only breached by the discovery of the keyholes. How ironic that, while other Primes had concentrated on developing ever more efficient technologies, they had developed the minds that mastered their use.

At last, all three of them seemed to return from that distant place where their mental skills had taken them. Ciela opened her eyes and blinked up at Caelyn. "I thought that was you in my head, Elder Brother."

"I serve, Elder Sister," he said, then nodded toward the Shantir. "But Shan Quine did all the heavy lifting."

She accepted his help to sit up and offered a grateful smile to the Shantir. "I feel almost new. The headache's gone. Will I be all right?"

Quine nodded. "The brain has a remarkable ability to heal itself and the body that supports it. We just need to offer a little encouragement."

Seth stood up, unsure if it was quite his place to intrude on this moment.

Ciela looked past Caelyn and jumped up from the couch

to throw her arms around Seth, as always unconcerned about Delphian propriety. "It's all well, Seth," she said. "My head's still where it's supposed to be. You can stop worrying now."

Seth held her closer than she probably expected and then mouthed a silent *Thank You* to Shan Quine over her shoulder. "You scared me," he said.

The Shantir also came to his feet. "And now I think we have other business." He gestured to Caelyn as if to a kitchen attendant. "I'll have *arooja* juice. Not too warm, please."

Caelyn went to busy himself at the small galley counter while the others took to the comfortable benches by the window.

Ciela peered out over the planet to watch its terminator slowly turn day to night for some of the people below. "What do I have to do to convince you to stay here for a few days?" she said to Seth.

He turned away from Shan Quine's line of sight and smirked meaningfully.

She sighed and accepted a cup of tea from Caelyn, but the eyes that met Seth's over its brim held considerable promise.

"Now then, this is what we have." Caelyn flipped a table surface from the floor and placed both his cup and a datasheet on it. Delphians had little use for idle chatter and neither Quine nor Caelyn seemed interested in catching up. Then again, the Shantir had not traveled from Delphi to hear about their adventures. Reluctantly, Seth turned his attention to the display, almost certain about what they had discovered in the data he had sent ahead of them.

"The incident in that span is disturbing not just for what it did to Ciela," Caelyn said. He tapped the interface to raise an image of a wave form into the air. "Shan Saias and her team took your recording apart. It wasn't hard to find something in there."

"What did you find?" Ciela said, startled by his matter-of-fact pronouncement.

Caelyn glanced at Seth. "Not only did we find *something*, we found something that Seth, no doubt, will recognize."

"What do you mean?" Ciela looked to Seth.

Seth frowned. It wasn't what he wanted to hear. Ever since their escape from subspace, since hearing her description of what she had felt in there, from his own vague memories and, most tellingly, because of her question about *Khoe*, he had both dreaded and anticipated this news. And of course it explained Shan Quine's presence, rather than another Shantir's, here on the orbiter. "Are you sure?"

"Yes. We compared the recording to the copy of the subspace resonance you gave us last year. It's nearly identical." A second wave, not quite as sinuous, appeared beside the original one.

"Resonance?" Ciela looked from one to the other. "What sort of resonance can exist in subspace?"

Seth frowned at the depiction of the frequencies. "This kind, if you forget about what we think we know about subspace."

"And we know very little," Shan Quine said. "Although some of us had occasion to enrich our knowledge these past few years."

"We also received some news from Targon," Caelyn said. "They've requested our astrophysics team to head out to the keyhole leading from Callas to Tor Ag. It seems that the reason they took the beacons down was because ships have been disappearing in that breach. Eleven, not counting the hitchhikers you lost."

Seth whistled under his breath. That occasionally a ship failed to emerge was a risk that any deep-space traveler took. But this tended to happen during keyhole breaches made by inexperienced spanners, not while traveling through the stable and well-charted jumpsites that took most commercial traffic along their designated routes. "Big loss?" he said.

"Yes. The first to disappear was a small research vessel destined for Aikhor some time ago. Then two commuters, some traders, a small military convoy sent to investigate. Two hundred people or so. Who knows how many unregistered ships. Rebels, smugglers, the sort that travels between Tor Ag and Callas."

"Not exactly the most law-abiding sub-sector," Seth said. "So likely quite a few."

Ciela scrutinized the display on the table. "Something tells me you three know something I don't. You think something in that breach is veering ships off course? Keeping them there, maybe?"

"Well," Caelyn leaned back and sipped his tea. "Yes."

She looked around the table, an uncertain smile on her face. "And you're not even joking."

"Nope," Seth said.

"You mean mathematically, right? Some aberration, something new we don't know about, maybe closing the span before the ships can reach the terminus. Or some failure by their processors to hang on to the exit."

Caelyn shook his head. "Something sentient."

"You've felt it," Seth said. "You told me so before. You said you feel watched sometimes during a jump. And you felt it again during this last one."

"Yes, but I was just..." Her eyes shifted to Shan Quine. "Is this possible?"

"Not just possible, but very much a fact." He gestured at the datasheet. "It's all there, although few people have access to this. We've always assumed that, unless we reach our exits before our mechanical protections, namely the shields and processors, get overwhelmed, our subspace breaches collapse, crushing anything caught inside. Imagine, then, that whatever particles result from this catastrophe dispersed over distances we cannot even fathom. They are not gone." His eyes followed the arc of a glittering satellite moving past the window. One of its facets caught Magra's sun and a flash of light briefly bounced off the wall behind them. "They are the building blocks of something entirely new."

"Something new? Something alive?"

"Nothing organic. But alive nonetheless."

"And you've encountered it?"

"We all did, among a few others. Seth more so than

most."

Seth smiled when she turned to him, wide-eyed with curiosity. "I was going to tell you about it someday," he said before she could ask. "It's not that easy." He glanced at Caelyn who did not meet his eyes. Of course he had meant to tell Ciela about that peculiar and ultimately destructive encounter. But something had held him back, as if it was something precious better kept to himself. As if talking about it might reduce it to nothing more than a fleeting case of First Contact that was never meant to be.

"So tell me now. It sounds fascinating."

He slid his hand over the datasheet on the table. A hologram of a compound particle appeared, turning slowly, looking like none she had ever seen. "Subspace particles," he said. "Subatomic, rare and incredibly far apart. But connected in ways we don't understand. We don't know how much space they encompass, but it's possible that one being, made up of connected but isolated particles, is spread out over an area larger than this solar system. Maybe larger than the entire Trans-Targon sector of this galaxy. Who knows?"

"And it's alive?"

"The resonance Caelyn mentioned is what brings these particles together. Some frequency excites them to join, creating something nearly sentient. Conscious, anyway. The compound particle that produces that resonance was named simply the Alpha entity. Once formed, they can then join others and come apart again, using existing energy sources to sustain themselves. I guess that's their life cycle. Each might live for a moment or a century. They can't be in that state for long without that Alpha."

"Um, what do they do in subspace? Just sort of float around?"

Caelyn chuckled before remembering his manners. Shan Quine, who was known to occasionally smile when among friends, appeared not to have noticed. "Yes, they do. But you can't think of them as the sort of thinking, feeling sentients we have here in real-space. They are quite content with how they live. It's all they know."

"Most of them," Seth said.

"What does that mean?"

"Well…" Seth said, out of habit rubbing his chin which was very smooth today. "That's what I've been meaning to tell you about."

"There's more?"

"There's a lot more," Seth said, not sure where to begin. It seemed so long ago. Or was it? "These… entities found their way into real-space. Mostly because we interfered with them. They were able to enter our ships during the leap through subspace, through the com receiver. From there, they set up shop in our heads." He tapped the neural node embedded in the skin of his temple. "When we linked to our ships, they moved into our brains."

Ciela blinked. "Like a virus? Or a parasite maybe?"

"Not a parasite!"

Caelyn leaned forward. "We don't call them that. For the most part, our contact with them was positive."

"Right," Seth said, a little stung by Ciela's response for no particular reason. A parasite was probably the right word to use but it sounded ugly to him. "They use living hosts, sentient hosts, to build a neural net in our heads at an astonishing speed, copied from the one that's already there. They draw energy from us here in real-space as well as thorium from our ships if they can get it. In the end, the host becomes two separate, sentient individuals within one body."

Ciela gaped, trying to comprehend what he was telling her. "It's like giving birth to someone inside your own head. That is so awesome!"

This time Caelyn did not suppress his laughter. "Somehow I thought you might think that. It took Seth a while."

She turned back to Seth. "You had one of those things? What was that like? Did it hurt? Why didn't you mention it before?"

"From what we understand," Shan Quine said. "It was a

highly personal experience for those who were hosts to these visitors. In effect, the combination gave rise to an entirely new species which, for now, we named Dyad."

"Dyad. Seems fitting."

"The subspace visitors do not have access to the hosts' memories and thoughts. But we found that they do share many of their host's personality traits, initially, and then grow from there. So, yes, like our own children. But once safe within the host brain they reached out to our information systems, using the neural nodes. Some had access to vast libraries, like the one Seth keeps aboard his ship, others had less success. From this, they learned about real-space and, in some cases, even manifested as one of us."

"What? How is that possible?"

"Manifested only to the host," Caelyn amended. "Because they have access to cerebral functions dealing with the main physical senses, touch, sight, sound, they can project these things so that their hosts perceives them in whatever way they choose to present themselves. They can appear like a real person, no different than any of us. In effect, a hallucination that feels utterly real to the host."

Ciela cocked her head to study Seth for a moment. "Why don't you like us talking about this?"

"What?" he said at once. "Why do you say that?"

"You don't often look like you'd rather be elsewhere."

"Do I?"

She poked his arm. "I get it, you know. Having someone live in your head must have been awful."

Seth glanced at Caelyn. "It was all right. She was easy to get along with."

"She?" Ciela said, suddenly looking a little less amused by this tale.

"Yeah. She decided to be female. I think she liked the braids they wear on Bellac." He inhaled deeply. "Her name was Khoe."

"Khoe."

"Yes, you asked me who that was, after we came out of

that jump."

Ciela nodded. "I remember now. You said that name just as we went in." Her eyebrows drew together as she tried to recall. "Or maybe it was something I... I felt in there. I couldn't have heard it. It was before I cut your link to the *Dutchman*."

"It's what she called herself."

"And you think she's back somehow?"

"Now let's be careful here," Shan Quine interjected. "We're talking about a being that existed for just a short time and that we don't fully understand. An entity took shape when it joined with Seth. It only became Khoe after that. When she left she may well have returned to a state that remembers neither him nor herself."

Ciela lifted her hands as if to slow the conversation. "All this aside, why would these entities hang around Callas and snatch planes? There is not even that much traffic out there."

"She has a point," Caelyn said.

Seth shrugged slowly. "Ships are disappearing. Exactly where our scanner picked up that frequency. It would seem that's connected somehow."

"Did you have one of those things?" Ciela asked Caelyn.

"They're not *things*!" Seth said and stood up. He walked away from them along the window to stare out into space, seeing nothing. She, the entity, had lived inside his head, becoming so completely a part of him that he, for some insane moments, had given himself to the fact that he was no longer Sethran Kada. He had become a Dyad, no longer Centauri and no longer a single individual. He had lost himself and done so willingly. The power of that lure still haunted him and he had hoped to never feel it again.

He heard the others resume their talk after a startled few moments.

"No," Caelyn said. "It doesn't seem that Delphians are suitable hosts. But I was able to communicate with her. See her, even, when I linked up with Seth. Shan Quine saw her, too."

"Do they... um, do they try to control their hosts?"

"They are completely individual. But not all of them get along with their hosts. I guess in the same way not all of us here in real-space get along. It is possible for them to compel their hosts into taking actions just like the ticker you removed does."

"By torturing them?" Ciela exclaimed.

"Yes, although most of them are just curious about us. But they, being neither wave nor really particle, can interact with our technology. Using electromagnetic radiation of any kind. As long as their host can handle it, they can manipulate it."

"Sounds dangerous."

"It is. Some Dyads..." He paused and Seth was fairly certain that he had cast a meaningful look in his direction. "Uh, weaponized this. Harmed others."

"Simply becoming a Dyad is dangerous," Quine said. "Some of the hosts died. Others suffered irreparable brain damage."

Seth closed his eyes for a moment, but that didn't shut them out or end this conversation. "We have orders," he said and turned around.

The others looked up, startled.

"What orders?" Caelyn said.

Seth leaned against the transparent wall. "Your team isn't aware of it, Caelyn. No one in Astrophysics is. The directive comes from the governors. Our esteemed Elected Ten Factors themselves. At this point, only the Vanguard division has the orders, should the Dyads reappear." He looked over to Shan Quine, who had worked tirelessly with the deep-space team for the past year and a half to learn more about the subspace entities. "Destroy on sight. They're not welcome in Trans-Targon."

"By the Gods," Quine whispered.

"How do you know this?" Ciela asked.

Seth shrugged. "Friends on the Vanguard."

"But that means killing their... their hosts as well? If

they're all joined up I mean," Ciela said. "Doesn't it?"

"It does."

"See?" she said to the others. "This is why I don't like Air Command. In the end everyone is collateral damage. At least the Arawaj are honest about it."

"That's why you have that subspace scanner," Caelyn said to Seth. "In case they turn up again."

Seth nodded. "I thought if we knew early enough we could warn them away. Or get your people working on some other solution. You Delphians have the ear of the Commonwealth, and you've acted as peacekeepers before. But mostly I just hoped we'd never see them again."

Shan Quine took a deep breath and exhaled it forcefully. "Unfortunately, us Delphians also sent a report to Air Command just yesterday. I informed them of the presence of the subspace resonance you picked up in the Callas-Tor Ag span. Intelligence will tie that to the Dyads as quickly as we did. I'm sorry. Had I known about this order I would have reconsidered making the report until we have more information."

Seth cursed silently. "Precisely why they didn't tell you about it, I'm sure."

Quine looked nearly amused. "We have made their governance a little difficult in the past, haven't we? We're becoming far too predictable, Shan Caelyn."

"What about Targon's exobiology labs?" Ciela said. "Would they not want to study these... Dyads? We need to know about them, don't we? Not just kill them and hope to eliminate them all. That makes no sense."

"No, but there are no specimen left. At least not in captivity. There is no evidence of aliens, no DNA, nothing left of the Dyads but the corpses of their hosts, which don't show anything unusual. Not a trace left. There were captive Dyads on Targon for a while. Xeno Lab took them apart after they died..." Seth frowned. "Probably *before* they died, to see how they work. Seems like the only conclusion they came to is that they must not infect our species."

"Infect!" Quine said, shaking his head.

"Targon doesn't see them as sentients. They're considered hostile, nothing more than some mind-altering pathogen, a parasite that needs to be destroyed. Even the reports from Delphians who actually made contact, who saw them for themselves, are suspect. Apparently, your visit with Khoe was just an extension of my hallucination, Caelyn." He smiled without humor. "Of course, few people knew I was a Dyad, myself, for which I thank you."

"I don't understand this," Ciela said. "I think everybody knows I don't have much love for Air Command, but the Commonwealth wouldn't just kill a whole lot of people rather than try to, well, cure them or something. Or even just try to get along, if they've been changed. We've learned to co-exist with others. Why not Dyads?"

"The Commonwealth doesn't know," Seth said. "This is classified. Air Command considers them a hazardous pathogen regardless of what the exobiologists found. They will wipe out any threat to Trans-Targon's future. Which it probably is. And they know that the Dyads will defend themselves if necessary."

"How dangerous can they possibly be?" Ciela said, sounding skeptical. "Air Command has many powerful enemies. They've managed so far."

"Khoe's people aren't dangerous at all," Caelyn said. "Dyads, however, are." He moved his hand through the holographic display hovering above the table. "Just by me touching these photons, a subspace entity in my head, merged with me to form a Dyad, could take out this entire orbiter. Not blow it up or something equally crude. It could destroy its electronic systems, the quantum computers, every last nanocircuit used in our processors. Their ability is only limited by the knowledge we allow them to access, through our information systems. And to do that I'd just need to establish an interface, as I'm doing now."

"Imagine if a Dyad were to infiltrate our military command," Seth said. "We've uncovered rebels in some pretty high places."

Ciela whistled, considering these facts. "Yeah, I can see how that'd be unpleasant." She held out her hand until Seth came to sit down beside her again. "Those people, Khoe's people, mean a lot to you," she said softly.

He scrubbed his face with both hands, feeling tired. When had he last slept for more than a few hours? "I was one of them. It… it was an amazing experience. I've never felt…" He frowned, unable to put words to the memory. "I don't know. Whole, I guess. Powerful, too. And utterly convinced that they have no interest in real-space. No interest in harming anyone."

"But they did," Caelyn reminded him.

"Not until they joined with us. On their own, they just exist. They want nothing, they are simply thought." He picked up his tea cup, found it empty, and just stared into it. "But I guess I was wrong."

"We just don't know enough," Quine said. "We know they are aware, that they can join with others of their kind until they are complex enough to be able to plan and communicate, to some extent, limited only by what is available to them. And out here, in real-space, that is limitless. They assimilate mass, energy and, then, knowledge at a phenomenal rate. We can only guess what could move them to intercept our ships. If that's what they're doing."

Seth felt Ciela's eyes on him and looked up to see that it was so. She observed him for a while longer, as if deciding something. "What?"

"We need to go back," she said.

Shan Quine and Caelyn both suddenly wore the same stunned look.

"Out of the question!" Quine said.

"Are you mad?" Caelyn added.

Seth's expression suggested that he shared Caelyn's suspicion. "Back into that breach?"

"Yes. *You* need to go back. The resonance on that recording could just be a fluke, but if you don't find out for sure it'll keep haunting you. And if those entities are doing something to those ships, we need to know."

"Going through there almost killed you," Quine reminded her.

"Because I fought it. Maybe I shouldn't have."

"You don't know that at all," Caelyn said. "In all likelihood, you saved Seth's life."

"This really isn't advisable," Shan Quine said.

Ciela's eyes were still on Seth. "But important, no?" she said to him.

Seth bit his lip. A year or so ago, he would have headed out immediately to poke around that breach, not giving a single thought to what came after that. But this was no longer just him. Without Ciela's skills, he'd find nothing. He would not even be able to enter the keyhole, with or without Air Command at the gate. But had he not so long ago berated himself yet again for placing her life in danger? Feeding his suspicion that she'd live a safer and more productive life without him? He shook his head. "I won't ask this of you."

"You're not asking," she said and the edge in her voice told him that her mind was set. "You worry about these Dyads. About Air Command treating them like some virus to be eradicated. You spent your whole life cruising around the sector, making friends of species most of us can't even talk to. But you're not practical. You never are. Think about this: What if they start snatching ships in other breaches? Subspace travel would become so dangerous that few could afford it. Imagine what that would mean to all of us in this sector."

Seth nodded. Without access to subspace, no one would get as far as the next solar system. By now so many worlds relied on interstellar travel that severing those roads would be simply catastrophic. The collapse the Commonwealth Union of Planets, existing primarily for interstellar commerce, was assured.

"So if those beings are involved somehow, let's find out

why this is happening before Air Command comes up with a whole set of new rules for everyone. You know how much I love that."

Seth smiled at her and resisted a sudden urge to kiss the tip of her nose. "I do," he said.

"You should run some experiments," Caelyn said. His long fingers already shuffled some symbols around on his datasheet. "Before you decide to return to Tor Ag and not live to regret it."

"What experiments?" Ciela said.

"Take a few jumps, safe ones. Send a few probes. Run the Alpha frequency while you're doing that. See if anything answers. We can configure your onboard scanner to look for a response, rather than send your findings here for analysis."

"Seems reasonable," Seth said.

"One of us has to be," Caelyn responded. "I'd advise you to stay off the neural link while jumping until we know more."

"Why?" Ciela said.

"So that he doesn't become re-infected. I'm sorry, Seth, that was a rude word choice. But when Khoe left she didn't exactly put your brain back the way it was. At this point, we don't know if you're immune to their invasion, or more susceptible than anyone."

"How's that?"

"Some leftover pieces of her neural net are still in my head," Seth said, shrugging. "Inactive, according to the Shantirs."

She smirked and poked his ribs to make him flinch. "And all this time I thought I was the one with an extra piece in my head." She turned back to Caelyn. "I think we should leave immediately. Before more ships get lost."

Caelyn nodded. "I admit that I'm itching to join you. It would allow us to jump more frequently. But both Shan Quine and I have already signed on to the research vessel about to leave for the Callas gate to Tor Ag."

"Tor Ag is locked down now?"

"Yes. Air Command sent a battlecruiser to guard that site on the Callas end as soon as they got our report. Everyone on the Tor Ag side is either stuck there or disappearing if they try to jump. I think the *Dutchman* was the last ship to make it out of there."

"That'll make it just a bit difficult for us to give that keyhole another try," Ciela said, looking disappointed.

"You should have a little faith in my proven talent for sweet-talking my way past the crustiest of cops," Seth said.

"You have a proven talent for getting shot at," she reminded him.

"She's well enough to do this?" Seth asked the Shantir, still troubled by Ciela's recent experience.

Quine nodded. "Run those tests during a few safe jumps, as Shan Caelyn suggests. I don't think you'll have any issues. If you meet up with us at Callas we can go over the results before you decide to try for Tor Ag. I do have misgivings about that, but no say in the matter. You've shown more than once that the sensible route is not the one you generally follow, Shan Sethran." He actually smiled at Ciela. "And Shan Ciela is every bit as adventurous as you are."

FOUR

"Nothing, nothing and then a little more nothing," Seth said in answer to Ciela's question.

She had just emerged from the crew cabin where she'd retreated to recover from their last jump into this sector. Since then Seth had sifted through the sensor readings, finding a whole lot of nothing. He had migrated to the lounger, surrounded by the remains of a meal and the tools he needed to manipulate the data gathered by the *Dutchman*'s subspace scanner.

This had been their fourth jump since leaving Magra. The first leap had been a safe trip through a charted and well-traveled jumpsite leading to Targon. Although Seth's ability would have sufficed for that gate, Ciela made the jump to let him keep his neural link disengaged from the *Dutchman*'s processors while they broadcasted the Dyad resonance. The next jump took them through an uncharted keyhole, ending up near Feyd. There, too, nothing responded to their unconventional hail. A few days' travel through real-space to the next keyhole brought them, again unmolested by subspace entities, to the massive Pelion Gate station, a busy crossroads sector connecting traffic from a stable jumpsites and two, more distant, keyholes. Finally, they jumped to Callas to meet the science vessel exploring the forbidden span leading to Tor Ag. Each time, nothing unusual happened during the subspace traverse and not even a single spike appeared on the scanner to show that anything at all existed in subspace. The way it should be.

Ciela looked at the large screen fixed to the bulkhead above the galley counter. "Four jumps are probably not enough for any conclusions," she said. "Where are we?"

"We just left Callas," Seth said and patted the spot beside him on the lounger. "I picked up some coolant and supplies at the lunar station. You'd sleep through anything. We're a few hours out from the keyhole to Tor Ag."

She stretched out beside him after removing a few food packages and several datasheets, and propped her head on his thigh. "Damn, I'd hoped we'd find something useful to bring to the expedition."

He handed her one of the screens. "I suppose *not* finding anything weird in the other spans does tell us something. It's only a sampling, but it supports the assumption that we don't need to worry so much about this happening elsewhere as well. That's worth something, I guess."

"Have you heard from Caelyn? Did they come up with anything yet?"

Seth tilted his head, his eyes on the monitor. "Wait a minute…"

"Hmm?"

He took the data tablet from her and shifted to sit on the edge of the lounger. "I think we're doing this all wrong."

"Doing what wrong?"

"Broadcasting the frequency. Of course that won't work! We're not going to get any answer. It's keeping them away."

"What? You said that they need this resonance. Why would they not at least check us out for broadcasting it?"

"Because the last time someone did that they ended up in a bad spot. They will have learned. We have nothing that'll perfectly duplicate that resonance so it's not fooling them one bit. This is just more or less sound, a copy, not something produced by the Alpha entity. All we're doing is telling them to stay away."

"Worth checking out, then," she said. "We'll go into the Tor Ag span without the broadcast and see what happens."

"You're all set on that? You got hurt."

"If this resonance is actually keeping them away we can use that to help us escape if we have to. Besides, we got out before. I know what to do now and I can just take us back to Caelyn's ship if we run into trouble."

He tried to look past her guileless expression to sort the logic of what she was proposing from the reckless streak that let her tread where other Delphians would not. "If you're sure…"

"Of course I'm not sure. Can you put that away and notice how suggestively I'm posed on this bed?"

He let his eyes roam where she meant them to. "Now that you mention it…"

* * *

What used to be the entry to the Callas jumpsite leading to Tor Ag looked a whole lot like what they had seen on the other end. Beacons shut down, now stationary and useless, guarding some invisible piece of nothing. Only the *Dutchman*'s sensors highlighted the quantum anomaly existing unnoticed until supplied with the massive burst of energy needed to expand it to a useful diameter.

Except that this time, the guns aboard the Air Command vessel guarding the site were not the type of short-range deterrents carried by patrols. The dark gray bulk of the Titan class military ship made clear its intention to keep traffic from passing through here. The sleek, sensor-studded Delphian science vessel *Laruel* hovered in her shadow, unconcerned by the goings-on nearby.

Seth, however, was unhappy with the goings-on. A Fleetfoot cruiser had reached the keyhole ahead of them, her captain already engaged in a heated debate with the battleship's com officer. Heated on the side of the Fleetfoot, in any case. The officer let the captain of the cruiser voice his

Chris Reher

opinions about the situation and Air Command in general and, like his counterpart at Tor Ag, merely apologized for the inconvenience. It was clear to all that the apology did not include standing down the weapons arranged to deliver a precise spread encompassing the space around the keyhole. Probably not a deadly spread, but designed to weaken shields enough to make the jump impossible.

"I'm sorry," the voice over the open com channel said, sounding bored. "The terminus for this site has become unstable. You may not proceed."

"That's the third time you've said that," the irate lisp of the Magran aboard the Fleetfoot returned. "We will take the chance. I have urgent business on Tor Ag."

"Do not proceed, Pilot."

"My spanner is the best in Trans-Targon. We can handle some backwater leap under any conditions. I insist that you let us through."

"Please return to Callas and await news from there."

"Who is your commanding officer?"

Ciela came into the cockpit and leaned over Seth to reduce the volume of the transmission. "Looks like he's using up all your excuses," she said.

"I can do better than that. Next there'll be an attempt to bribe. I'll leave them to it." He directed the *Dutchman*, via his neural interface, to move around the Air Command vessel and head instead to the research ship. An alert on his screen showed military scanners poking through his cruising shields and he allowed this, for once not worried about anything aboard that might rouse their interest. The scan passed over them and they proceeded without hail from the larger vessel.

He sent his own hail to the *Laruel*, requesting to speak with Caelyn. Ciela snickered when he identified them as the Scoutship *Dutchman*. Only moments passed before the Delphian appeared on their screen. He wore a formal lab vest and his blue hair was pulled back tightly into a braid, adding an even more severe look to his angular features.

"You made it," he said as if they hadn't been chatting

60

since the *Dutchman* dropped out of the other keyhole into this sector. "Begin data transfer."

Seth complied, transmitting the inconclusive reports, aware that other ears were listening to their exchange, made deliberately over an open com link. "The breaches we tested all came up negative for any unusual disturbance, Shan Caelyn. We're ready to deploy." Seth's monotone suggested that they were all engaged in the most routine of research projects. "Stand clear."

"We're ready also, Shan Sethran," Caelyn said, his eyes on something before him. "Please ask your spanner to prepare for entry."

Seth winked at Ciela when a signal indicated that someone else wanted to join their conversation.

"*Laruel* please confirm your intention to enter the keyhole?" This was not the com officer they had heard before and this voice sounded a little incredulous. The screen divided to show a Centauri woman with a major's insignia on her sleeve.

Caelyn looked up, his expression blank. "Not the *Laruel*," he said. "The Scout will enter for additional readings. We can only do so much with probes."

"Negative, *Laruel. Dutchman*, please do not attempt to enter the breach."

"Major, why did you think we were sent out here by Targon?" Caelyn said. "So far we have not detected any anomaly that you could not also gather by probing the fissure. This Scout has delivered a most competent Level Three spanner. Please move out of range so that we can begin our operation."

"Shan Caelyn, I have no clearance from Targon for this."

"Please contact Astrophysics, not Command. I assure you this is standard operating procedure."

Ciela's expression, less capable of restraint than Caelyn's, nearly made Seth laugh. Nothing here was standard operating procedure, given a complete lack of precedent for any of this. The major was on her own out here. The only way to contact Targon was by sending a message packet back through several jumpsites equipped with the sort of relay beacon needed to forward it to Targon. A reply could take hours to return.

Ciela made a surprised sound when Shan Quine wandered past Caelyn, imperious in his Delphian garb. "Shan Caelyn…" he began, then looked at the screen as if just realizing that a conversation was taking place. "If you please, we need to proceed. I understand that complaints about the delayed traffic are reaching all the way to Targon. Callas is demanding that we complete this operation and be on our way." Apparently not expecting a reply to this, he strolled away.

Seth powered up the *Dutchman*'s shields as if the officer's objections no longer applied.

"Shan Caelyn, I strongly advise you to reconsider," she tried again, apparently unaware that most Delphians would not give a damn about traffic snarls in a remote location. "This span is extremely hazardous."

"Thank you for your concern, Major," Caelyn said. "Please ensure that the other vessel here does not attempt to follow. *Dutchman*, please proceed."

Seth shut down the open com channel and left only the direct link to Caelyn. The major's face disappeared. "And there you have it," he said.

"I can't believe you kept a straight face through all that, Caelyn," Ciela said.

"Not that hard for a Delphian," he replied. "If you attended the enclave more often you, too, could learn a little decorum." Only the bright blue of his eyes revealed the humor behind his words.

She stuck her tongue out at him, knowing how much he enjoyed this game. Were it not for his desire to see his hundredth solstice without being shot again, he would have joined Seth aboard the *Dutchman* long ago.

But then Caelyn's eyes darkened again. "Be careful," he said. "I have all sorts of doubts about this."

"The moment it feels like trouble I'm taking the nearest exit out," Ciela promised. "I know what to expect now."

He nodded and looked to Seth. "Be well."

Seth made a gesture used by Delphians to indicate an absence too short to merit a formal farewell. Then he shut the com down.

"Ciela," Ciela said, lowering her voice. "Are you sure you want to do this?"

Seth blinked, startled.

"You were going to say that, weren't you?"

"Well, yes."

"Thought I'd save you the trouble." She pulled up the restraints on her bench. "Am I sure I want to jump in there? Yes. Am I sure we're not about to get into a big fight in there? Nope. Let's just hope we come out somewhere not deadly."

"I have faith in you," he said and removed his headset. "You're scrappy."

"Kiss me," she said.

"Huh?"

"Just in case."

He sat up on his bench when she leaned toward him from hers. When he touched those sweet, soft lips he felt the weight of this decision creep back into this mind, threatening to cancel the whole damn idea. He pushed his hands through her thick hair, holding her closer, banishing all doubt to think of nothing but her in this moment. Had any kiss ever felt as good, and as frightening, as this one?

"All right," she said finally and dropped back into her couch. "Let's do this."

Seth turned his attention to the *Dutchman*'s controls, working them manually to direct the ship's energy to the keyhole. Their sensors showed an echo and soon a space large enough to enter. He increased their velocity, holding back for her signal.

"Looks solid enough," she said in that faraway tone that told him she had reached a deep state of khamal. The console indicators showed all processors fully engaged with her neural link, a state that few Prime species withstood without damage. "I've got the exit," she added after a while. "Go."

He accelerated into the aperture, reaching top speed as they passed the threshold. Some unnamable dread took hold of him at once and he told himself that it always felt that way. A reasonable response by a brain that suddenly lost all senses when even the gravity generated by his own ship disappeared. Nothing new here, he assured himself as every instinct told him that they were making a very big mistake.

And then they were through. Seth felt weirdly disappointed when, as usual, the *Dutchman* chattered to itself as it checked for damage, waiting patiently for its pilot to set a course to somewhere. Had they actually made the jump to Tor Ag without incident? His heart also settled happily into its usual routines. "Ciela?" he said.

"I'm here," she gasped. "Gods, I'm here!"

He sat up to see her frightened face, eyes huge as she looked around the cabin as if to assure herself that they were safe. "Are you all right?"

She exhaled forcefully and closed her eyes in search for equilibrium. "All's well. I just had a scare. We're not near Tor Ag, are we?"

He reached up to reconnect the headset to his neural nodes and stabilized the ship, slowing it to nearly a full stop. "No."

She pushed herself up. Whatever shock she had sustained was wearing off, leaving her simply fatigued, as always after a jump. "I didn't think so. I lost the terminus the moment we jumped. Something grabbed for us. It was almost as frightening *not* to fight it this time as it felt when I did."

A proximity alarm sounded when the *Dutchman* automatically ramped up its shielding again. The ship shuddered when something impacted on the port side. Seth engaged the real-vid displays showing their surroundings. "Debris," he said and tapped the sensors for an analysis.

"Dust?"

He raised both eyebrows. "Bloody graveyard. Metal, fuel rods leaking radiation, organics. Body parts! Looks like a ship didn't make it through the jump. More than one. That's a Magran hull."

"Where are we?"

Seth recast the scanners, this time farther to find mechanical beacons, and triangulated their position. After a moment the onboard navigator confirmed their position in an unpopulated and barely-explored margin of what they called Trans-Targon. "We're in the Badlands. Long way from home." He regarded her for a moment, thinking she looked a little wilted. "I didn't feel a thing this time. Are you sure you're all right?"

"Yes, don't fuss. Just tired."

"I think I'm allowed a certain amount of fuss."

"Well, fuss about where we are, then," she said, but softened her words with a smile.

He directed his frown at the *Dutchman*'s reports. "Solar system nearby. Oh, lovely. Chitta Moor."

Information moved over an overhead screen, showing details about the solar system a few hours from here. "Mining, mostly," Ciela murmured. She curled up on her narrow bench, too engrossed in their current problem to seek the sleep she needed. "No indigenous population. No history of rebel activity, therefore no real Air Command presence in this sector. At least we ended up somewhere habitable. What are the odds of that?"

"Some military ships over there, though. Second planet." Seth sent a hail when he recognized an Air Command signature. "And that one looks like a Feydan trader."

"Are they drifting?" she asked when his call received no response.

"Most of them are on the surface. One transport in orbit, stationary. Looks pretty organized." He shifted his gaze to another display when more data arrived. "Some of them are on the list of the lost ships. The *Chidix*, *Zera-36N*, the two tugs from Callas, Targon's *Odin,* a few others."

"Maybe our doctor is here. Why aren't they answering?"

"We'll try again when we clear this radiation bath." He read the pale color of her eyes – a Delphian barometer of mood and health. "Why don't you grab a few hours of sleep? I'll try to wake you if anything interesting happens."

She sat up but, instead of heading to bed, scrutinized one of the data displays. "That keyhole is pretty stable. We should take a look to see what shape it's in from this end."

Seth checked their power supply and decided that they could afford to crack the keyhole for another look. He targeted the breach and incited it to open enough for a quick scan. "This keyhole is supposed to lead to and from the Mrak system. Not Callas. I can't tell from this if that terminus is still available."

She kept up with the incoming reports, mumbling to herself. "Still got that resonance singing away in there. Slightly higher frequency. I'd guess jumping in there will just get us sucked back into this space again."

He pointed to another screen still showing the debris field outside. "Or worse, maybe."

She kept her eyes on the main screen but he saw her chew her lower lip as she considered what might have happened here. "There's no sign of a battle. Those ships ripped up during the jump. We haven't seen that happen in about a hundred years. You either emerge, or you don't."

"Doesn't mean it can't happen. I've seen some traders, pirates, jaunt around in relics you wouldn't set foot in."

She nodded only after a thoughtful moment, probably just to acknowledge his attempt to reassure her. "There isn't another keyhole in this entire sector. Not within a lifetime at top speed, anyway. The only way out, back home, is through this one. But with all that interference I can't even tell if this naturally leads to Mrak, like it's supposed to, or now leads back to either Tor Ag or Callas."

"Shouldn't matter. We we've got that Alpha resonance. It seems to work to keep us on course. We only got here when we shut it down. We should be able to use that to get back. Somewhere." He hesitated a moment, well aware that she thought him far too protective of her. "That interference is thick here, though. What if you end up in another battle like before? We almost didn't make it out."

"Scared, Kada?" She grinned, perhaps trying to appear braver than she felt.

He returned his attention to his monitors. "I wasn't thinking about me," he said, sounding sullen even to himself.

She tipped her bench forward to ease her way out of it. He felt her fingers move through his hair to caress the back of his head and leaned into her hand, enjoying the contact. "Thanks for worrying about me," she said. "I think I'd be worried, too, if I wasn't so tired." She slouched off to the main cabin. "Sleep. Must sleep."

Seth worried for both of them. If necessary, they would make the attempt to return to Trans-Targon. But what awaited them down there, near that star? Other than completely losing their way in subspace, both he and Ciela had come through no worse for the experience. Surely others would have, too. And yet, the silence on all com channels felt like they were about to encounter ghost ships.

* * *

"Seth, wake up."

Seth groaned and rolled away from the hand gripping his shoulder. At some point during these past hours he had gotten bored with sending unanswered hails and waiting for Ciela to wake up and so he had nodded off beside her. He wanted to sleep more.

"Seth!"

"What?"

"And they say it's hard to wake a Delphian. Someone's calling from the planet."

Seth opened his eyes and turned to see Ciela standing over him. She had evidently been up for a while, looking freshly bathed, as far as the ship's decon chamber was capable of actually bathing anyone, and well-rested. He sat up, feeling rumpled. "What did they say?"

"I didn't answer yet. Come on."

He followed her into the cockpit where a blinking light vied for his attention along with the occasional squawk from the console. "Video?"

"Yes." She reached up to run her fingers through his hair in some effort to make him look a little more presentable.

He sat sideways on the pilot bench and faced the overhead camera before opening the receiver. "*Dutchman*," he said, not willing to offer more identification than that. Both he and Ciela winced when the squeal from a poorly calibrated com system rang through the cockpit.

"Queta Station tower," a garbled voice came from the speaker. The video image of the Magran that greeted them was no less mangled. They heard other voices in the background. A Centauri woman leaned over a console behind the Magran, speaking to another. Someone else hurried past the camera. Whatever had shut down the keyhole had apparently not induced them to suspend their mining operations. "Proceed to these landing coordinates."

"I'm not sure that's really what I'd like to do at this point," Seth said.

"Then keep floating around out there. Suit yourself. We have enough to deal with."

Ciela pursed her lips. Any contact with a remote location usually started off quite cordially, mainly because such places saw few visitors from other parts of Trans-Targon. Guests brought a change of routine, gossip, and often gifts for isolated communities.

"What happened here?" Seth said.

"A subspace anomaly, obviously," the controller said. "We've had one-way traffic for a while now, but we can't enter that keyhole. I don't suggest you try. We've set up a support facility at the coordinates I sent." He turned when the Centauri approached his station. She ducked down to peer into the camera.

"Another new one?" she said. There was a lieutenant's insignia on her sleeve. "Hello out there. We had hoped that we'd seen the last of new arrivals. I'm glad you made it through in one piece."

"Almost didn't," Seth said. "Any idea about this, uh, anomaly?"

"None," she said cheerfully. Her eyes darted to her right as if someone else stood there. She gave a small nod before looking again into the camera. "Did you encounter anything unusual on your way through? Since arriving here, maybe?"

"You mean the body parts bouncing off my shields?"

Again the exchange of furtive looks with someone unseen. "You are in no immediate danger. It takes a while to get used to things. Do come down if you wish." She smiled and moved off-screen.

The Magran looked after her for a moment before turning back to Seth. "A landing area has been cleared at the mouth of the canyon. You will remain in the emergency facilities set aside for the arrivals. The production areas and the town are not safe for visitors. Air Command is managing the camp."

Seth nodded, taking this as a warning, should Seth's affiliations lean toward the rebel side of things. The military had little jurisdiction out here as most of Queta Station was operated by private companies dealing directly with Commonwealth interests. But Air Command would be far better equipped to deal with what would become a survival situation as soon as the supply ships stopped coming from the Mrak system. "I'll keep that in mind."

"Also keep in mind that this is not a Union planet. You're on your own for supplies but we've got water. We barely scrape by with what the company sends us but you might be able to barter." The controller cut their transmission without another word.

"Welcome to Queta Station," Seth said. He turned to Ciela. "What did you get?"

She brought up the voice and visual analysis on the main

screen, having amused herself once again with testing Targon's newest update. "Nothing unusual with the Magran. The officer is definitely Centauri. But look at that." She leaned forward to tap the screen. "Those spikes don't register as Centauri at all. Don't register as any known species."

Seth had to agree. Centauri were the most common non-native species in Trans-Targon and any voice recognition program would identify them within seconds. He leaned over to look at the display more clearly. "I don't think those are speech patterns at all. Looks like interference of some sort." He tugged on his bottom lip as he pondered this. "Does that frequency look familiar to you?"

She nodded after a moment. "I'll bet you a bag of *teela* nuts that's our Dyad resonance, unless my memory fails, which it never does."

"I won't take that bet. I thought the way she was looking around a little odd. It's probably the way I looked when I talked to Khoe. After a while you learn to interact with them without people noticing. It's all just in your head."

"You think that might be what she meant by getting used to things? Getting used to being a Dyad?"

"Could be. It took me a while to even grasp what Khoe was. And it took Khoe a few hours to go through my archives. That's how they become who they are. They grab whatever information is available to learn how to extrapolate and then interact. Pretty much like an AI system but with a better sense of humor."

Ciela nodded to the now inactive screen. "That woman didn't seem bothered by it. By being a Dyad, I mean."

"It's not objectionable," he admitted.

"So what are we going to do?"

He shrugged. "I'm going to get cleaned up. Then we'll go down. That's what we're here for. But for now let's not tell them that we know what Dyads are." He leaned down to kiss her, not aiming for any particular part of her face. "And say nothing about that special little brain you have."

He ducked out of the cockpit before she found something to throw at him and spent a good while enjoying the steam cycle of the decon chamber. The meal he had hoped for upon emerging was not waiting for him and so he puttered around the small galley, glad that they had not only stocked up on coolant but also on food before leaving Callas. "You want some of this?" he called to her.

After a moment, Ciela came into the main cabin, her eyes on a datasheet in her hands. "Got more readings. I'm pretty sure that keyhole does lead to Ud Mrak, as always. But getting a grip on that terminus through all that interference is just about impossible." She looked up to where he stood behind the counter. "Are you wearing anything at all behind there?"

"If I say 'no', will you take me to bed?"

She peered over the counter before sitting on one of the stools next to it. "I'll have some baraberry tea, please."

He sighed and sifted through a jumble of tea packets in a cabinet. "Copy the resonance to your scanner," he said. "Maybe it'll come in handy."

She went to a shelf by the lounge to retrieve her data sleeve. "A siren call for your Khoe?"

He cocked his head. "*My* Khoe?"

Ciela did not look at him while she transferred the file to her system. "You've been a little evasive about what happened. About her. You had feelings for her."

He placed her cup in front of her. "Yeah."

She looked up as if surprised by his admission. "You did? For an alien living in your head?"

"Want me to lie?"

"No, I guess not." She slipped her data sleeve over her wrist, fussing with some small wrinkle even though she would soon remove it again to put it over her jacket sleeve.

Seth waited for her to say something more, but she only sipped her tea and returned her attention to the datasheet in front of her. He supposed that he could have been a little less honest about Khoe. He walked around the counter to find some clothes, no longer hungry. "That resonance is evidence of the subspace entities, not any one of them specifically. She's long gone, Ciela."

FIVE

The *Dutchman* threaded its way through jagged walls of rocks guarding deep canyons that seemed hacked into the surface by some giant's axe, following some faults of the planet's crust. The resulting fractal fissures had exposed the valuable minerals, attracting prospectors who soon set up their operations here on Chitta Moor and called it Queta Station. Despite the dreariness of the place, its atmospheric conditions meant that most visitors moved about unfettered by protective gear, improving mobility and cost effectiveness. Even in Trans-Targon, the most crowded sector of explored space, such planets were rare. To also find a pleasant view was against most odds.

Seth had not been here before. The planet was merely a destination for transport ships and the supply haulers making life on this barren wasteland tolerable. It held nothing of interest to explorers, smugglers, pirates or rebels in search of new territory. Chitta Moor's destructive storms made most surface habitation a futile venture and so the deep canyons provided shelter as well as ore.

He eased the *Dutchman* down onto a bare expanse of rock on the bottom of a canyon where several of the lost ships already vied for space. Ciela busied herself with the scanners, reporting a dozen or so people of various Prime species inside and among those ships, and a cluster of individuals in a hangar near the edge of the airfield.

"Now let's see if we can find something interesting," she said, tapping into the public communications system. Seth watched her as she worked to find her way into more private channels to dig around recent and current conversations. "Nothing," she said after a while. "Nobody up there knows what's going on. Once in a while they send probes and message packets into the keyhole but no one's answering. They've decided to keep the town busy and at work so everyone thinks rescue is going to happen any moment."

"Seems wise."

"They're worried about the extra people arriving, but we knew that. They've doubled security around their supply depots. Probably figure there'll be a riot."

"Numbers?"

"About five hundred in total that actually belong here. Workers, some families, support staff, couple of businesses. Ugh, prison labor. Did you know that?"

Seth shrugged. He'd come close, once or twice, to doing a stint here.

"And then there are a hundred and thirty survivors from the lost ships, not counting whoever is still in orbit."

Seth whistled. "More than I thought. What about elsewhere?"

"Nothing, really. Couple of test sites looking for more ore. Queta Station is the only real town, if you want to call it that. Staff is rotated out every six months when the supply ships get here from Mrak. The rest don't get to leave until their sentence is up." She closed her tap into the station's inner workings. "That's three in a row, Kada. Three trips to places that don't serve breakfast in bed. If we ever get out of this place, we're going somewhere pretty. Some place with beaches and green things or maybe air that doesn't smell like someone just threw up."

He grinned. "Promise."

The conditions outside called for a layer of heated clothes

and so they dressed for that, glad that this allowed them to conceal their weapons. A cold wind whipped along the canyon, tugging on their wraps as they exited. Down here, where the towering rift walls blocked the planet's sun, the false twilight seemed perpetual. Globes of lights strung together by untidy ropes of cabling showed the way along the single street snaking through the bottom of the ravine. Seth glanced at his scanners to check for radiation leaks, too common in outpost settlements. After another look around, he turned back to add another security protocol to the ship's locks. It would require his or Ciela's live hand print and a scan of their eyes to re-enter the *Dutchman*.

The other ships parked here, all of them small craft cruisers, didn't appear launch ready. Open gates and doors hinted at shoddy contamination protocols and, given the prison population, even shoddier security measures. One ramp actually served to support some sort of heater set up for cooking, and tarps were strung from another's crossdrive to fashion a shelter. The side of its hull gaped to reveal the engine access as if someone had walked away in the middle of a repair.

"Looks like they've been here a while," Ciela murmured, tipping her chin toward a line of laundry hung out to dry.

Seth nodded absently, his eyes on the cliffs looming above them. Mine entrances pockmarked the bare, dark rock, connected by rails attached precariously to the walls. Carts and workers moved between them and he saw the bright, unnatural light of their tools blasting from some of the openings.

The canyon narrowed to the north where a scatter of pre-fab buildings followed a listless creek. Metal bridges connected the two banks of mobile habitats and service buildings. Light shone from some of them; perhaps they were residences. Other buildings clung to the walls of the massive rock face where steel beams seem to have been driven into the stone with little thought behind the engineering. Their stingy, barred windows hinted that those housed the prison population while not attending to their slave labor. Rust and decay marked a lack of care by those made to live and work here. The noise of the mine carts and distant machinery blocked out the sound of people and even the ceaseless wind. Above them, metal bridges spanned the canyon but from here it was impossible to see what went on at the surface. Something more pleasant than this, he hoped.

Ciela nudged his hand to get his attention. The Centauri officer who had spoken with them aboard the *Dutchman*, accompanied by two armed Humans, walked toward them with hands stretched out in greeting. Ciela ducked behind Seth, looking suspicious and frightened. She put her hand on his back and tilted the screen of her data sleeve toward herself.

"I'm glad you decided to join us," the woman said. "My name is Lieutenant Zire, and this is Tel Randan and Viko. I'm acting as liaison between Queta Station and, well, those of us who drifted out here for some reason."

"Sethran Kada," Seth said. "And Ciela. We have many questions."

"Yes," Ciela said, sounding distraught. "Why did we get pulled through this terminus? We were going to Tor Ag. Why is everyone still here? How are we going to get back?"

"I know this is frightening," the Human male said. "And disorienting. We've all experienced it."

"Experienced what?" Seth said. He felt Ciela tap his back twice. The subspace frequency heard only by the scanner radiated from the man as well. Another Dyad.

Zire tilted her head as if appraising him. "Are you... alone?"

"Yes," Seth said as if he didn't understand her question. "Just us two. Ciela's a little shaken by all this."

An odd silence followed. The Human beside her started to say something but then didn't. Seth recognized the expression. It had taken him a while to learn how to silently communicate as a Dyad without looking like an utter lunatic.

"Of course she is," the Centauri said. "We were fortunate

to emerge here, so close to a hospitable planet. But the news is not all good." She pointed skyward. "We can't re-enter the keyhole. We will not be able to leave this place."

"What?" Ciela cried. "There must be a way!" She gripped Seth's arm and added another note of despair to her voice. "Seth, I want to go back!"

Seth patted her hand. "Let's try to stay calm." He frowned at the Centauri. "You've tried to return, I assume?"

"Of course. We've sent a ship back up for scans. The *Kietha*, out of Callas, tried to re-enter and failed. So did one of the private ships. We can't even get an emergency message through to warn Targon. Or to call for help." She peered more closely at Ciela. "You are Delphian?" Her expression suggested that she found Ciela's public display of emotion puzzling.

"My navigator," Seth said, offering no more than that.

"Not much need for navigators now," Zire said. "Even Delphian ones. But there are other ways you can make yourself useful. We are dealing with some casualties. It will likely become necessary for us to pool our supplies and resources. There may be difficulties and the local residents are unhappy to have us add to their burden. There are many Mrakis among them and the thought of having lost all contact with their homeworld is making them a little edgy."

"Nothing more fun than an edgy Mraki," Seth said. The inhabitants of both Mraki planets tended to possess short tempers and massive bodies, useful to Air Command's infantry ranks and dangerous when they decided to join rebel forces instead. Out here most of the non-convicts would be of that species.

"It's probably best if we try not to involve ourselves with them if we don't have to." Zire gestured toward the long metal shed at the end of the airfield. "You'll find more of our people in there. It might of course be safer for you to remain aboard your ship for now."

"Are there any Delphians here?" Ciela asked.

Zire glanced at her companions. "There were. Two pilots,

I think. They did not survive the jump here. I'm sorry." She turned to walk away. "Stay with the others. This is not the sort of place to wander around and get lost. There've been some hostilities already."

Seth watched them go. "I've seen people marooned in some pretty weird places. No one's ever seemed happy about it before."

"Are the Dyads doing something to make them act this way?" Ciela said as they began to walk toward the shelter. She shivered despite the heated layers she wore.

"Possible," he said. "And they *are* the Dyads now. Together. A whole new life form. Two beings in one body. We don't have a name for them when they're still in their own space." He slowed his steps to work with the sensors on his forearm. "That frequency they're exuding wasn't something we noticed before. The Alpha resonance was produced by just one specific subspace particle. Now it seems to radiate directly from them. That is bad news for us."

"Why?"

"Because what was keeping them in their own space was that Alpha entity. If they no longer need it, they'll be able to exist out here. Exactly what Air Command is afraid of."

"Are there more of them here?"

He gave up on his scanner, which told him nothing more. "Yes, but I can't tell what sort of range we're seeing with this. We'll analyze this when we have more to go on."

They passed a Centauri in dusty Air Command uniform sitting in the open doorway of a defunct Trident cruiser. The cold did not seem to bother him as he dug listlessly into the bottom of a ration bag. Seth nodded to him. "Evening, officer."

The man only scowled.

Ciela pointed to the entrance of the metal shed, perhaps some sort of hanger. "That looks ominous." A smaller door at the base was guarded by two armed men. The Centauri sported a lieutenant's uniform while the Feydan beside him wore civilian garb in relatively good repair. Both of them carried Air Command weapons.

Seth raised his hand in greeting. "Nice day for a walk." He surveyed the canyon as if in judgment of it. "Although we seem to be a long way from planet Home."

"Something we all have in common," the Feydan said, tinting the Union mainvoice with the thick accent of his people. "Who would you be?"

"Traders out of Callas. Missed our exit at the Tor Ag terminus."

"You're not the only one," the Centauri lieutenant said, showing far less enthusiasm about this than Lieutenant Zire had. "Looks like we're all here to stay."

"What are you trading?" the Feydan wanted to know.

"Nothing right now. What is going on here?"

"Nothing we've figured out. Go see the captain if you're interested in sitting around making guesses." He pushed the metal door on its track to allow them to enter.

"I am," Seth said. He pointed to the man's weapons. "Something to fear here?"

"Fucking rebels everywhere, pretending they're civilians. Getting hard to deal with but the captain says we have to play nice, this being a survival situation." He laughed unpleasantly. "Maybe he's thinking we'll need them for dinner someday. So far most are behaving. Gods help'em if they don't."

"Shri-Lan?"

He shrugged. "And Arawaj, but what's the difference."

"There's most definitely a difference," Ciela said. "Most Arawaj still respect civilians and won't sacrifice bystanders to achieve their objective. If you'd pay attention..." she trailed off when the guard looked at her as if he'd just noticed her for the first time.

"You Delphians have to be experts on everything, don't you?" he growled. "Rebel scum, the lot of them and I don't lose sleep over where they belong. They're here, they bear watching, and now that they're stuck here with us they suddenly all get along with each other. That's never a good sign, if you ask me."

"Is that your captain there?" Seth asked.

The soldier turned to see a uniformed man at the opening of one of the evac shelters set up to divide the cavernous hangar and contain the heat generated by small portables. He stood with hands on hips, watching them by the door. "Aye," the lieutenant said and spat close enough by Ciela's feet to earn her most irate glare. "We've to thank him for ordering us to Tor Ag when he did. Could have stayed healthier on Callas."

Ciela checked her scanner when they left the guards to enter the shed, holding it up as if exploring their new environment. "Neither of them are Dyads, if we're going by that Alpha resonance," she reported.

Weak pockets of light illuminated the interior of the hangar where groups of castaways gathered to share warmth, a little food and conversation. More of the evac shelters lined the far wall; in other areas pallets were set up among crates and ration bins of the sort stocked by long distance transports. This too, looked like a camp that had been run for a while.

"Why don't they just stay on their ships?" Ciela said.

"No idea. Although some of the long distance haulers I've seen are not the sort of ship you want to spend a lot of time in. Maybe that tub in orbit is an immigrant transport. They're not fun."

Ciela nodded politely, in a reserved Delphian sort of way, when the Air Command captain walked toward them. The Human's uniform collar was unbuttoned despite the cold air and looked in need of cleaning. The rolled-up sleeves and grime-covered hands made it clear that he had joined his squad in maintaining their camp of castaways.

He stopped to scrutinize them as if trying to look beyond their bland greeting. "New arrivals?" he said.

"Seems that way," Seth said, feeling Ciela's hand on his back, informing him that this officer, too, came up negative on her scanner. "It's been a confusing few hours."

"No doubt! Some of us have been here for three weeks, Targon time. I'm Captain Thierry Bryn, out of Base Callas. Got caught up in this thing when we got reports of some overdue transports. I guess you could say we found them." He didn't bother to hide his visual survey of their weapons. "I'm not interested in dealing with rebel nonsense."

"We're not rebels," Seth said, although the officer had little cause to believe him. "We're looking for someone that got lost in that span."

The captain waved them inside one of the shelters, a simple knockdown box made of plastics. Some storage crates served as furniture and several pallets lined the walls. On one of them, a Human woman sat with her legs drawn up and her head lowered onto her knees, arms wrapped around them. She did not look up.

Bryn gestured for them to sit on the crates. "Starting to feel like home." He grunted as he also sat, perhaps in pain, or perhaps just relieved to be off his feet. "We haven't seen new ships coming through in a few days now. I thought perhaps this madness was over. Our probes still show a whole lot of turbulence at the keyhole. I was about to send someone up to try to take another run at it."

Ciela shook her head. "Don't bother," she said. Seth noticed her effort to remain civil in the officer's presence. Although she had now worked with him for a year or more, she had not lost her contempt for the Commonwealth expansions or her distrust of anyone in uniform. Usually she just ignored them. "The keyhole is still exhibiting that anomaly."

The woman on the pallet mumbled a monotonous stream of words, apparently directed at no one. Seth thought he recognized a Human language that was rarely heard in Trans-Targon.

He peered out of the open door before leaning closer to the captain. "My name is Kada, special ops. We are here by orders of Colonel Carras, Targon," he said, barely audible.

"Investigating the disappearance of these ships. We are also looking for a passenger aboard one of the vessels."

Bryn looked from one to the other, clearly not convinced. "Targon?"

"Yes. Be assured they're working on finding a solution. They've even turned to the Delphians for support. They'll get here long before any rebels bother to look for their people."

"You're here on purpose, then? Or just really reckless?"

"Both, actually," Seth said. "The keyhole failure may not be a random or even natural anomaly." He glanced at the catatonic woman. "We know about the changes some of the survivors have experienced. It is a…" He paused, looking for the simplest version of this without revealing too much. "It's a sort of infestation. An alien parasite. When they have merged with a sentient host we call them Dyads. Targon wants to avoid importing it into Trans-Targon."

"And we're infected?" The captain's expression suggested that he understood well that his chance of returning to Trans-Targon had suddenly diminished.

"Those who are will know by now. And it's not contagious. I'm guessing you've noticed unusual behavior among some of the survivors?"

Bryn nodded and tipped his head toward the woman. "Varying degrees of it. We've got a transport in orbit where a dozen or so crewmen are being cared for. The med team reports extreme stress responses, psychosis, a few of them in some sort of stupor. Hallucinations, hearing voices, talking to invisible spooks. Dozens have died. We don't know why."

"They were all linked to their ships during the jump? Pilots? Engineers? Com officers?"

The captain shifted over to crouch beside the woman on the makeshift bed. "Yes. This is my com officer." He raised his hand, hesitating briefly before touching her hair. She flinched but then allowed the contact. It was not the touch of a senior officer and the pain and concern on his face told the story. "Larris?" he said gently. "Are you here today?"

"What's wrong with her?" Ciela whispered.

Seth sighed. "I've seen this. They're not... not suitable, I guess. Or something happened during the merge." He nudged her with his elbow. "You could try to take a look."

She gasped. "I don't know..."

Bryn also turned to her. "You're Delphian. You've got the..." He searched for words that would show neither his ignorance nor his prejudice of Delphian abilities. Like most of their society, the extent of those talents was shrouded in mystery and the subject of a ridiculous amount of nearly superstitious speculation. "Could you help her?"

"I'm not trained as a healer," she objected. "I don't know if there is anything I can do. This isn't even something we know anything about."

"Just take a look," Seth said. "They can't hurt you."

She looked down at her hands and then finally nodded. The captain moved aside when she came to sit beside the woman whose voice had dropped to a mere whisper. Slowly, she reached out, stroking back the dark hair until she found the officer's neural node above her ear. With another glance at Seth, she touched the implant and closed her eyes.

"Think it'll help?" the captain said.

Seth touched a finger to his lips and watched as Ciela attempted to connect with the woman. He never failed to be awed by this gift shared by all Delphians, hinting at greater things for the rest of the Prime species as they continued to evolve. He had spent years of his life, alone aboard his *Dutchman* before Ciela joined him, studying the interconnected Prime species of Trans-Targon. He learned their languages rather than rely on his translator, studied their customs, history and politics, making him not only a valuable mercenary and sometime profiteer, but also an expert xenologist. This education had served him well over the years. To be able to work and travel freely among the intriguing species that populated this sector was, to him, a privilege as well as a profession. Ciela shared this passion, unaware that her own species held the greatest fascination for him.

She stared at nothing for a long while, a small groove etched between her brows. Time passed in silence until, at last, the Human raised her head. Ciela guided her gently to lie down on the pallet and waited until the woman closed her eyes before breaking their mental link.

"A lot of noise in her head," she said, still looking at nothing. Seth knew that by now she would be suffering a headache. "I think I saw… it. It felt like a small animal in a cage. Frightened. Wanting to get out. Not understanding how it got there." She looked up at Seth. "Alone."

He put his arm around her shoulders when she moved over to sit beside him again. "She looks calmer."

"Yes, I think I was able to let her know she'll be fine. The thing inside her head slowed down, somehow." She glanced at the captain. "She's pregnant. That might have confused the entity trying to merge."

Seth exhaled sharply but decided not to voice his opinion of people who needlessly took their unborn into subspace.

The captain dropped his head to run both hands over his shaved pate, unsurprised by Ciela's announcement. "Will she be all right?"

Seth looked at their expectant faces for a moment before shaking his head. "I don't think so. I'm sorry, Captain, but none of the failed mergers survived. If the entity dies, so will the host. If we could get her to a Shantir, maybe something can be done. We know it's possible to separate the Dyad again but it's not clear how. There are some theories."

"How do you know all this?"

"It happened before. Most of it is classified."

Bryn's head snapped back. "Classified? How about a little warning? How about letting us know about subspace creatures ripping your brain to shreds when they don't like it there? Your damn special ops and your damn secrets…" He closed his eyes in some attempt to recapture his composure. "I'm tired," he said by way of apology. "Damn tired."

"We'll get out," Ciela said. "Air Command's working on

it. Targon is working on it."

The captain barked a short laugh. "Out of here? Is that likely?"

"We have to believe that," Ciela said.

Bryn looked from one to the other. "You do, huh? Is that why you're here? To lead us all home again?"

"Well, no," she said, shaking off the gentle tone as if she suddenly remembered that she was talking to an Air Command officer. "We're looking for a Union biologist. Her name is Lara Hedvig. Human, about, uh, forty, blond going gray. Thin. She'd look ill or exhausted."

The captain pondered this for a while and then shook his head. "No one comes to mind. She might be aboard the transport. We transferred some of the sick up there with our medics to look after them." He scratched several days' growth on his cheek. "It hard to keep track of the survivors. We've lost a few people since we got here. Struck out on their own, maybe, if they're short a few brain cells. Or maybe just in the whorehouse down the canyon way. Some we're suspecting of being rebels seem to be falling into their own groups." He cursed softly. "All I need is for Shri-Lan to start pushing back. Like alien parasites aren't enough to deal with."

"How long can you hold this together?" Seth asked, meaning the camp.

The captain shook his head like a man out of options, hope and strength. "Not had to deal with this before. My crew's been pretty good following protocol. Most of the civilians are allowing that. For now. We're trying to work with the locals to find ways to deal with the extra population here. Things are tight. Supplies won't last for long but we have water here. Looks like some of the vegetation is edible, if you like chewing sticks. The next supply convoy from Mrak isn't due for three months and I'm starting to think they're not going to make it."

Seth nodded, reading the signs of exhaustion on the man's face. From the looks of the camp, so far his leadership skills had served him well in keeping this motley collection of survivors out of trouble. But he had seen places like these, where those with nothing in common needed more than Air Command crisis management training to keep from murdering each other over the least provocation. Isolation and lack of essentials challenged even the most prepared outpost community. And having a bunch of bored rebels among them would not help matters.

"How many here can we suspect of being Dyads?" he asked.

"I don't know. Some of them are visibly affected. Others just seem a little odd but we're all dealing with stress here. But people are starting to look each other with distrust. Fear, even."

"We have to keep in mind that the turbulence at the keyhole may well be a temporary phenomenon," Seth said. "The Dyad formation might just be a side effect of that. You continue to send probes?"

"Yes, and we've got a research vessel here. They've set up an observatory in the lowlands trying to get a grip on it. There must be a reason for the keyhole to act this way."

"Observatory? On the surface?" Seth asked.

"Maybe our doctor is there," Ciela said.

The captain shrugged. "Worth checking out. Targon sent them. Astrophysics, as I understand it. They've been here longer than any of us. They must have known something was going to happen with that keyhole. Some others joined them since." He tapped his data sleeve and squinted at it. "The engineer of the second transport. A missionary from Feyd." He rolled his eyes to show his opinion of missionaries jaunting around rebel-infested sub-sectors. "Some others. I've lost track. But I've sent a few of my men to keep them safe."

"Any ideas what they're doing out there?"

"None. We're staying out of their way. I've given them one of our long-range scanners and as much thorium and coolant as we can spare. They seem to be bouncing some signals off the transport in orbit. I just hope they come up with something helpful soon."

"Are any of them acting... differently? Showing any odd behavior?"

Captain Bryn looked up with narrowed eyes. "You think they might have been infected?"

"It's possible. Anyone with a neural implant could be. Some might hide it."

"Dangerous?"

Seth glanced at Ciela. "Some of them can be. They can augment the host body in some ways. The Dyads take on the host's personality. Or certain aspects of them. Attitudes, intellect. If any of our rebel friends are affected they won't be the friendly sort of Dyad. I'd be careful when dealing with any that seem hostile."

The captain snarled. "I have no appetite for exercising group dynamics, Kada. We have rebels here in camp, along with pirates and whatever trash was floating around that span. So far they're behaving because they understand that they better get along. If a bunch of aliens now want to cause trouble I've got a gun for that."

"Right," Seth said and came to his feet. "We'll nose around a bit."

"Be sure not to interfere with them. Or with Queta Station. All I want is to have as many folks alive as possible by the time someone gets here. Are we clear on that part?"

"Clear." Ciela also rose and pulled her scarf over her head before checking the weapon at her hip.

"You're not taking the girl, are you?" the captain said.

Seth caught Ciela's arm when she rounded on the officer, irked by his comment. "The *woman*," he said before she could voice her opinion, "can trim your eyebrows with that knife of hers before you even see her move. I try to stay on her good side whenever possible."

The officer looked from him to Ciela. Something in the blue eyes blazing defiance at him made him shrug. "Not my business, I guess."

SIX

The two guards at the hangar door greeted Seth and Ciela with broad and unpleasant smirks. "Looks like you're contributing to the cause," the Feydan said and gestured toward the motley collection of ships parked near the camp.

The *Dutchman* seemed to have drawn the attention of several individuals now standing near its gate. Someone else was crouched beneath the landing structure, a common location for a secondary hatch on ships of this class.

"What are they doing?" Ciela said as they hurried toward the ship. A skimmer was parked nearby, watched over by a hulking Mraki male. A few others slouched at the north end of the parking area as if to guard the town from the newcomers stranded here. Their layers of patched and ill-used clothes looked improvised from whatever materials were on hand. Seth supposed the only way to distinguish the prisoners from the guards was to look for their weapons.

"Looting, I guess," he said, noticing a small cart among them. "Not that they have the means to actually get inside." He had to reconsider that statement when a worrying thought struck him. "Unless they're Dyads. If so, there isn't much that can stop them."

Ciela drew her gun as they approached. "Step away from that," she snapped, aiming at a woman who was busy tapping the cargo gate's key plate. Two people nearby also raised their weapons, apparently prepared for a confrontation.

Seth put a hand on Ciela's arm until she lowered her gun. "We weren't expecting visitors," he said, keeping his tone carefully neutral.

A Centauri in soot-stained coveralls stepped forward. The shift of his eyes reflected nervous flickers of violet light in the near dark. "You best put that gun away. We're here by orders of Queta Station's directors. All visitors are to relinquish unnecessary thorium and all coolant to the Targon team for their work. We'll need to take a look at your accelerator as well."

Seth bent to peer beneath the *Dutchman*'s belly to see that the Human under there also had no success with breaking into the ship. "Seeing how I can't fly my ship without the cubes, I'd say they're fairly necessary."

"You don't even have a full crew. If we get back to civilization you can ride aboard the transport. That's why they're called transports. They need more power out there at the site, so we're collecting it." The Centauri gestured an invitation for Seth to open the *Dutchman*'s gate. The gun in his hand suggested that he did not expect him to decline.

Seth pushed the long lapels of his coat aside when he put his hands on his hips. "Going to shoot me? You can't get into this boat unless you lob something big enough at it to make a mess of my drives and the thorium in them."

Ciela shifted restlessly as everyone stood around and stared angrily for a while. Finally, one of the men, a pale Human wearing a long Caspian kilt, reached out for her arm. "We'll take the girl till you change your mind," he said with an unpleasant sneer.

Seth's arm shot out to grasp his throat, slamming him back against the *Dutchman*'s gate with a hollow bong. His other hand whipped forward to thrust a pistol under their leader's nose. "Don't move even one degree," he said. The others stared, stunned, at the smear of blood on the door when Seth let the Human drop to the ground.

"Let me talk to your bosses," Seth said.

"Easy, Centauri," a woman among them said. "No need to get hostile. They're busy."

"Unbusy them." Seth forced the man at the end of his gun back until he, too, was pinned to the *Dutchman*.

"Go, dammit," the Centauri said. Blood flowed from his nose under the pressure of Seth's barrel. "What are you standing around for?"

The woman offered an angry glare but then turned and stomped off to their skimmer. The others moved away also, leaving their cart behind.

Seth glanced at the gore on the *Dutchman*'s gate. "I really don't like people touching my ship," he said to his victim.

Ciela watched the crew now standing around the air car, visibly arguing. "I don't like giving up thorium."

Seth relaxed his gun a little. "Why do they need so much power?" he said.

The crew leader grunted something that might have been a curse. "Don't know."

"They took everyone's?"

"Not Air Command's. Just the private ships. You might as well give them up now. It's the only thing that'll get you food here. Unless you work the mines." He nodded to Ciela. "Or her."

Seth heard something like a low growl coming from Ciela but she said nothing. "They're taking coolant, too?"

"That, too."

Ciela turned when the woman among the ground crew returned to them.

"Got your wish, Pilot," she said when she reached them. "You're expected up there." She pointed up along the canyon wall. "That catwalk'll take you to the bridge. Don't go inside the mines. Don't talk to the workers. Boss is waiting for you at the top. He says he doesn't appreciate you giving his crew a hard time."

"Then maybe you shouldn't try boarding ships without asking nicely," Seth said and shoved the man with the bloody nose toward her. "Take that with you," he added, pointing with his gun to the unconscious Human on the ground.

Ciela hurried after him as he strode away, her eyes on the proximity scanner at her wrist. None of the ground crew followed. As Seth hoped, the job didn't seem important enough for them to collect more damage on their quest for spare parts.

"It's scary how quick you are," Ciela said. "I didn't even see you move. Considering those gangly legs of yours, you might be defying some laws of nature."

"Gangly?" He looked up a narrow metal stairway leading in precarious switchbacks to the top of the cliff. At intervals, wider landings accommodated the ore carts hauled away along cables and rails to the depot. He motioned her to walk ahead of him. "I prefer to think I'm elegantly proportioned."

"Why are we going up there?" she said. "Are you sure they can't get into the *Dutchman*?"

"A Dyad could. Did you get any readings from those thugs?"

"Nothing. They're all clear. I've also scanned some of the others in range. I don't think there are very many Dyads here at all."

"I wonder what Targon team everyone keeps talking about. Did Caelyn mention any crew from there?"

"No. He said a research vessel is assumed lost, but it belongs to Azon Corp. Targon barely allowed us to jump out here. Someone would have said something if they'd sent a team already. Caelyn would have known, I'm sure."

They stopped to make room for a trio of miners shoving their cart of greenish ore onto one of the platforms. In other worlds these functions were automated, reducing the size of work-crews to technicians monitoring from a safe distance. In a penal colony, Seth supposed, efficiency was hardly the main priority. "See if you can hack into whatever mainframe they have here. Grab whatever is most encrypted. I want to get something we can use as leverage to keep the *Dutchman* in one piece." He walked close to her to steer her up the uneven treads, allowing her to work with her data sleeve. "I might be pretty," he sighed. "But you've got the brains, lady."

She glanced up at him, pleased by the peculiar compliment. "Only for numbers," she said. "And you're definitely not prettier than me."

"Leave me my conceits, please."

She winked and returned her attention to her work, walking ahead of him. They collected suspicious looks, and heads turned to watch them as they passed but Seth supposed that, short of some sort of armed conflict, no one really had any grasp on who bore watching around here. The raw shriek of someone in sudden pain echoed up from a lower level, immediately silenced again. Seth looked down to see a guard hurry along a catwalk but no one else, including Ciela, paid much attention. They moved at a steady pace and were out of breath when they reached the top of the canyon wall.

"I'm not good with heights," Ciela said when Seth stepped out onto a narrow walkway spanning the chasm. She peered over the edge and then quickly closed her eyes.

He bounced lightly on the balls of his feet, grinning when she gasped and gripped a handrail. "I've been watching people cross this thing. It seems safe."

"You said that tavern in Talan An was safe, too. You ended up with a broken clavicle."

"I did not start that fight."

She experimented by putting one foot onto the bridge. It did not sway but the wind cut through the metal supports like the strings of an instrument, if far less melodious.

"Want me to carry you?"

"And that's safer?" She took a deep breath and walked toward him, her eyes on his face.

He moved backwards until she seemed comfortable and then led them across at a quick pace. What seemed less safe was a hulking tank of a Mraki waiting for them on the other side. Seth relied on speed and technique to overcome his opponents in close combat. Neither of these would have much impact on the unmovable force glaring at them through a burnoose wrapped around his head.

"Take me to your leader," Seth said, saluting in the peculiar way of the Caspians.

The guard refused to be amused by Seth's antics. "That way." He pointed to their left. "Gray building at the top with two lights out front."

"What isn't gray here," Seth murmured to Ciela as they continued, the guard walking close behind. "Did you get anything useful?"

She nodded, shivering in the sharp breeze, and pulled her thick cloak more tightly around herself. It was also gray, as were her trousers and the weapon at her side. Someday a vacation somewhere pretty was definitely called for, he contemplated, out of habit scanning the cliff for cameras, weapons and com gear. Blue skies in place of this dull cloud cover, green fields and forests, like those of Feyd or Magra, would do both of them much good.

He shook his head to rid himself of his sentimental woolgathering when they came to a plateau just below the rim of the canyon. A row of pre-fab buildings, mere boxes with openings for doors and windows, lined the wall here. Some of them were stacked atop others to create multi-story dwellings, like those they had seen on the valley floor. It seemed that these were of better quality. Above them, but still within the shelter of the rock walls, a receiver and other com gear told that this area also housed the town's communication and traffic control station.

Instead of being allowed inside, they stopped when a short Human emerged, clothed in all-weather gear that was probably as warm as it was expensive, followed by two women. They recognized one of them as Lieutenant Zire, who had greeted them earlier today. The Human didn't look overly pleased by this meeting. Although he reached barely to Seth's elbow, he drew himself up as if ready for some physical confrontation.

"We're all very busy up here," he said, dispensing with greetings. "Too busy to deal with refugees. Captain Bryn is managing the situation quite efficiently, including complaints about our hospitality."

"Your hospitality includes stealing vital components from our ships?" Seth said.

"Captain Bryn should have informed you. I'll ask Lieutenant Zire to remind him that we will expect cooperation from everyone here. And that means contributing what is needed to help us though this crisis." He gestured down toward the landing area. "Your assault on my ground crew is uncalled-for. We have enough capable planes to evacuate everyone when the time comes."

"Air Command ships," Seth said.

The Human struggled to keep a few long wisps of hair from blowing around his otherwise bald head. "Our relationship with Air Command, here at Queta Station, is valued, as always. All of us are aware that their authority is what keeps us safe for now."

"Why do they need so much thorium?"

"To restore our contact with Trans-Targon of course. One of their science vessels arrived here about three months ago, Targon time. They brought specific orders with them that Queta Station is to offer every support. Said that the keyhole had become unstable, whatever that means. They set up some sort of experiment to the east, so that didn't bother us. They keep to themselves. But when all these other ships started to come we found that the keyhole isn't even working."

Seth frowned. "It took you that long to notice?"

The man's arm swept over the canyon. "We have little to do with the outside world. Every six months we get new supplies, new prisoners, and we send back our products and rotate our personnel. Even that is expensive. No one is due to return to the Mrak sector for months."

"So that research crew out there has requested thorium and coolant from the lost ships?"

"Where else would they find that? Our power supply here is limited. Fissile thorium is expensive. We augment what we can with wind turbines on the surface."

Seth glanced at the lieutenant and then tilted his body toward the Human. "Can we speak privately?" he said with a wag of his brow toward the officer.

"What?" the director said, looking around. "Well, all right. But make it fast. I have a mine to run."

Not really caring what the Dyad heard, Seth led the man further along the cliff, away from the ledge to keep the guards from worrying too much. "I suggest a trade," he said.

"Oh?"

Seth nodded to Ciela.

She smiled sweetly. "Mister Shild, you're mining twenty percent more rhodium than you've reported to the mine's investors. It's going to Magra to fund rebel operations out of Torley. You've recently discovered gold and are diverting some of the operation to reach those deposits. Your remaining personal wealth is gleaned from reselling materials and supplies meant for the prisoners sent here by Mraki and Aikhor governors."

"Those are lies!" the director exclaimed.

"Would be a shame if Captain Bryn or Lieutenant Zire were made aware of those lies," Seth said. "Not worth a few more cubes for your little science project, is it?"

Shild glared from Seth to Ciela for a moment before stomping back to his guards. "Let them keep their ship," he snapped.

"Director," Seth caught up to him. "We'd like to visit that science team. Did you say they're east of here?"

Shild was already heading for the shelter of the administrative building. "Yes. There's nothing there for you, but do what you like. Just look for their energy emissions. They've got some sort of transmitter out there."

Seth watched him go, amused by the man's temper. "Nice work," he said to Ciela.

When they turned to walk back to the bridge they found

that Lieutenant Zire had remained behind. "I wonder if you could lend a hand," she said. She pointed to a path leading upward. "There are some skimmers up there you can use to reach the site. The energy emissions out there are unannounced and unpredictable so taking your ship out there wouldn't be wise. We have some supplies ready to be delivered. If you like, you can use that skimmer to take it to them."

"Thank you," Seth said.

She walked with them along the steep trail. "We really can't spare any of our troops to make delivery runs, so you'll be doing us a favor. You're with Air Command, are you not?"

He smiled. "How did you guess?"

"We've already taken a look at your ship. It's got secrets you don't find aboard a smuggler's vessel. I'm sorry that the ground crew overstepped their assignment."

Seth peered at her. "What is going on here, Lieutenant?"

Her gaze shifted but she managed a puzzled expression. "Just what you see. An emergency. We're doing our best to manage it. Queta Station has been less than welcoming but at least they consider us the lesser evil over some of the crews that have been landing here. Their cooperation, such as it is, is important to our safety and the work being done at the site."

"What *is* being done out there?"

"I'm assuming they're trying to clear out that turbulence or whatever has happened in subspace."

"You do not know?" he said, somewhat pointedly.

Zire hesitated. "No, I do not," she said at last.

She remained silent until they reached the top of the canyon wall. A brisk wind moved over the featureless surface, powering turbines and blasting them with gusts of fine grit. The colorless ground undulated in edgeless swells and channels scoured by the ceaseless abrasion of dusty air. A cluster of parked skimmers huddled in the lee of ventilation conduits rising from the ground, looking as utilitarian and misused as all of the equipment they'd seen here so far. Two unmarked cases were already stowed aboard one of them. Zire pointed downhill. "Follow the canyon edge to the lowlands, past the airfield. Then just head east. You won't miss them."

* * *

Ciela turned on the skimmer's noisy heater the moment the vehicle's dome closed over them. "Think she's lying?"

"I do." Seth let the skimmer rise from the ground. He steered away from the dreary mining town to follow the canyon as instructed. He heard Ciela take a deep breath as if the open space here offered a physical relief from the oppression below. Strange, he thought, given that both of them spent much of their time confined on his small ship. But he felt it, too, and he let the skimmer cruise at top speed away from the edge of the canyon toward a horizon so unobstructed that he could see its curvature.

They did not need their scanners to find the location of the research team. Indicators on the skimmer's panel warned of energy fluctuations that would soon force them to continue their journey on foot. It also warned of abandoned test pits and boreholes as well as geothermal taps left unmarked and unguarded. Seth engaged the ground sensors to search below the surface for anything that might trip up the skimmer.

"I wonder why they've set up so remotely," he said. "And not on high ground. The com station back there would have made a better platform, if they're looking at the sky."

"Interference from all that machinery maybe," she guessed.

They drove in comfortable silence across the flat, featureless expanse of rock and dried mud flats that sloped like frozen rivers toward the lowlands. Chitta Moor had no oceans but surface water existed, as did a network of underground aquifers, giving life to tough grasses and the occasional thick-stemmed shrub. Some parts of the planet offered more fertile environments. This was not one of them.

New readings forced Seth to swing around the north side of the source of the emissions to avoid some of the radiation drifting south. None of it registered as harmful to living beings but the unshielded electronics on this vessel would not deal well with it. Before giving up on its job, the ground scanner warned of a large depression just ahead of them.

Once parked, Seth unfastened the cases from their restraints, glad to have another excuse to come out this way. They walked to the edge of the drop to look down into a vast cauldron. Old tracks led from here into the pit and equipment sat abandoned along the way. A lake at the bottom of the crater reflected the gray sky, and taller vegetation crowded the rock-strewn shore. The hulls of three interstellar cruisers sat near the rim, apparently being dismantled for some purpose. It was not difficult to spot the research vessel perched on the opposite side of the hole. The Outrider class served as a smaller scout version of the mobile labs used by deep-space researchers. This gleaming specimen did not look abandoned and they saw two people near its open gate.

"Tapped-out surface mine, I'm guessing," Seth said, looking down.

Ciela checked for information on her sleeve. "That water is deep. Cold." She hummed to herself. "Too cold for what's around here, so that explains that pressing need for coolant. There's something at the bottom."

He looked at her wrist, at first not sure what he was seeing but the data was coming together despite the interference. "That's a ship. In the water."

She nodded. "Powered up, too. Think they crashed into there?"

"Not with this much precision. It's almost the size of this pit. It would have come down vertical to land right side up."

"Who would put a ship on the bottom of a lake?"

"Not Targon." He gestured to the Outrider parked on the

other side of the pit. "That ship isn't out of Targon. Astrophysics would have UCB symbols on the crossdrives. It's not Delphian, either. Delphi uses Union-owned ships."

"Look, people down that way. Near the water."

He set the crates on the ground and placed a scanner over his eyes to survey the cauldron. "Someone by those shrubs," he said. "Three heat signatures, near that outcropping with the pink rocks."

"Another one over there," Ciela said, also looking through her eyepiece.

Seth's sensors swept the valley to look for anything out of the ordinary for the terrain. He pointed across the lake. "Something mechanical over there, by the shore. Could just be for water purification. Not operational. At least I'm not getting any energy readings from it." But when he continued his scan, this no longer seemed likely. "And another. No, two more."

She had found them, too. "Evenly spaced around the lake. Could be some sort of lifting device to get the ship back out. Or maybe that's how they dropped it in."

"Maybe," he said, not convinced. "Those turret things look more like transmitters."

Two more shapes moved among the rocks. Nothing about their movements seemed furtive. Apparently, no one here worried about anyone watching from the sidelines.

She indicated the Outrider across the mine. "Should we go talk to them?"

Seth picked up the crates again and looked down along the slope to find a safe path to the water's edge. "Nah, let's pretend we didn't see them. I want to look at one of those contraptions before we need to apply for a guided tour."

"You think they're up to something they shouldn't?"

"I always think that. Step carefully. The slope looks pretty loose. Don't look like you're trying to hide."

She grinned. "Tourist mode active."

They scrambled down the steep side of the hill, at times reaching for rocks and undergrowth to keep from slipping, until they reached level ground. The bottom of the valley presented a challenge of broken boulders from a long-ago slide. Their scanners sorted organic from synthetic substances to lead them to one of the devices near the water.

"Quick," he said.

Ciela circled the mechanism, tapping her lips with a finger as she identified its components from memory. "Union issue. Those conduits could be from anywhere but the shield wraps are from a Trident cruiser." She looked up at what they assumed to be a transmitter. "Those look an awful lot like cannons from a Titan class transport."

He nodded. Titans tended to carry only minimum armament designed to ward off pirates or even debris as they delivered cargo and passengers. The laser cannons were crude but effective. "That grid there is for plasma conversion."

"Yep." She whistled and crouched on her heels to take a closer look at a bank of gray boxes, designed to be replaced without having to be opened. "Not just one, but six thorium cubes. That's some power they're playing with."

Seth switched his scanner. "No leaks," he said, relieved.

Ciela tried to get past the access panel but finally shook her head. "Locked up tight. Nice work."

"Look over there," he said.

She straightened up and lowered the visor over her eyes again. The three people he had detected earlier stood at the shore, one of them dressed in a pressure suit, the sort kept aboard any interstellar vessel. The nicknamed weather gear was used to avoid contamination in hostile environments and could even be used for short spacewalks if necessary. By removing excess air from the interior, it could also serve to protect the wearer in a liquid environment. They watched the person in the suit walk into the water and disappear below the surface.

"Isn't that interesting," Seth said.

"Someone's coming. Looks like they spotted us."

A woman walked toward them, picking her way over the

boulders strewn along the shore. A tall man, possibly Feydan, followed her. "I think that's the doctor."

"Oh, that's good news. She made it."

"She shouldn't be hurrying like that," Seth said, remembering that the woman had barely stood steady on her feet when they last saw her on Tor Ag.

The doctor reached them just a few minutes later, a happy smile on her face. "Sethran," she said. "Ciela. I thought that was you! I'm so glad to see you safe. And sorry to see you here at all. It's quite a situation we've found ourselves."

"Isn't it," he said, peering into her face when she pushed back the hood of her jacket. She was flushed from the scramble but it was a healthy dose of color. The dark smudges beneath her eyes were gone and she stood firmly on the uneven ground. "You look well," he added, a question in his tone.

"Yes! What luck that we have a science vessel among us. Their med lab is outstanding. I'm practically one hundred percent again."

"I'm glad to hear that," Ciela said doubtfully. She tapped her data sleeve to run a medical check. Hedvig indulged her. A brief glance at Ciela's display told Seth that the doctor was no longer merely Human. The man who had followed her also came into scanner range but had no words of greeting for them, not unusual for a Feydan among strangers.

"This is Skoth. He's been a great help to the team," Hedvig said.

Seth nodded to the Feydan and received little in reply. The man's bronzed and tattooed skin bore scars spanning many years, some embellished by more drawings, more recent ones obscured older writings. One of his eyes had a strange cast, as if artificial. Seth put a hand on Ciela's shoulder to draw her attention. She looked up from her work to study the man, her eyes on the tattooed tales decorating his neck and face.

"What are you doing all the way out here?" Seth gestured

over the water. "It's safer in the camp, don't you think?"

"Oh, we're quite safe, have no fear."

He tipped his head meaningfully toward the cobbled-together piece of machinery not far behind them, waiting for her to answer his question.

She smiled. "We've got some ideas about calming the interference at the keyhole," she said. "It may not work. But we must try, don't we?"

"You'd need an awful lot of energy to even reach it from here, never mind open it," Ciela said. "How is this thing going to work?"

"I don't know!" Hedvig's laughter seemed forced and a little nervous. "So far we're just experimenting with various wave forms. There is something about that ship they drowned down there. I'm no expert."

"Do you need help? Ciela is a wiz with most processors."

"Oh, no, we have experts. Engineers, the research team, and an Air Command pilot with an interest in astrophysics. I'm probably the odd one out, just being a biologist. But I suppose someone needs to make sure we don't eat the wrong things out here. All I know is that we need a whole lot more thorium for the next shot at that keyhole."

"Queta sent this for you." Seth gestured to the cases they had brought. "Are you sure you're all right? Nothing unusual? The voyage here must have been stressful."

"All is well," she insisted, quite firmly. "That pirate crew did not mistreat me. They had me resting and hooked up to a medical monitor when we made the jump to whatever this place is." She looked from him to Ciela. "There is nothing to worry about," she said.

Seth felt Ciela's eyes on him, waiting for direction. He looked out over the water, an unmoving, dark surface where not even insects darted the way insects tended to. The air lay still on his ears but something reverberated through the silence that he had not noticed before. Something from the ship down in the water perhaps. He looked back at the doctor and decided she was lying.

"I suppose this is more interesting than what's going on in that miserable camp," he said lightly. "In a way I envy you out here, with your project. Others seem to be suffering with boredom as much as the dread of being stuck out here."

"Yes, we're comfortable here. There is room for us to overnight in that ship. I'll put together a report for the officers looking after the camp about possible edible plants out here. I've already identified several. It will help."

"I'm sure it'll be appreciated."

She smiled her nervous smile again and half-turned away from them already. "Please stay optimistic. We are doing all we can to get off this planet. We'll send word soon."

Seth nodded. "Just call if you need help with your invention. Surely you can use extra hands?"

"We may," she said and began to make her way back along the shore.

The Feydan finally spoke up. "That's a fine weapon." He gestured to Seth's sidearm. "Air Command issue, isn't it?" His question seemed to suggest more than just the gun was military issue here.

"Borrowed it," Seth said.

Skoth looked more closely at Ciela. "The female is Delphian?"

She returned his gaze without flinching. Her eyes scanned over the tightly packed tattoos describing, in words and images, his deeds and affiliations. "That is correct. I see your pledge to the Pyron, Kytra Skoth. Your clan is well known to my friends on Tadonna, and some will remember your presence on Ganbel Nine."

Seth stifled a smile when the Feydan stepped back from her, his head lowered. By mentioning those names, she had let him know that she recognized him as a Shri-Lan rebel and that she was quite capable of deciphering the complex Feydan language system. The standoff at Ganbel had just recently brought Shri-Lan and Arawaj rebels together for one of their uneasy alliances.

"It is an old clan," he mumbled. "And well-traveled."

Seth waved casually and motioned to Ciela to walk ahead of him, back up the steep incline to their skimmer.

"What's on your mind," she said when they reached the top. "Why didn't you ask the doctor about the Dyads? Aren't we're going to take her with us?"

Seth looked back across the pit to the science vessel parked there. "That Fedan's a Dyad, too, isn't he? Why would Doctor Helvig not tell us about being a Dyad? She's an exobiologist. You don't get more exo than that. She should be pretty excited about sharing that. Something's not right here. She knows damn well what they're up to. Wave forms? Even she'd be more precise than that."

SEVEN

Something had changed in the mining town when they returned to the confines of the camp. The distant clank and thunder of the operation continued but fewer people walked about and fires had been lit along the river. As if someone had called it a night, Seth thought, although the sun had not moved much since they arrived. The planet's slow rotation was at odds with most Prime species' natural cycle and here, like elsewhere, people had to set their own clocks. And here, also, telling night from day was done by mutual agreement.

They made their way back to the *Dutchman*, eager to leave this dank wasteland for the cluttered and cozy confines of their ship and their bed. Seth ached for a hot bath, an indulgence often mocked by Ciela who cared nothing about such luxury, as long as it resulted in cleanliness. The steam cycle aboard the *Dutchman* would have to do. He decided not to think about the possibility that they, too, were stuck on this dismal rock and might soon have to do without it. The ribbon of water trickling along beside them did not inspire thoughts of bathing or staying healthfully hydrated, for that matter.

"What?" Ciela said when he tugged on her arm to stop her.

"I'm getting Alpha readings but they're really hard to

pinpoint. Let's take a look over there." Seth nodded toward the river he had just viewed with a skeptical eye. Some of the castaways, perhaps unwilling to live under the watchful eye of Air Command inside the hangar, had set up their camp there. "See if we can find more Dyads."

"Now?" she replied but changed direction away from the ships and to the bank.

"Sleepy?"

"I can put in a day's work as much as you can, Kada," she said. "But how tired do you want me to be at the end of it, that's my question."

"We'll hurry," he said, answering her lewd grin with one of his own.

They found a fire burning unattended and paused there to look around the people huddled on a patch of meager grassland near the river. None wore the colors of their respective rebel factions but here, as elsewhere, the Shri-Lan would dominate their less powerful rival gangs. There were others, too: civilians untrained and in despair, Air Command soldiers looking for drink or women, outlaws equally armed and preferring the dark.

"This is going to get ugly," Seth said, his head turned toward Ciela but his eyes on the camp beyond her shoulder.

"It's ugly now." She peered up at the hulking, twisted shapes of the mining superstructure climbing the canyon walls.

"When supplies start running low people are going to turn on each other, if not before. There aren't enough soldiers here to keep running the place like it says in the manual."

"Nothing to do in this place but wait for rescue." She watched a small company of men loitering by a fire, by the sound of their voices inebriated. A Centauri among them laughed and slapped another's shoulder hard enough to shove him off his camp chair. The man's foot landed in the embers and his curses rang in their ears. "You think some of these are Dyads? Don't they care who they inhabit?"

"They don't have a choice. And they're as limited as their hosts, so this wouldn't seem odd to them. It's their life now. They'd be careful about hiding their new state, I guess. Like Doctor Hedvig did. You don't want to start acting peculiar when everyone's already on edge."

"Well, that whole Dyad thing is kind of creepy." She smirked. "Not you, of course. I'm sure you weren't creepy at all when you were one of them."

"I probably was." Something caught his eye near the far end of the camp. A Feydan had joined a small group of others of his species near the creek in some attempt to catch something living in there. Feydans judged each other by their size and bearing; this one did not seem particularly impressive. Their facial tattoos recounted their deeds and histories; his were still rather sparse. And yet, the others moved away when he approached without making eye contact.

Seth put his hand on Ciela's arm when the newcomer to the group touched another to catapult him from his perch upon a boulder as effectively as if he'd been given an electrical shock. There was no raucous laughter this time. The others just stared as if unsure how to respond.

"What?" Ciela said.

"I think we've got us a Dyad over there," Seth said.

She turned. "Which one?"

"The Feydan in the blue coat. He just zapped someone."

"So?"

"Without a gun. Come on."

They walked along a meandering path through the camp, occasionally exchanging nods with some of the civilians, aware of suspicious glances from the soldiers. Eventually, they made their way to the edge of the creek where some campers were testing and processing drinking water. At last, they approached the Feydans near the bank.

Seth watched two of them as they continued their fishing, which seemed to be much less fun now than it was only a short while ago. He sat on another boulder near the man he suspected of being a Dyad. Ciela remained standing behind him as was the custom among their strict Feydan patriarchal society, her hand placed loosely on his shoulder.

"Anything edible in there?" Seth asked, gesturing to the water.

The Feydan shifted his eyes to appraise the newcomers, barely acknowledging Ciela. The lines tattooed along his jaw told of his clan originating in the islands of a Nordic region, a minor race with little influence on the planet. "Not likely we'll find out any time soon," he replied. "You're useless, Yase!"

There was no good-natured laughter to follow the insult. The men exchanged a few furtive glances among themselves before returning to their task. Seth felt Ciela's thumb press twice against his shoulder. Her scanner had confirmed the Alpha resonance emitting from this man.

"Name's Kada," Seth said. "Looks like Air Command's got the rule of the place. Anything being done about that?"

The Feydan took another look at Seth. "You're Shri-Lan?" he guessed.

"Arawaj."

The man spat on the ground. "I don't give a damn about Air Command," he said. "They can keep busy dividing up rations and coddling the sick. My name's Tuyen. Narr's Tuyen," he added his clan name with some pride. "We're not putting up with this much longer."

"What else can we do? There's no way out of here."

Tuyen turned his head, staring at nothing for a moment. The pressure of Ciela's hand told Seth that she saw it, too. The Dyad's expression did not change but he seemed to be listening to something. "There's nothing for us here. Those idiots up there keep digging in the rock like someone's actually going to come get it. That's no way to live." He looked over the camp. "*This* is no way to live."

Seth tilted his head toward the others. "Make them go away. Let's talk."

Tuyen's narrowed eyes glared at him. "You heard him,"

he said after a moment and without taking his eyes off Seth. "Get lost."

It seemed to Seth that his people removed themselves with nearly grateful haste. "I know about your friend," Seth said, nodding to the empty space beside the Feydan, hoping that his counterpart was actually still manifesting there. "We call them Dyads."

"Oh?" Tuyen said, momentarily taken aback. The aggressive façade faded for an instant, showing surprise and curiosity. "Dyads, huh? How would you know?"

"I just do," Seth said, deciding against informing the man that *he* was the Dyad now, an entirely new species, and no longer a Feydan at all. "What did you mean when you said you weren't sticking around?"

Tuyen scooped a handful of pebbles from the ground and began to throw them, one by one, into the creek without much enthusiasm. "Them Dyads have some useful tricks," he said. "You know about them?"

Seth nodded. "They have a way with energy transfer. As long as it's conductive, they can use anything to channel electromagnetic radiation pretty much as they want." Not certain if the Feydan had gone beyond inflicting pain on his fellow castaways, he said nothing about their ability to infiltrate most computer systems as easily as if they were actually crawling around in them. In a way, he supposed, they were.

Tuyen's face suddenly lit up when an idea seemed to strike him. Or perhaps it struck the individual living inside his brain. "Watch." He got up from his perch to crouch by the water's edge. Grinning, he touched the surface. Only a second later, an anguished cry reached their ears. They turned to see a woman on the ground not far away, part of the crew fetching water. Her companions bent over her, astonished by her collapse. Tuyen chuckled when dead aquatic creatures rose to the surface to float downstream. "I guess that's the way to do some fishing around here," he said and returned to his rock after a quick scan over the camp to see if any Air Command soldiers had noticed the commotion.

Ciela's hand had tightened on Seth's shoulders but she held her tongue. At any other time, the Feydan would by now find himself soundly cursed or perhaps with a knife in his throat, depending on her mood.

"We could run the planet if we wanted to," Tuyen said, still looking pleased with his feat. "But this isn't the place for us. They can have it if they want."

"You're planning to do something?"

"Tuyen!" a voice rang out behind Ciela.

All of them turned to see a tall Feydan move out of the shadows. Ciela's small intake of air told Seth that she, too, recognized him as Skoth whom they had met earlier in the doctor's company.

Skoth glared at Tuyen. "No need for showing off, brother," he said in their own language. They watched someone carry the woman to the makeshift med-station in the hangar. "I'll not see that again."

Tuyen stood up, eyes averted, and gave up his seat on the boulder to the larger man but did not leave, as the others had.

"Idiot," Skoth said comfortably. He scrutinized Seth as if judging a cut of meat for dinner. "You're Arawaj, then?" he asked.

Seth nodded. "Out of Magra Torley. We were going for some caps on Tor Ag when we got lost. The doctor was a passenger."

Skoth looked up at Ciela. "You have a sharp eye, woman. Not many can appreciate our scripts." He rubbed his hand over his neck. While none of the tattoos actually declared him a rebel, the list of deeds and locations told their own story to those able to decipher it.

She did not reply, as was expected.

Having bestowed her with his notice, Skoth turned back to Seth. "You know about us, then?"

Seth nodded. "I have met others like you. You are

working with that… project going on in that pit?"

"No. But I heard rumors. So I went out there to offer my help, see what they're doing. Taking a few of the ships apart to build their transmitters." The Feydan glanced around although there was no one else in earshot. "They're not done bringing ships down here. They changed the exit from Callas to funnel people here. Doesn't matter what people. They're hoping to get more turned into… What did you call them?"

"Dyads."

"Yes. Dyads."

"For what reason?"

Skoth ran a hand over his decorated head as if to feel the creature inside. "They want to settle here, I guess. In real-space. Tired of living in the Nothing and want to see how we live out here."

"On Chitta Moor?"

"No. They plan to move on. Far from Trans-Targon somewhere. Except things aren't going quite right yet."

Seth frowned. "Did your Dyad tell you that?"

"It doesn't talk much. I don't want things talking at me in my head so it's shut up now, most of the time. It doesn't like them other Dyads, I can tell, though. No more than I do." He leaned back to order Tuyen to fetch some food. The Feydan slipped away without demur.

Seth glanced up at Ciela. Skoth's words made a strange sort of sense. Was it possible that the subspace entities simply wanted to experience a corporeal existence? Snatching ships full of people would ensure that at least some of them would merge into a Dyad. Preventing everyone else from leaving again would keep their secret.

"How many are at the crater? Dyads, I mean."

"Just nine or ten of them. They won't say much to us grunts but it looks like they've figured out how to open a keyhole. Right there. In the ground."

"What?" Ciela was unable to stop her exclamation.

"Can you believe it? Who does that? A new keyhole will let them find a better place than this, I guess. Away from Air

Command and other meddlers."

"Inconceivable," Seth said, mostly to himself. Keyholes existed anywhere in space, regardless of what might already be there, or get in the way. There were two known instances where a planet's orbit took it directly through a keyhole location, passing unnoticed as it rolled by. Opening such a keyhole at that moment, however, was equivalent to a meteor strike, at the very least. Creating a keyhole where one did not exist wasn't even something that real-space inhabitants had the means or the energy to attempt. But then, no one knew the extent of the Dyad's capabilities. "You said they were having problems with making things work?"

Skoth chuckled. The sound reminded Seth of someone breathing heavily at the end of a drain pipe. "They were sent here by some fool on Pelion to get set up. He's supposed to be here by now to make it all happen. Except he hasn't arrived yet."

"Why would Pelion bother with this sewer?" Seth asked, trying to sound like he didn't really much care. "Not another Dyad, is it?"

"Damn right it is." Skoth laughed. "Some really big brain working on the Azon Corp orbiter, judging by the way they talk about him. He sent them here months ago to start hijacking ships."

"That seems to be working well for them." Seth felt a sudden urge to get away from this place this very moment and find a way to warn Colonel Carras. Whatever the reason for sending a science vessel out here, the fact that a Dyad wielded such authority in real-space was an alarming bit of news. If Azon Corp's administration was compromised it would not take much to also invade Air Command echelons.

"I guess he's not coming, though," Skoth said. "Way overdue now. For all I know he's floating around the keyhole with the other junk that didn't make it through."

"That might be a good thing," Seth said. "If that really is a keyhole they're playing with, it's not far enough away from this place. They'd have to release an unbelievable amount of energy to create a spacetime fissure." He looked up at the forbidding canyon walls. "This place looks ready to collapse at the first earthquake anyway."

Skoth shrugged. "I hope to be away by then. There are about a dozen of us here, some from other places. I'm damn sure the bosses are going to be very interested in us when we get back."

"A dozen Shri-Lan with Dyads?"

"Some're Arawaj. And I've got almost thirty men in my group that haven't turned into Dyads. You mean to join us?" Skoth glanced briefly at Ciela. "Don't need women around, unless you're willing to share."

"She's my navigator," Seth said. "I have a good ship and some skills you need. And I don't share."

Skoth shrugged. "Can always use a navigator." He raised his hands and studied them with an undisguised expression of awe. "I've seen them do things out there in that pit we haven't even figured out yet. With a proper power source these Dyads are weapons like no one's ever seen. The kind that'll catch the eye of the Brothers. We can get into some fancy positions right at the top of the Shri-Lan. All we have to do is get off this rock."

"How?"

The Feydan looked at Seth as if judging him as simple-minded as Tuyan, who still hadn't returned with the food he wanted. "Get them to stop interfering with the damn keyhole back to Callas. It's all we want. They damn well know how to do that because they're making that happen. I don't care why, or what they want to do with this place. If they don't stop it long enough for us to get out we'll blow their little project into bits. That should do it."

Seth raised his eyebrows. "You're going to need ships."

"We have a ship. They took our coolant so we won't be jumping with it, but we kept the thorium. In a few more days the captain's fine cruisers will be ours, too. We just need to get used to our new talents. Some of us have been practicing. The whole town is made of metal. They won't put up a fight when they see what we can do with that."

Seth stood up. "We're in. Let me know when things are ready to go down. I'm itching to get out of this dump."

"Just stay clear of Air Command. They think they got us bossed so that's what we'll let them believe."

Seth laughed and clapped the man's shoulder. "You just say the word."

Ciela scanned the metal terraces lining both sides of the rift as they walked from the rebel camp back to the stranded cruisers. Not just workers moved up there but the guards also, gripping their weapons, their eyes more on the strangers down here than their prisoners. "Looks like this place is going to implode sooner than we think," she said.

"Yes. We're leaving. Now."

"Now?" she said, surprised. "Hmm, I guess that's the thing to do. There's not much we can do here."

"We've got Dyads in real-space. Creating far too many casualties in their quest for a new place to live. That's a high price to pay. And if our friend Skoth rejoins his comrades we'll have even bigger problems. Dyad Shri-Lan? What a nightmare that would be."

"So what can we do? He was probably bragging but even a handful of them could turn this place upside down."

"Air Command will have to head out here to clean up. A single Ghoster will have the firepower to take out that keyhole-making operation from orbit. Not even a Dyad can stop that if they don't expect it. If we use Delphian spanners to make the jump we should be able to get back here in one piece."

"You'll risk the civilians."

"They're already at risk. If that rebel is right, taking out those transmitters might end the keyhole problem. For now."

She said nothing for a while, like him keeping her pace leisurely as if they had nothing else to do on this bleak evening. Finally, she took his hand. "Seth…"

He turned to see what might have caught her attention.

She tipped her chin toward the hangar where the survivors were crowded together. "We could take her," she said. "We've got room."

Seth frowned, quite aware whom she meant. "I'm not sure that's such a great idea. We'd have to..." He scratched his chin. "On the other hand, I think that's pretty brilliant."

"Huh? Of course it is." Puzzled, she hurried after him to the shed.

He passed the guards with a casual wave and muscled the door aside. People seemed to have turned in for the night, as much as that meant crawling into whatever bedrolls were available and shutting out the sounds of the hall as much as possible. A dim light still shone from the captain's shelter.

Seth scratched on the door and looked inside. "Captain Bryn," he whispered. "A word, please."

The captain sat on his pallet, little more than a thin mattress on the ground, a display tablet in his hand. It did not look like he had rested since they had left him earlier this day. The woman in his care lolled listlessly on her side, staring at nothing, blinking slowly.

He looked up at Seth's call and squinted through the gloom inside the hut. "Kada," he said and nodded for them to enter. "Find anything out there?"

Seth crouched before the officer, keeping his voice as low as possible. "Yes, we did. Not enough but too much to get into." He looked up at Ciela, wondering how much he could tell the captain. One did not have to be a rebel to harbor a distrust of Air Command's methods and the scruples of its officers. "Listen, there is hope. We may have the means to get out of here." He raised a hand to forestall the captain's immediate reply. "No, we can't get everyone out with us. But we'll return as soon as Air Command can pull an extraction mission together." He nodded toward the other bed. "We have room for her, if you like."

The captain's dull and red-rimmed eyes stared at him for a moment as if not quite comprehending Seth's words. "Yes," he said finally. "Take her."

Ciela picked up a blanket and went to the woman, speaking soothingly as she convinced her to sit up.

"While we are gone I think you should transfer as many of your people as you can to the transport in orbit. Tell them Cazun Himself told you to lead your people to freedom, stuffed-up keyhole or not. Or that they've found some treatment up there to help the... the injured, like her. No one here will care as long as you're not drawing on their food supplies."

Bryn nodded. "I'll have to leave the troops. Queta Station is counting on us to keep things calm."

Seth rose to give Ciela room to walk the woman to the door. "Right now you don't owe this town a damn thing, Captain. And no one knows who's a rebel here, who's just pissed, and who used to be a rebel before realizing their only hope to get out is to play along with Air Command because there's no damn way the Shri-Lan are mounting a rescue." He turned to follow Ciela. "Get them ready, Captain."

They moved as quickly as the woman's shambling gait allowed, past the guards and then to the small airfield. It was not long before Seth stopped, realizing that someone followed. He gestured to Ciela to keep moving.

"What do you want?" he said to Tuyen, the skinny Feydan underling from the camp.

The rebel crept from the shadows, ducking in that ingratiating way of their people's lower caste. Seth fought an urge to shake the man.

"Heard you're leaving," Tuyen said.

"Not going too far," Seth said. "We're taking that woman up to the transport. They've got a better med-station than anything to be had in this dump."

"Thinking that's not what you told the captain."

Seth turned to walk away, moving to his left and into the shadows cast by an abandoned Trident cruiser. "Think what you like."

"I heard you. You're going to make a run for it and you know how. I say you'll be taking us along instead of her."

Seth spun to deliver a high kick to Tuyen's face, slamming him into the struts of the Trident before the Dyad had time to react. He followed up with a few quick punches, dropping the man within seconds. "Crap," he whispered when he saw the open com link on his wrist. Not bothering to drag the body into the deeper shadows he sprinted after Ciela who had just reached the *Dutchman*'s gate. He slapped the keyplate and then waited breathlessly while his eye was scanned. "We're now in a big hurry," he said.

"What happened?"

"That little runt heard us talk to the captain in the hangar. Must have been spying." Seth waited while Ciela led the woman into the cargo hold and then slammed the gate. "Get her strapped down. No time for wind-up." He crossed the main cabin and engaged a bare minimum pre-flight sequence.

Ciela shoved their patient into the small crew cabin to belt her into the lower of the two bunks in which few people had ever slept. The woman made some small sounds of protest which she ignored.

"Won't be long before they'll want to know who left," Seth said when she joined him in the cockpit. He performed a soft launch, hovering the *Dutchman* vertically to rise out of the canyon and then away from the ragged ledge for some distance before pushing the ship to reach escape velocity within minutes.

"And here they are now," Ciela said when the com console chirped at them. She silenced the hail from the ground. There was nothing they needed to say to whoever was calling.

No one contacted them from the transport still in stationary orbit when they passed them on their way to the keyhole. *The Dutchman* reported over fifty persons aboard. "I hope Captain Bryn finds a way to get more of his people out of harm's way before Air Command gets here." Ciela watched Seth lay in their course to the keyhole. "If they get here."

He let the autopilot take the helm. "They only need to

make the jump to Tor Ag to find their way here."

"You think they will? Once we tell them that some ships didn't make it?"

Seth pushed himself out of his bench and left the cockpit. He pulled his shirt over his head, feeling the need to spend some time in the *Dutchman*'s cargo hold with his exercise equipment. His knuckles ached where he had abraded them on the Feydan's head and Ciela's question wasn't one that he felt like examining just now. "I don't know, babe. We're going to give them what we have and let them decide. What else is there?"

* * *

"I think you should come up now," Seth heard Ciela's voice from above. He had squeezed his long limbs into the tricky space behind the coolant manifold where he stored extra tubes. For the jump ahead of them, he wanted to make sure a full supply kept their processors happy. He cursed when his knee got in the way of something sharp as he backed out.

"Are we there?" He stood up and pulled himself through the hatch and into the main cabin.

"Yes. But there's a ship up ahead."

Seth entered the cockpit to study the display. "New arrival to this vacation destination?"

"I don't think so. They've been hiding in the junk field by the keyhole."

Both sensors and real-vid screens showed a live engine signature among the slowly spreading pieces of debris floating away from the keyhole. As they watched, the ship switched into full power mode and boosted its engines to move toward them. "I think you're right. The *Dutchman* wouldn't have noticed them with all this interference."

Ciela opened a com channel to receive their hail.

"Hello, Pilot," they were greeted. "That's some hurry you're in."

Seth dropped into his bench and engaged his headset.

"Just taking a look at this balky keyhole," Ciela replied. "Things are tiresome down at the station."

"Drop your speed," was the reply to that. "Let's have a talk about what you're really up to."

"Nothing to talk about. Up to nothing but a little scavenging. Isn't that what you're doing?"

"You won't pick up much at that speed." The other ship now angled toward them, also pushing their velocity. "We heard you might be leaving us. How about a little company?"

Ciela looked to Seth. He swiped a thumb across his throat and then pointed forward.

"That's all right, we're not lonely," she said and closed the com link.

"Something tells me that when Skoth said he still had a ship, he didn't mean it was actually on the ground," Seth said.

"Think they'll open fire?"

"Not if they think we know how to get out of here. Let them follow. We'll either lose them in the breach, like we lost those pirates at Tor Ag, or they'll come through with us and run into that Air Command ship near Callas. Either one is fine by me."

She shook her head. "This jump's going to be tough enough as it is. Both ships in the span will cause a lot of interference with the resonance. And if that resonance fails we might just end up back here. Only we won't be friends with Skoth anymore."

Seth cursed. "Is Larris secured?"

"She was last time I checked."

"Going marginal," he said and pulled the restraints over his shoulders. Ciela did the same when he rerouted most of the *Dutchman*'s resources. The gravity spinners wound down, life support dwindled to minimal temperature, even the cabin lights dimmed as the ship switched into maximum power conservation.

"They're pursuing," she said. She checked their velocity. "Can we outrun them? That's a Trident. We'll need to slow to open the keyhole. They don't."

"I'll look after that. Get ready to jump."

She gave him a worried look but, as so often before, put her faith in his ability to command his ship. Closing her eyes, she blocked out all distraction, trusting that, when joined by his neural interface, Seth and the *Dutchman* were able to work in perfect unison, relaying commands and feedback as instantly as if the ship were part of his body.

He locked onto the keyhole and rallied resources to channel a little more power into the converters. A glance at the displays made clear that the rebel ship prepared to ride their wake into the keyhole. "Hang on," he said but she was by now so deeply immersed in her khamal that nothing but the task at hand mattered.

Seth reigned the *Dutchman* to perform a sharp turn and swooped back toward the pursuing ship, using a missile spread designed more to look impressive than harm. The surprise worked and the Trident veered aside, likely more by reflex than alarm. Seth rolled and came at them from the side, placing a careful line of fire, again calculated to avoid taxing his reserves, along their shield seam. His familiarity with that class of ship paid off; theirs did not. The *Dutchman* appeared as tired and commonplace as thousands of private cruisers but the heart of this mongrel, the engines and defensive systems, were highly tuned Eagle class military issue. He dove up and delivered a devastating blow into the Trident's exposed and weakened belly and then shot away, back to the keyhole, leaving her bleeding in his wake.

"They're lame," he said. "We'll leave them to it."

"Ready for jump," she said. "Take your headset off."

Seth did so, not willing to admit that he had forgotten all about it, and also start the transmission of the Alpha resonance. He was even less willing to admit, even just to himself, that the most likely scenario was for them to end up precisely back in this spot, and even more likely in very tiny pieces. He slowed the ship and began to feed the site until the aperture appeared on his sensors, widening gradually.

A shockwave slammed into the *Dutchman*'s shields hard enough to throw both of them into their belts. Another blast followed.

"They don't know when to give up," Seth snapped. There was no room to dodge now. Unable to return their fire, he fed every last bit of power to the *Dutchman*'s shields to see them safely through the jump. "Ten seconds."

"I don't see it. I don't feel the terminus!"

"Abort?"

She lifted a finger, asking for more time.

"Pick another exit! Any exit. Five seconds."

"Go go go," she urged. "I can do this."

Seth closed his eyes when he raced into the still-widening keyhole. His mind tumbled into the Big Nothing, divorced from all sensation as always, aware only that, again, this was taking far longer than it should. Without his link to the ship he could not feel Ciela's presence any better than he could feel his hands gripping the bench. She was not ready for this, he knew, and he doubted that he would ever be.

"Damn!" he shouted in a glorious release of pent-up terror and breath when the ship's familiar sounds rushed back into his awareness, along with the stab of light into his eyes. Too much light, actually. And too many sounds. The *Dutchman*'s alarm systems were fully engaged, alerting him to several systems failing the routine post-span checks. "Damn," he said again, less joyfully, and righted the ship manually before leading it into a more organized diagnostic.

"Ciela?" he said, his hands still flying over the controls. He looked over to her bench. "Talk to me!" He leaned over and shook her arm, still nervously scanning the sensor displays.

She frowned, always a good sign at this point.

He finally had enough systems in check to let the *Dutchman* continue on its own. She opened her eyes when he shook her shoulder, more gently this time. He exhaled sharply, not sure when he had held his breath. "Awake, sweety?"

"Are we there?"

He looked at the mapper. "No. Not near Callas. That's all right. You did it. You're amazing."

"This one hurt," she said, barely above a whisper. "They... someting tried to get at me again. I don't think that resonance is working so well, after all."

"Seems that way. Come, let's get you comfortable." He helped her out of her bench and into the main cabin where she curled up on the lounger.

"Where are we?"

"We're actually in the Mrak sector, where that keyhole is supposed to be leading. There's a Union jumpsite at Ud Mrak but right now there's no one around here for days in any direction. I doubt anyone comes out this way unless they're shipping to Chitta Moor. We're safe and all you need to do now is sleep." He ran a medical scan, just to assure himself that he wasn't lying. She closed her eyes and smiled when he kissed her.

Seth watched her for a moment and then returned to the cockpit to complete the diagnostic. The *Dutchman* rarely balked at even the deepest of subspace jumps and yet some of the systems still complained about the rough treatment they had just received.

"Let's see what's got you in a tizzy." He took the pilot seat and attached his headset to work more directly with the ship's processors.

The pain in his head was instant and absolute, knifing through his skull in a sheet of cold, black agony. Then there was nothing.

EIGHT

He awoke as abruptly and wide-awake as if he had closed his eyes for just a few seconds. The pain was gone. Had there even been pain? For how long had he been passed out?

His eyes shifted when a small movement caught his attention. A slow smile tugged on his lips. "Khoe," he said. "Didn't I tell you not to sit on the console?"

The small woman on the cockpit controls tilted her head when he spoke. Her shape at first seemed a little nebulous but the longer he looked, the more she came into focus. The wild tangle of white braids surrounding an impish face, the odd assembly of clothes, the bare feet; all of it familiar as their memories put her together in front of him. Nothing about this seemed disconcerting, even when she slid off the console to float horizontally above his bench.

"Seth." Her voice sounded as sweet as his memory of it.

"You remember."

"I remember. Your ship does, too. It was easy this time. Does your head hurt?"

"Not now." He glanced over the *Dutchman*'s displays. All systems had resumed their usual routines – apparently the ship had gotten over its objections to this strange creature invading its circuits and, from there, Seth's brain.

She raised her hand to touch his face and it took just a

moment for her to align their senses, allowing her to feel with his touch, just as she saw through his eyes.

"I'd forgotten how real this seems," he said and watched his fingers run along her arm, feeling her skin and then the woven fabric of her blouse, knowing that all of this was simply an illusion. "How did you find me?"

She laughed. "You've been singing my song. I woke and there you were. The others are frightened by it. Did you know that?"

"I suspected."

"So I came to see why you make such noise." She smiled. No, he reminded himself. She let him believe that she had smiled, likely in response to something he wanted. Together, as before, they created her to suit them both. "It wasn't easy! It felt like something was blocking me, but then I got through. Have you done something to your ship to keep us out?"

"Sort of. Not to the ship, though." He sat up, feeling a touch of vertigo as he had before. Nothing else alerted him of the new presence inside his head, still busily using the cells of his own body to rebuild an entirely separate neural net. "Let me show you something."

She followed him into the main cabin, walking although her feet did not touch the floor.

"Look." He let his eyes travel over Ciela on the lounger. She slept with her hands tucked under her cheek, her loose shirt slightly bunched up, showing the pale skin of her belly. As usual on a long trip, she wore a snug, soft pair of shorts reaching only to mid-thigh.

"A Delphian," Khoe said, whispering for some reason. Her voice existed only in his mind. "That's what was blocking me."

Seth nodded while Khoe shifted her focus, likely accessing the *Dutchman*'s archive for whatever she didn't already know about Delphians. "Don't bother," he said. "She not really a lot like her people. Didn't grow up on Delphi."

Ciela shifted when he spoke, a sign that she was close to

waking. The Delphian sleep state was deep and they rarely moved when immersed in it. "Ciela?"

"She's beautiful," Khoe said when Seth bent over the sleeping woman.

"Yeah, I think so, too," he said and touched Ciela's cheek.

Khoe sighed.

"What?"

"She feels beautiful, too. Touch her again."

Seth put his hand on Ciela's shoulder. "Sweety? Wake up."

"Sweety?" Khoe said. "She's your woman?"

He grinned. "That's probably not the way she'd want it put."

"Look how pretty that hair. It's much darker blue than other Delphians. Is she very old?"

"No, she just likes it that way. It also doesn't stand out so much."

Khoe moved across Ciela to sit beside her on the lounger. "Wake her up. I want to see what she looks like awake."

Seth withdrew his hand, suddenly unsure. Khoe's return to his head and mind had been effortless and easily accepted. It felt comfortable and soothing and like something that he'd been missing for a long time. But he wondered if Ciela would welcome Khoe's presence as unquestioningly as he had. Nor was he quite prepared to have these two women actually in the same room together. "Maybe I should explain this to her."

"I suspected that was the plan," Khoe said. "Unless you want her to think you've suffered some damage during that jump and are now talking to yourself."

"You know what I mean. This isn't easy to explain to people."

"Hmm?" Ciela turned onto her back and rubbed her face. "What?"

Seth smiled and sat down on the edge of the lounger. "Did you sleep well?" he asked, feeling weirdly nervous.

She stretched her long limbs and then held her arms out to him.

He caught her hands. "Ciela, I need to talk to you. I mean I need to tell you something."

She frowned, instantly alert. "Tell me what?"

He glanced at Khoe for no particular reason. Her face was tilted toward the wall but she observed Ciela curiously through his eyes.

"Seth?" Ciela sat up.

"What pretty eyes," Khoe said. "I should change my eyes to that color. Let me feel her hair."

He sighed and decided to jump in with both feet. "Ciela, it looks like we've picked up a hitchhiker during that jump."

"What? How? That resonance wasn't working."

"It did. It scared them away, but Khoe recognized it. She came for it."

Ciela's eyes widened. "Your subspace entity? It's here? On the *Dutchman*?"

He ran his hand over his eyes, but that didn't help find some not-insane way to explain this. "Not just in the *Dutchman*. I linked to the ship and she found me."

"She's back in your head?" Ciela exclaimed. "You're a Dyad again?"

"Dyad. Right," Khoe said. "That's what they called us."

Seth nodded at Ciela. "Yes. She's here."

She looked around. "Here? You can see her?"

"Come on, let *her* see me," Khoe said.

"Yes, I can," Seth said. "She's sitting beside you. There. She wants to meet you."

Ciela looked at the empty space and then surprised them both by scrambling from the lounger to put some space between herself and whatever Seth was hallucinating.

"Ciela…" he began.

She crossed her arms over her chest and backed up until she was stopped by the edge of the galley counter. For a brief, irrational moment, Seth wondered if a knife was at hand there. She had never looked at him quite this way before.

"There is nothing to fear," he said, making no move to get up. "I'm still here. Nothing's changed. They're not really parasites."

"That's not very polite, calling us that," Khoe said.

"I didn't call you that," he replied.

"You're talking to her?" Ciela said.

"She has pretty legs, too," Khoe decided.

"Will you stop that?"

Ciela's brows drew together, looking less shocked now than just confused.

He held his hand out toward her. "Come sit. It's nothing to fear. Caelyn and Shan Quine met her, remember? They weren't worried one bit."

Her tense shoulders dropped when he reminded her of this. She had become very fond of Quine during the time he spent tutoring her in the ways of her people, both of them less constrained by convention at the lab on Magra than on their home planet. Caelyn had also become a trusted friend. Neither of them had expressed any fear of Khoe.

She stared at nothing for a moment, ignoring his request. "I'm going to check on Larris," she said finally and left for the crew quarters.

"She seems frightened," Khoe said.

"She just needs a moment. It takes more than this to scare her. She's far too curious to pass up a chance to see how you and I fit together." He regarded Khoe for a moment, wishing she had not decided to jump into their bed. Hallucination or not, the woman's projection of herself looked undeniably real. "Could you cover up a little?"

A high-collared body shirt appeared under her loose blouse to hide the appealing curves she had found somewhere in his database and liked enough to emulate. Until today he had appreciated the choice. "Your other passenger is in trouble," she said.

"Huh?"

"Ciela is running a scan. I'm following it. That's a Dyad,

but very fragmented. It's not meeting up very well at all."

"Yes, we're hoping to get her some help. Is there anything you can do?"

She shook her head.

When Ciela returned she looked as downhearted as Khoe. "Physically, Larris is fine," she said. "But her mind is in an uproar. I've managed to calm her a little." Instead of sitting again on the lounger, she perched in the bucket chair next to it. "Can you do that…that thing the rebel did? When he hurt that woman by the river?"

"Yes," he said after a moment.

"What does she want? Your Khoe, I mean."

"We called her. With the resonance. So she came." He watched her reach for her data sleeve to scan him for the Dyad signature, hopefully more out of curiosity than suspicion. "I want to talk to her about what's going on in subspace. It'd be helpful if you joined us."

"Join you?"

"She can't harm you," he reminded her again. "I think it was you who kept the Dyads out of the *Dutchman* to begin with. You were able to block their intrusion into the ship itself."

"For a while."

"Yes, she's clever." He held his hand out again. "Please trust me. I'd rather rip my own head off than hurt you."

She looked at his hand, then his face. A silent moment passed. At last, she put her data sleeve aside and rose to touch her fingers to his neural node.

He exhaled the breath he had held, deciding not to share his moment of sudden and absolute dread that she might actually doubt him. She concentrated, frowning slightly, as she overcame the unnatural means by which Delphians established a mental connection with those not of their species. His neural taps allowed her into his thoughts and now also his perceptions of the being living inside his head.

"Ciela," he said when she had completed the link. "Meet Khoe."

Ciela looked around until she saw the white-haired woman sitting on the lounger, arms wrapped around her drawn-up knees.

Khoe grinned broadly and raised a hand. "Hello."

Ciela closed her eyes briefly and shook her head as if trying to rid herself of a peculiar vision. When she opened them again she took a long moment to study the apparition before her. "That's your Dyad?"

"*I* am the Dyad," Seth reminded her.

"Why is she not looking at me?"

"She tries to look in the proper direction when she remembers. She's seeing you through my eyes. She can only see what I see." He tapped the data sleeve that communicated with the *Dutchman*. "Or what the ship's sensors and cameras see."

Khoe turned to face Ciela directly. "Sorry! I don't mean to be weird."

Ciela blinked. "Uh… that's okay." She looked to Seth. "So am I looking at her now, or you?"

"Both of us. We share my senses. What you see there is just how she looks."

She tilted her head, again looking at the apparition. "So if your… if Khoe is an extension of you, your personality, why'd you pick this? It looks like a short Centauri, sort of. But with Bellac hair? Not some fierce warrior? Or someone a little taller?" A small smile appeared on her lips. "Or even just male?"

"She picked this. They only start out like us. After that they go their own way. She found some things in my database that she liked. She thinks you're pretty," he added, hoping to ease the tension he saw in the tilt of Ciela's body.

"Oh, yes," Khoe said. "Would you mind if I got eyes like yours?"

"Uh, no." Ciela watched, fascinated, as the woman's eyes turned from violet to sapphire blue.

"There is something different with you," Khoe said, looking thoughtful. "You're not like Caelyn. Not like I understand Delphians to be."

"Ciela is a GenMod," Seth said. "Part of an experimental series that didn't go so well. The Delphians don't really want people to know about her. Altered her hippocampus. It's a bit of a secret."

"Who would I tell?" Khoe said. "Can I look? Please?"

Ciela nodded, not with any great enthusiasm. "Careful."

"You have a third lobe there," Khoe said only seconds later. "No wonder he's got you working as a navigator. Your spatial perception must be phenomenal."

"And you wouldn't believe her memory," Seth said. "She never lets me forget anything."

Ciela wrinkled her nose at him.

Seth got up and went to the galley. "Is anyone else hungry?"

Ciela frowned. "She eats?"

"No. She tastes what I do. But you and I haven't eaten in a while. She's burning up my energy." He poked through the ship's storage bins and found some pouches of *tarind* seeds. Combined with a suitable helping of flavored nutrient sauce, it made for a fine meal. Peering past the edge of the cabinet he saw Ciela still looking at Khoe in wonder. And, seeing through his eyes, Khoe realized this, too, and smiled at Ciela. "It takes a while to get used to," he said, unsure of how Ciela felt about any of this. Although unschooled in many of her people's traditions, she seemed to have a knack for the Delphian way of keeping their thoughts to themselves when they felt like it.

Ciela nodded. "Must be strange to be two people in one body." She moved to touch Khoe's knee with one extended finger. When it made contact she jerked it back immediately. "Gods, I felt that! How is that possible?"

"You didn't," Seth said as he retrieved the packets from the heater. "I did. But only because I was watching your hand. What do you want on this?"

"Just some *yaro*," she replied absently. "Did she feel that?"

"I did," Khoe said. She leaned forward and stroked Ciela's arm. "But it's all just in our heads." The tips of her fingers touched Ciela's cheek and then passed through it like a mirage.

"Khoe can't actually feel that." Seth returned to them and handed Ciela a bowl of the gruel. Unsure of how Khoe perceived stimuli from both of them, he had chosen the same seasoning for himself, deciding to put up with the sweet flavor. He sat down on the opposite side on the lounger from where Khoe perched. "So, Khoe, what's going on in your space?"

"We're dying."

Ciela coughed around a spoonful of food at the sudden declaration. "What?"

"How? Why?" Seth said.

"I don't know. We're very tired."

Ciela frowned. "You don't seem very upset."

"They don't really get that whole being-dead idea," Seth said. "In subspace, they are made up of compound particles, far apart but somehow connected, tangled together to form a consciousness. Sometimes they come apart and rejoin. They don't actually die because they're not actually alive. Is that right?" he added the question for Khoe.

"As you understand it, yes," she said. "But now we're not able to reform very well. There seem to be fewer of us all the time."

Seth stirred around his bowl, wishing he had chosen another sauce but both women seemed to enjoy it. "Is it possible some of you are escaping subspace?"

"Yes," she said without hesitation. "Did you find some?"

"You could say that."

It was Khoe's turn to frown. "That's not supposed to happen. We don't belong here."

"Is it possible that you're evolving somehow?" Seth said. "We have detected the Alpha resonance out here, in real-space. And I'm not talking about the copy we've been broadcasting."

Khoe tilted her head. "The Alpha entity is still in my space. Weakening, too, but there."

Ciela set her bowl aside to pick up the scanner instead. "Look at this." She started to tilt the display toward Khoe but then, remembering, held it before Seth's eyes instead. "It's right here, coming off Seth now. We met a few people on Chitta Moor that also radiate this."

Khoe closed her eyes and held up a hand as if asking them to let her concentrate on something. Ciela glanced at Seth, who shrugged. A few moments passed before the apparition opened her eyes again. "Yes," she said. "I carry the particle. I hadn't even noticed. We're so used to it. Something has changed in the way we... we merge, transition into a Dyad. We bring the Alpha with us now."

"And Air Command isn't happy about that," Seth said. "We, uh, won't be tolerated out here. You can imagine the consequences."

Khoe shrugged. "Evolution's a funny thing." She winked at Ciela when Ciela gasped at her indifference to all of this. "That was a joke. Sort of. Things change. We change. Unfortunately, your people have a hard time with that. It's because you have so many *things* that don't stand up well to change. We don't have things. So we can change when we have to."

Ciela looked down at the steady readings on her scanner. "There is a difference between drifting around in a big vacuum and getting executed out here because you're too dangerous to live. You might have to get used to that whole being-dead thing."

"Why do you think you're dying in subspace?" Seth asked Khoe.

"I don't know. I wasn't aware of it until I felt your presence and came for it."

"Maybe that's why your people are coming out here. Just to survive."

"They won't survive long if their presence becomes known," Ciela said.

Seth nodded. "Maybe their idea of jumping to some faraway place where people aren't going to hunt them down isn't such a bad idea. So far, things are still contained on Chitta Moor."

"*You're* not contained. And we know there's at least one more out there." Ciela held up the scanner. "And now you're pretty easy to detect, at least at close proximity. This can't be contained."

He sighed. "No, I guess not. Not while there are rebels making their own plans on Chitta Moor. I think we'll need to update the colonel."

"What are you going to tell him?"

Seth took the screen from Ciela and engaged the *Dutchman*'s com system. Using an encryption employed by a handful of special ops agents, he created a message packet to Colonel Carras, one of the few contacts at Air Command who knew he was not just a smuggler and rebel sympathizer. The mode he used also scrambled and resynthesized his voice, hopefully obscuring any traces of the Dyad signature. He stared at the symbols waiting patiently for him to begin his recording and then tipped his head back to look up at the ceiling. Nothing up there, among the exposed pipes, light strips and ventilation ducts, offered any clues as to what to tell the Intelligence officer.

He took a long breath and tapped the panel. "Good morning," he said, not having bothered to check what time it would be on Targon when this message arrived. "Lovely weather we're having in subspace. By now you and Astrophysics will know that we've picked up the Dyad signature in the Callas-Tor Ag span. The cause of the problem is not Tor Ag." He combed his fingers through his hair, pondering his next sentence. "The keyhole now terminates in the Chitta Moor sub-sector, which is cut off from the outside now. We were able to get out only by sheer luck."

Ciela rolled her eyes. This was not the first time that they had to create some explanation for their ability to travel where others could not. Some day, they both supposed, they'd have to trust the colonel with their secret but neither Seth nor Ciela worried about a future that seemed to change with every new assignment.

Seth winked at her. "We encountered Dyads at Queta Station. We think they're creating a new keyhole out there, possibly to leave the Trans-Targon sector. They know we don't want them here. Unfortunately there are rebels among the Dyads, mostly Shri-Lan, that are planning to stay in Trans-Targon and rejoin their factions. If the keyhole is restored, and there are indications that it might be, you can expect them to emerge at Ud Mrak, so you might want to intercept."

Seth was glad that this was not a two-way conversation. The colonel had a way of asking questions that even the wiliest agents were unable to dodge. "Well, long story much shortened, we've located some of the lost ships on Chitta Moor, but there've been casualties that require evacuation and medical support." He paused again. Carras would need to know to quarantine these victims under very tight security. "Many are Dyad casualties. You know what that means. Unfortunately, Doctor Hedvig is now one of them, although she appears unharmed. We can probably expect more ships to be intercepted and rerouted to the Moor."

He scratched his chin and then realized that his little habits were telling the colonel that he was less than forthcoming with his report. By the time Carras heard these words, he'd be cursing Seth's birth for keeping so many details to himself. Seth walked a fine line between acting as a Union agent loyal to Air Command, and a mercenary looking to get paid for his work. It was not a relationship that the colonel much cared for but the value Seth brought to the Intelligence team outweighed his occasional delinquencies. "We have information about at least one Dyad currently elsewhere in Trans-Targon. We'll investigate and report back when we know more. Kada out."

Ciela regarded him in silent astonishment. "He's going to

resort to foul language when he gets that message."

Seth grinned as he sent the packet to the Union relay at Ud Mrak's stable jumpsite, from where it would be forwarded to Targon. "No doubt. But he's got enough to get busy here, in case our pal Skoth and his posse actually get the Dyads to stop their interference with the keyhole. We should probably leave before any of them arrive here. It's not something I want to get in the middle of."

"Let's jump to Callas from here, then. Larris needs help. And, really, I would love to get Caelyn's thoughts on all this." Ciela waved her hand vaguely in Khoe's direction. "It's all a bit much."

"Can I jump us?" Khoe said. "Please?"

"She's a spanner, too?" Ciela said.

"Yeah, although not your kind of spanner."

"There are other kinds?" Khoe asked.

"That little squiggle in Ciela's brain lets her get around the mapped exits in subspace," Seth said. "She can emerge anywhere. This keyhole here doesn't naturally span to Callas, not even for the best of the Delphian navigators. It only leads to the Chitta Moor sub-sector. It takes weeks to travel from here to Callas using the commercial jumpsite near Ud Mrak. In fact, it would take us three days just to get to the jumpsite from here to make the first leap. But Ciela can re-map the ship's path inside subspace using this keyhole."

"What? How's that even possible?"

"Ask the Delphians who designed me," Ciela said. "Or that part of my brain, anyway."

"It's also a secret," Seth said. "Imagine if she fell into rebel hands with this gift of hers. Or if Air Command decided they didn't want her working with me anymore."

Ciela scowled at him. "I think I can decide for myself who I want to work with."

He got up and headed for the cockpit. "Yeah, I worry too much."

"Well, don't."

Khoe drifted across Ciela to approximate standing on the

cabin floor. "I think it's sweet that he worries. Don't you?"

"Worries too much," Ciela said, loud enough for Seth to hear. "We've done fine so far keeping our heads down. I can handle this without hiding on Delphi for the rest of my life in fear of someone snatching me away."

"I'd be worried, too," Khoe said. "I'm sure Air Command wouldn't dilly-dally to make you part of whatever crew they thought was more important than this one."

"*This* crew is important," Ciela said. "And Colonel Carras knows it." She threw up her hands. "Now look at me, arguing with a hallucination." She got up and followed Seth into the cockpit. "Your Dyad is taking sides," she said.

"Mine, fortunately." He engaged his mental link to the ship and set a course to return to the keyhole.

"Know what's interesting?" Ciela said as she took to her bench beside him. "My head doesn't hurt very much. I wouldn't want to keep this khamal open for very long, but it's bearable right now."

"Really? That's great!" As her practice of her innate Delphian talents had led her to explore the khamal, they had tried a few times to maintain a mind link between them. But he was not Delphian and using his neural interface to create the connection inevitably ended up with a troublesome headache for Ciela. "Is that something you're doing, Khoe?" He looked around to see her sitting cross-legged on top of the com console.

"Yeah. Can I watch you jump?"

Seth waited for Ciela to respond, unsure if she would allow having all three of them linked in a khamal during what was not a simple jump.

"Be my guest," Ciela said, already feeling her way into the *Dutchman*'s subspace navigational system. "But you're showing me later how I can get around that headache myself."

The ship responded to her mental touch, ramping up shields and processors while Seth accelerated toward the keyhole coordinates. The aperture opened when he projected the energy upon which it fed. At a mental nod from Ciela, he punched the ship into the breach and once more their world disappeared into nothing.

* * *

"Dutchman? Is that you? I cannot believe my eyes!"

Seth relaxed his grip on the pilot bench when the voice cut through the silence of the cockpit at what felt like the very moment they emerged in real-space. He opened his eyes and, as always after a jump, immediately checked the overhead diagnostic reports for any emergency caused by the traverse. His second check was for his co-pilot who smiled back at him, apparently unaffected by this jump.

"Amazing," she said. "I think Khoe lent a hand in there somewhere. This didn't hurt at all."

"Not tired?"

"Not even a bit!"

"Dutchman? Come in."

"I remember that voice," Khoe said. "Is that Caelyn? I liked him."

Khoe beamed so happily at Ciela that Ciela responded with a smile of her own before turning to Seth. "*How* long were you two joined?"

Seth replied to the hail by opening a video link. Caelyn's face blinked onto the screen and Seth and Ciela exchanged an amused glance when they saw the smile on his normally motionless face. "Yes, it's us. What are you doing there?" Seth scanned the vicinity of the Callas system. It had only the one habitable planet and the second keyhole, the restricted one leading to Tor Ag, lay beyond its outer planet, several hours from this one. Caelyn's research ship had left its position and now stood in orbit over Callas. A military cruiser hovered protectively nearby but did not contact the *Dutchman*.

"Air Command ordered us away when some ships arrived, insisting on passing with the threat of guns. Nobody's saying so but we're guessing they're rebels, worried about something going down on Tor Ag. Some of them actually made it past Air Command and entered the breach. Who knows what's become of them. It appears to be a combat situation now. We're about to be recalled to Targon, I'm sure. Did I mention how happy I am to see you, Centauri?"

"We're happy to be seen, Delphi," Seth replied with a grin. He focused the *Dutchman*'s sensors on the distant keyhole to Tor Ag to see the Air Command fleet surrounded by a swarm of private ships. Their open com transmissions sounded a lot like nobody was about to give way in the situation.

Ciela had Larris on her feet by the time they approached the *Laruel* above Callas. As before, both Caelyn and Shan Quine awaited them at the docks. Their serene expressions did not change but Caelyn's eyes brightened with joy when the arrivals stepped through the airlock. A third Delphian accompanied them and immediately took the catatonic woman into her care. Larris, looking no more or less confused than she had all along, allowed herself to be led away.

Ciela watched them go. "I hope she's all right."

Shan Quine sighed. "We were not able to help them before, but we have learned from our observations. We will do what we can." He lowered his voice. "No one else here is aware of her condition. If necessary, we will remove her to Delphi." With a nod to Caelyn, he hurried after his colleague to begin his work.

Seth and Ciela followed Caelyn along the curved passage matching the *Laruel*'s graceful contours until they reached a small lab, more private than the large observation hub at the ship's center.

"We've got a bit more information, but nothing conclusive," he said when they settled around a hologram board. "I'm anxious to hear about your findings."

"Oh, we've got findings, all right," Ciela said, glancing at Khoe who was waiting to be recognized by Caelyn, looking like she'd burst if that didn't happen soon.

Seth pointed at the interface node at his temple. "Take a look."

Puzzled, Caelyn reached over to initiate a khamal between himself and Seth, taking a sharp breath when he realized that Ciela was already linked. When he then saw the white-haired woman standing behind Ciela a surprised smile lit his face. "Gods!" he exhaled. "How did you manage to find Khoe?"

"The resonance," Seth said. "Or, rather, our version of it. Frightened away everyone but her. That's how we made it back here. Good thing she's nosy. She gets that from me."

"Hello, Caelyn," Khoe said. "How's the hand?"

The Delphian automatically flexed the prosthetic that served as his hand, almost indistinguishable from the other. "Close to perfect. You're aware of what's happening in subspace?"

She shook her head. "Something sad, I think. Some of us are lost again. Everything seems so slow. Dark."

"Dark? In subspace?" Caelyn smiled. "I do suppose that's a good analogy of what we're theorizing." He manipulated a few symbols on the data screen before them. It showed a standard image of what represented a subspace span, looking like little more than a thin funnel between two or three endpoints outside of which nothing existed. This, all of them knew, was no longer true. "We've been chasing probes through that span since you left. Some were lost, some returned. We're detecting a discrepancy in the strength of the resonance that we're finding now. When compared to your recording, I mean."

"But that is just a facsimile," Ciela said. "Isn't it?"

"Yes, but not where it counts. It allowed us to make comparative measurements."

"Compare what?" Seth said.

"Well, time. We've found that what we call subspace is likely very old. Perhaps older than we assume our own universe to be. And it's in decline."

"How can it decline?" Ciela said. "It's the Big Nothing."

Chris Reher

Caelyn shook his head. "Another misnomer. It has mass, although very little. Khoe herself possibly encompasses more space than this solar system but out here she fits into Seth's head without even causing physical discomfort."

Khoe snickered.

"Rather broadly scattered but nevertheless entangled in ways we don't really understand," Caelyn amended. "Gravity is most likely, but drawn together by the Alpha resonance. Therefore subspace has energy and time, which is what we assumed *not* to be the case before we encountered the Dyads."

"Khoe said that they were dying," Seth said.

Caelyn's face showed no surprise. "She is likely correct. Her space, her world, is basically winding down. With such weak fields, so little energy, it is ending."

"Ending how? It's already nothing." Ciela said. "Sorry, Khoe, but it really does seem empty."

"Entropy," Khoe said and looked to Caelyn for confirmation. He nodded. "They think that we've reached a point of equilibrium. What energy we have is now dissipated so evenly that it cannot provide us with what we need to maintain our connections. We are finite. We can reform from existing entities that have lost their cohesion but we don't multiply."

Ciela blinked. "Entropy." She seemed to taste the word as she spoke it. "Everything just stops?"

"Energy yes. Mass no," Caelyn said. "Khoe's particles in a vacuum will keep moving. She'll just fly apart without the energy she needs to maintain cohesion. And without that they are just that. Particles floating around in a vacuum."

"That's terrible," Ciela said. "It'd be the end of an entire species."

Seth studied the keyhole model which told them absolutely nothing of what was really going on. "This isn't just the end of the subspace entities," he said. The others watched him change the interface and then flick his finger across the string that connected one terminus to the other.

The line crumpled and then reformed. "This is going to change how we travel through subspace. If we can travel at all."

"That, my friend, is the conclusion we've come to." Caelyn changed the display to show a map of the sector, including the location of several gated jumpsites and known keyholes. "We've now had reports from navigators here, there, and at those two locations that they are unable to find the expected terminus at all. One military ship reported a very rough jump coming out of Aikhor. But the navigator is Delphian and held it together. Said that he lost his grip on the exit during the jump but then found it again."

"You can't just move a keyhole," Ciela said. "Or delete it out of space."

"The terminus hasn't moved for those keyholes. But the path we use to connect them can dissipate, which is new to us. Or switch to another keyhole, which Ciela's talent has proven. We occasionally lose ships during a leap. Some of them may have emerged in some distant spot well outside Trans-Targon. Who knows, maybe outside this galaxy. We all know that it's a very bad idea to jump if you don't know where you're going to land."

Seth watched holographic display for a moment. It looked less real than Khoe's very tangible shape beyond it. "When is this going to happen? Their energy fizzling out like that."

Caelyn winced like the bearer of bad news. "Her people are already falling apart and even failing to merge, which is probably the only thing that made them aware that this is even happening. Without even gravity, the Alpha resonance that brings them together is weakening and will stop. We're seeing the results in the way some subspace spans are failing for us. We'll soon see more, making travel impossible. In this part of our galaxy, the end has already begun."

Khoe poked his arm and then pointed at the interface to the *Laruel*'s data system. "Can I take a look? Seth says I have to ask first."

"Of course. Look for the files we've put together on the span from here to Tor Ag."

Seth put his hand on the interface panel. Khoe's image faltered for a moment as she turned her focus onto the machine to feed her unending thirst for knowledge. Not for the first time, Seth wished she had the means to pass what she learned on to him.

Caelyn observed her for a moment. "She seems different," he said. "I'm not sure how, though."

Seth shrugged. "*I* am different." He looked to Ciela. "*Things* are different. Khoe just sort of slipped into that difference without missing a beat." He grinned. "I think she's taken a bit of a shine to Ciela, actually."

"I think Ciela is very shiny," Khoe said with a smile, but her attention seemed elsewhere.

"What a peculiar situation," Caelyn said, shifting his eyes meaningfully from Ciela to Seth. Delphians weren't famed for their empathy, especially when reading the emotions of other species, but Caelyn knew how inextricably Seth and Khoe now entangled, and what it meant to his friend. The worry on his face was undisguised.

Ciela pointed to the displays before them. "I think we were discussing the end of our civilization as we know it? You two are so easily distracted."

Seth chuckled. "Yes, but that's an unpleasant subject. And not something we can change. It'll be up to Astrophysics to find a way to at least try to stabilize the jumpsites. We may have to reinvent the way we move around Trans-Targon."

Caelyn nodded. "I have the feeling we're about to be recalled to Targon. And I'm not sure how happy I am about taking any subspace jump right now. Better navigators than me are losing their exits."

"This span here between Tor Ag and Callas holds some answers," Seth said. "It's a bit of an exception. It looks passable until you try it. But both keyholes now lead to Chitta Moor."

"Say that again?"

Seth nodded. "We found the lost ships on Chitta Moore, *not* having a good time at Queta Station. Some crew members have turned into Dyads. Not only that, some of them have told the locals that they're on Chitta Moor by Targon's orders. I'm fairly sure they're not, even if they have a shiny new Outrider vessel."

"Why would they pretend to be from Targon?"

"Because even on Chitta Moor no one's going to question an expedition sent out from Targon. Anyone else would be a civilian outfit, and be suspected of trying to muscle in on the mineral rights there or something. Our maybe-scientists said they're working on some sort of experiment. Ciela had a look at what they're building – she'll give you some details. They told us that they're just trying to figure a way to get everyone home."

"But you don't believe that?"

"No. It sounded to me like they arrived long before the trouble with the Callas-Tor Ag span started. I think the entities stole the vessel in subspace, merged with the crew to create Dyads, and diverted the usual terminus to Chitta Moor. Now they're causing more ships to end up in the wrong place. Making more Dyads."

Ciela scowled. "Apparently killing a lot of other crew and passengers while they do that doesn't bother them a whole lot. That woman we brought here might lose her baby as well as her mind. All that just so a few of them can get out?"

"Even subspace has laws of nature," Caelyn said. "What species would allow itself to become extinct if it has the means to prevent it? Everyone wants to survive. But why would they decide on Chitta Moor?"

"That's the big question," Seth said. "Someone there, another Dyad, told us that they're trying to form a keyhole on the planet to go somewhere else entirely. Away from the Trans-Targon sector. After what you just told us, I'm guessing they just want to escape subspace before it's too late. Hopefully far away from us."

Caelyn frowned. "They're forming a new keyhole? We haven't been able to figure that out in half a millennium of space travel. Even if they knew how, keyholes are a point in space and unaffected by gravity. They would not be tied to a solid object, like a planet orbiting a star. Of course, the Dyads could be waiting for the planet to move over the keyhole for some event to happen. But that would be easier in space. And far less damaging. Are they hostile?"

"Not the ones doing the experiments, except for the part about trying to blow up the planet. They're using a lot of energy and a number of accelerators. Parts of them, anyway."

Caelyn's eyes widened. "Accelerators?"

Ciela leaned forward and placed her hand on Seth's. "Are you going to tell them the bad part of that, or should I?"

He sighed. "I was just thinking that."

"Thinking what?" Khoe said.

"There are rebels among the Dyads. More than we assumed because the Shri-Lan aren't about to report lost ships to Air Command. Those rebels have as much interest in subspace as the average *greval* worm. They plan to rejoin their factions here, precisely what Air Command doesn't want happening. They think the mechanism being built out there is what's keeping them imprisoned on the planet. They'll try to take control of it, destroy it, even, if it means getting home again."

"When?" Caelyn said.

"As soon as they get tired of waiting for the others to assemble enough new Dyads to start their little colony," Seth said. "We *were* going to bring Air Command back with us to deal with them. Ciela can lead only one ship back at a time, we think, considering what we saw happening before, but a Ghoster would do the job nicely."

"I'm not sure if they'd bother with Chitta Moor right now," Caelyn said. "The Dyads on Chitta Moor are a threat. But so far they're cut off from the rest of Trans-Targon, apparently by design, if that rebel you spoke to was truthful. Targon's priority is the subspace entropy, now that other spans are failing. They won't risk their ships to make a jump that may well be one-way, as far as they know. That colony is on its own for now."

"We could go back," Ciela said. "You and me, Seth. Maybe try to bring out the transport ship, like you promised. If the captain gets his wits together, he will have followed your advice to move his people aboard. You know they'll end up in the collateral damage category otherwise."

Seth nodded.

"That's a big risk to take," Caelyn said. "You know, sometimes I think Delphians are the only reasonable-thinking people in this entire sector." He tipped his chin toward Ciela. "Not counting that one, of course."

"Probably," Seth said. "But are you having fun with all that reasonable-thinking?"

The Delphian raised his prosthetic hand to aim a rude gesture at Seth, one of which he had been unaware until Seth had shown him. Ciela laughed.

"Let's wait to hear back from the colonel," Seth said. "I'm hoping you folks will invite us for some real food and maybe let me have enough water for a hot bath."

Khoe glanced at Ciela. "I'll rest a while." Her image faded and then disappeared from view.

"Where did she go?" Ciela touched Seth's interface to break their mental link.

He frowned briefly, only now realizing how pleasurable her touch in his mind felt when she did not have to contend with the headache it normally brought on. Caelyn, too, closed their khamal. Seth didn't miss him quite as much.

"She sort of withdraws where I can't perceive her," he said. "Something we agreed on to give me a break from constantly having someone around."

"I didn't know you minded that," she said, a little disturbed by his revelation, given the many hours they spent together aboard the *Dutchman*.

"Sometimes," he said dramatically, "a man's got to do what a man's got to do without an audience."

* * *

Caelyn invited them to the *Laruel*'s dining lounge for a pleasant meal that included a wonderful selection of fresh food brought up from the surface. Shan Quine joined them, not with any good news about Larris, but, as he had promised, she was to be transferred into the care of the Shantir healers on Delphi. A few comfortable hours passed before Seth and Ciela retired to the *Dutchman*.

Rest, however, did not seem foremost on Ciela's mind when the pressure door sealed behind them. She stood by the lounger, watching Seth move around the cabin, randomly dropping his clothes, and it took a moment before he noticed the languid way in which she unfastened her shirt. Her eyes had darkened to nearly black when she let them linger on his bare torso before turning to pull back the covers.

He came to stand behind her to stroke the hair from her neck. She sighed happily when she felt his lips on her skin and then his arms wrap around her body. He savored her heady scent and the feel of her under his fingers. She let him lift her blouse over her head before she climbed onto the lounger, pulling him along with her.

Seth stretched out, losing himself in their kiss, resolving to take his time but knowing damn well he'd soon lose his patience. She understood too well how and where to touch him, showing him wordlessly what she needed from him and so lift them both to ever more passionate heights. It was never the same and it never disappointed.

But then her body stiffened beneath his. "Seth?" she said, her lips still on his.

"Hmm?"

"Is Khoe here?"

He opened his eyes and raised his head, confused. "Khoe?"

"Don't stop," Khoe said. "This feels so good!"

Ciela took his hand away from her breast. "She's here,

isn't she?"

"No, don't stop," Khoe said. "I won't be a bother. This is so wonderful. Touch her there again."

Seth flopped onto his back with a loud groan. "Khoe!"

She faded into view, visible only to him. "I'll be quiet," she said. "Ask her to turn over."

"What?" he gasped.

"I want to feel that ridge they have down their backs."

Ciela sat up, looking around as if to see Khoe in their bed. "No way," she said. "Not like this."

"Ciela, don't," he said, utterly at a loss. Had anyone ever experienced something quite like this? "She can go dormant again, if I ask her. I should have told her…"

Ciela rose from the lounger, looking more exasperated than angry, he hoped. "You figure it out, Seth, but I'm not doing this." With that, she stalked out of the cabin and slammed the door to the crew quarters behind her.

"Oops," Khoe said.

He placed his forearm over his eyes. "Was this really necessary?"

"It's a little hard to ignore you when you're in such a state." She smiled happily. "If you care to remember."

"I remember," he said, somewhat reluctantly. "This isn't the same."

"Exactly! I just had to know what it feels like to kiss like this. It was better than I imagined." She sighed. "She is so exciting. I guess we botched that now, though."

"We?"

"She'll be all right when she gets up. I'll tell her I'm sorry for peeking." They both felt the touch of her hand on the skin of his chest. "Want to, uh, finish what you started?"

He cursed and got off the lounger to walk to Ciela's door. "Ciela?" he said, leaning his forehead against the cold metal. "Look, I'm sorry. She's sorry. This is all so complicated. Let's talk about this."

"Go to sleep."

"Should I beg?"

"Don't make fun of this."

He sighed and turned to lean on the door, fairly sure that his troubles had only begun.

NINE

Perhaps it was possible, in some alternate universe, to remain asleep, or perhaps pretend to be asleep while Ciela went about her morning routines. But the banging of doors and the *Dutchman*'s traitorous obedience to her pre-flight commands would wake even a Delphian. Seth pulled his blanket over his head, aware that he hadn't slept alone in well over a year. He didn't like it.

"I think she wants you to get up," Khoe said.

"Thank you. I hadn't noticed."

The overhead lights blinked into their daytime settings, bright even through his blanket. He heard Ciela talking to someone over the com, probably Caelyn.

"Aren't you going to?"

He eventually pulled the cover back to see Ciela standing beside the lounger. "Are you getting up?" she said.

He groaned. Two women in his life and both of them nagging at the same time. Did any man deserve this?

"Message came in from Targon." Ciela went into the galley.

"Carras?" Seth sat up and ran his hands through his hair.

She nodded. He smelled the sweet aroma of her tea. She hadn't asked if he wanted any.

He fumbled for the datasheet near the lounger and

relayed the message to the screen above the counter. Ciela looked up to watch it as well. The colonel's face appeared, looking not at all like someone about to send a cheerful message. Ostensibly retired after that unfortunate incident over Shaddallam, Carras now headed Targon's Intelligence community, including the team of officially non-existent operatives to which Seth and Ciela belonged. Centauri, like Seth, he seemed more Human in height and considerable girth but the violet eyes gave away his origin, as did the dense shadow of black stubble on his head. The recording seemed to have been made in his private quarters rather than down in the sleek dungeons of the Intelligence department.

"*Cazun* curse your damnable shiftiness, Kada," he began. "Your report has more holes in it than the Talisa asteroid."

Seth stopped the recording. "He doesn't say Good Morning, either. See how I get treated?"

"Are you talking to me or Khoe?"

He resumed the message. "I don't even want to know how you got yourself involved in this," the colonel said, "but I'm sure you're aware that we're losing cohesion in a number of subspace exits now. Aikhor is cut off, so is Bellac and Delphi. We were able to chart the second keyhole to Magra but the processors are barely able to keep a grip on the terminus. Targon is putting all resources into Astrophysics to deal with the subspace catastrophe. The *Laruel* has been recalled to Targon. We need every Delphian we've got on this." Carras shook his head, looking resigned. "There is too much at stake to worry about the Callas-Tor Ag span."

"I guess Caelyn was right about that," Ciela said. "They'll just abandon everyone stuck at Queta Station. Typical Air Command."

"We'll dispatch a battle cruiser from our base on Ud Mrak to guard the keyhole to Chitta Moor," Carras continued. "If there is a chance to get those missing ships back, we might get some priority. Especially if Dyads are involved." He leaned toward the camera as if to make sure he had Seth's attention. "We have detected the Alpha resonance here in real-space. Vanguard agents are on their way to three hotspots right now. We cannot allow Dyads into this sector. You, more than anyone, understand the danger of that. I'll expect you to focus your attention on tracking down the one you reported." He seemed to want to say something more, but then just reached for the com panel. "Be well, Kada. I'll trust you to make the right call."

"Since when?" Ciela said when the screen had gone blank.

"He's being polite."

"He'll be less polite when he finds out that he just ordered you to murder yourself."

Seth untangled himself from his blankets and pulled a shirt over his head. His morning steam bath would have to wait. Khoe hovered nearby when he came to sit on one of the stools by the galley counter. "Let's talk about this, Ciela."

She sipped from her bowl of tea. "About what?"

"About me being a Dyad. About Khoe."

"What's there to talk about? She's in your head, I get that. But that doesn't mean she should be in your bed, too. Not while I'm in there."

"She's sorry about that. Truly. It didn't really occur to her that you'd mind."

"Well, I do."

Khoe tugged on Seth sleeve. "She's not breaking up with you, is she? That'd be terrible!"

He frowned at her. At another time he might have been amused by her wide-eyed expression of apprehension. "Nobody's breaking up," he said.

Ciela looked at the spot he had just spoken to. "Is she here?"

"Yes." He watched her turn away to work with the food processor. A good sign, perhaps, if she made his breakfast as well. "I can't lock her away. Like that rebel does, back there on Chitta Moor. She's not a toy you can put aside. She's as real as—"

She held up her hand. "I get that, Seth. It's not that hard

to understand. Doesn't mean I have to like it." She extended her hand toward him, a silent request to join him in a khamal. He nodded. Her eyes shifted to Khoe after a few moments of concentration.

Khoe smiled at her. "Hello."

Ciela's lips tightened. Seth wondered if this meant a deepening disapproval or some effort to suppress the smile that she'd otherwise offer in response to Khoe's sunny disposition. "Hello," she said, which still held no clues.

"Don't be mad at him," Khoe said. "I can stay out of your way. Honest."

Ciela's brilliant blue eyes turned to him, looking dangerously moist. "So what happens now? Is this it? You're staying a Dyad forever? On the run from Air Command's hounds?"

Seth looked over to Khoe, who seemed equally taken aback by the question. "Hadn't even thought of that, to be honest. We can't separate here in real-space. She'll die."

"She'll die if she returns to subspace, the way things are going there," Ciela said with deadpan Delphian pragmatism. "It's why those Dyads on Chitta Moor are bugging out, remember?"

"Can I have some tea, please?"

She stabbed a finger at the food processor's control panel. "You have to consider this, Seth." Ciela leaned against the cabinets and looked up at the ceiling. "Maybe my people on Delphi aren't so wrong about keeping to themselves and letting the rest of us meddle with things we shouldn't. Maybe we're not meant to jump through subspace as if it's no distance at all. It would end the rebel wars, that's certain. Maybe the thing to do is to find some pretty planet and just take up farming. Forget there's trouble among the stars. How's that?"

Seth, by now, knew her well enough to see that she might actually be serious. Unlike him, without roots or destiny, Ciela could call one of the most beautiful planets in the sector home. One that would welcome her as family. Maybe

Khoe's fear that a breakup was imminent was not that unreasonable. He had endured more spectacular breakups over lesser reasons that having an alien join them in bed. He felt a queasy stab of unease at the thought that Ciela might actually leave him.

"Come on, Arawaj," he said, forcing a bounce into his voice that he didn't feel. "You were practically born on a spaceship. There isn't a planet that can keep you for long and you know it." He turned when some unclear sound came from Khoe's direction. Ciela, too, saw that her face had lost its beguiling expression and she now seemed close to tears. "Khoe?"

"This is my fault," she said, barely audible. "I should have stayed away." She looked from him to Ciela. "I'll go away if you want me to. I can probably separate next time we jump."

"It's not what I want," Ciela said. She allowed a softer note into her voice. "This is your life, too, now."

"I'm making trouble for Seth."

"Yeah, you are," Ciela said, biting back a half-smile. "But he's used to that."

Seth sighed, starting to see a light at the end of this tunnel in that tiny twitch of her lip.

"I can be useful," Khoe said with renewed enthusiasm. "You'll need help if you're going to Pelion. I can be very handy. Ask Seth."

He frowned, puzzled, as he accepted a cup from Ciela. "We're going to Pelion?"

Ciela looked sternly at Khoe. "You were watching me?"

Khoe shrugged. "I noticed you in the database so I followed what you were doing. You have no idea how boring Seth is when he's sleeping."

"I do, actually."

"What's going on?" Seth said.

"I couldn't sleep so I went to see about that Outrider we saw on Chitta Moor. If we can find where it came from, we'll be closer to finding the Dyad that sent it out there. I traced its hull ID back to Pelion. Or, rather, the Azon Corp orbiter over Pelion. They own the ship. It was dispatched from there two months ago."

"By Azon Corp?"

"That's the interesting part," Ciela said. Khoe nodded, eager for Seth to hear these findings. "The orders could not be verified. The original dispatch was falsified by someone who hacked into Azon's system to release the ship. It was supposed to be heading to Aikhor, not Tor Ag. It jumped and disappeared. Azon assumes it stolen or pirated, the crew lost now with everyone else that went through that keyhole."

"I guess in a way it is," Khoe said.

Seth nodded. "At least we know the crew is all right. Mostly," he added with a look to Khoe. "Any idea who could have hacked into Azon? That's quite the feat."

"Not without going there," Ciela said. "The order appears to have been relayed from the orbiter's flight control. If I can get there I could poke around to see where it came from."

"I can help," Khoe reminded them. "But they've upped security there now, worried about inside jobs."

"I'm not surprised," Seth said. Although Azon operated independently, it supplied a vast amount of technology and arms to Air Command. Their contracts included new tech and medical innovations, new weapons, new propulsion systems, some carried out secretly in remote locations. As far as Seth knew, the corporation dealt only with Commonwealth interests and had no need or appetite for working with rebels. The orbiter over Pelion housed vast commercial ventures and a major administrative division along with more people than most of the cities on the planet below. "Let's shove off then."

"Can I—" Khoe began.

"No," he said at once. "Let's not take chances with these keyholes. Ciela will jump in case she has to grab another exit."

Khoe pursed her lips.

"She can pout?" Ciela said. "Where'd she learn that?"

"She likes girly fiction."

Ciela looked amused and very much surprised. "You have romance stories in your library?"

He shifted in his seat. "Came with the set."

"You have any new ones?" Khoe asked.

Seth cleared his throat. "I'll go get dressed." He stood up to head for the hygiene chamber.

"I'll tell Caelyn what we're doing," Ciela said. She went to open the pressure door to the *Dutchman*'s cargo hold when she turned back to see Khoe still standing by the galley counter. "Um, you run pre-flight," she said and briefly touched Seth's neural node to sever their khamal.

"She doesn't want us showering together," he said and ducked around the red-hot glare Ciela aimed at him.

* * *

When Air Command nudged the governors of Pelion to turn one of the sub-sector's three keyholes into a fully charted jumpsite, the rebels that once found refuge here were forced out and commerce moved in. The Commonwealth Union arrived with lucrative offers of trade and protection, and now the easily monitored jumpsite subjected suspect travelers to close surveillance by Air Command. Despite strident objections by anti-Union factions, it meant a far safer and cheaper subspace traverse for everyone else.

Azon Corp was quick to take advantage of the suddenly very busy crossroads and set up their largest operation in orbit over the planet. Accessible, movable, and defendable because of Air Command's close proximity at the jumpsite, it was easily supplied with workers and water from the surface.

"Look how big that is!" Khoe marveled when Seth brought the *Dutchman* around to the primary loop of the station. From there, long jetties reached out as if into an invisible sea to platter-docks for cruisers of this size. Farther along the massive ring, platforms received transports delivering raw materials or removing manufactured goods, others served commuters and visitors from the surface. A central spindle rose above them to a disc housing the administration of the company. "It must take days to walk around that ring."

"They use shuttle rails that run through the center," Seth said. "Ciela? You're up."

She nodded sleepily, still curled up on her bench where she had dozed since their leap from Callas. The jump had taxed her more than usual as she had spanned directly from there to Pelion along the increasingly vague subspace matrix, but they had emerged without incident.

"She looks so tired," Khoe said. She raised a hand as if to touch Ciela's pale cheek but then withdrew it and twisted her fingers together. Seth was again amazed at how easily this ethereal creature, knowing nothing but the information she had gleaned from his archives and their interactions, had amassed such a complex catalog of expressions.

"Yes, she's tired," Seth said for Ciela's benefit. "She'll need to sleep."

Ciela sat up. "No, let's do this." She straightened the crisp blouse she had put on earlier and smoothed her hair, looking to Seth for approval rather than find a mirror. He reached over to arrange a few wayward strands.

"You look like a Delphian," he said when she settled her face into the expressionless façade her people used when dealing with strangers. They reserved their smiles, as well as the tears of which they were quite capable, for their kin and those they held dear. It had nothing to do with their physiology and everything with their preference to remain pointedly aloof from the bewildering assortment of foreigners mixing on other worlds. Ciela had not benefited from this lifelong conditioning and Seth was glad for that.

"Thank you. I've been practicing." She touched his neural node and then nodded when Khoe appeared before her.

He switched the com channel from traffic control to station operations after double-checking the *Dutchman*'s ID. He had the ship scrubbed so often and Air Command deleted his records so frequently that he had trouble remembering it from one trip to the next. Ciela saw him display the current information and smirked to show what she thought of his inferior memory.

"Dinesh *Dutchman* PK-3, out of Aikhor, permission to dock," he said in a monotone.

It took a while before the overhead screen flicked on to show a Feydan controller at his board, waiting for reports about the station's newest visitors. He glanced at his displays and then looked again when he saw the Delphian beside the pilot, a rare crewmember aboard a private vessel. As had other officials on other occasions, this one spent little time checking the reports upon seeing Ciela – Delphi's reputation for being incorruptible had opened many doors for them before. Even Seth had never encountered a Delphian rebel before she had entered his life.

"What brings you to Azon Corp Station?" the operator said.

Ciela maintained her disinterested expression while her fingers tapped over a manual control board attached to the com panel, silently making her way along the open channel and into the controller's board. From there, her long experience with most technology of this type let her arrive at the main firewalls to the station's systems. Khoe followed her progress, ready to slip inside.

"Please check your records," Ciela said, perfectly adopting that cold mix of condescension and detachment that informed the operator of his irrelevance in greater matters. Delphians invited few outsiders into their world and so this exterior was all anyone ever saw. Seth watched the performance with awed amusement. "An invitation has been extended for me to tour your cartography labs," she said. "Shan Quine from the Delphian astrophysics lab on Magra Alaric sent his recommendation less than a turn ago." She left it at that although most traffic in Trans-Targon measured time by Targon's rotation to create a standard.

"Huh? Oh, yes. Here it is. Shan Quine did indeed make the arrangement. We do not often see Delphian navigators on this station."

She did not reply as nothing he said required the effort.

He cleared his throat. "Permission granted, *Dutchman*. Decon and iris scan mandatory. How many aboard?" The last question was a formality; the station's scanners had already inventoried the unshielded part of the ship.

Ciela regarded him silently, as if taken aback that he'd involve her in something as menial as docking the ship. She shifted her attention away from the camera to continue her infiltration into the station's inner workings.

"Two crew," Seth replied to let the flustered operator off the hook. "What's your recommendation for a place to get a good meal?"

"Not the small craft docks, if you value your stomach. Head to the twenty block. Pretty much anything there's edible if you have the coin."

Seth peered at the screen to catch the operator's name. "Thanks, Afael. I'll try my luck over there." He saw Ciela gesturing that she needed more time. "I'm hoping you folks have a good price on coolant. I'm running a little low."

"You're kidding, right? If you want cheap, try the surface. We're regulated beyond belief up here."

Ciela now tapped Khoe's arm although it was Seth who leaned forward and placed his hand on the panel. Khoe's shape flickered momentarily as she extended herself into the *Dutchman*'s circuits. It took mere moments.

"I'm in," she said, creating a profile for herself within the station's security settings. "Easy."

"Isn't that just the way," Seth commiserated with the operator. He kept his eyes on the Feydan's face, waiting for him to notice that someone had hacked his board. Nothing seemed to catch his attention. "At least you don't get leaky tubes that way. *Dutchman* out." He turned to Ciela and then winked at Khoe. "We make quite a team, don't we?"

Ciela slumped back into her bench, exhausted. "Good thing Shan Quine is so well connected. I need to sleep. How long do you think we have before they realize we're not showing up at that lab?"

"We never said we'd go right away." He focused on bringing the *Dutchman* to their assigned port amidst a ridiculous amount of traffic. The sky bosses running the operation did so efficiently but it still felt like threading his way through an insect hive. He waited for a disk-shaped passenger cruiser to clear his path and then sidled his way into the locks. The ship shuddered when the pogs closed, and then started to wind down the gravity generators to let the station's own take over.

"It's here," Khoe said.

"Huh?" Ciela blinked tiredly at the screens to see what might have drawn her attention.

"A Dyad. I'm feeling traces of the Alpha resonance nearby. Here on the station."

Seth tugged on his lower lip, considering this. "Are you sure? If this is our Dyad, he'd be a fool to stick around after stealing an Outrider vessel."

"I am."

Ciela tipped her bench forward and came to her feet. Seth walked her back into the main cabin and waited until she dropped her blouse onto a chair and snuggled into the blankets on the lounger as she always did.

He wondered if she'd be sleeping there tonight and pushed the thought aside. The past few hours had been a strain on both of them. She no longer seemed angry at Khoe's little indiscretion but something had changed, of this he was certain. He tried not to think of what lay ahead for them if she could not reconcile herself with what he had become. After a moment's hesitation, he bent to kiss her cheek, as he often did when she needed to rest after a jump. "We'll just have a look around."

"Be careful," she said. "This isn't some backwater outpost. They're using the best of Air Command security."

"No one's more careful than I am," he assured her as he stepped into his boots. Truly, this was one of the few places where a clear escape route existed for any contingency. Here his Air Command ID code ensured that, even if someone caught him nosing around, he'd be cleared by Targon and on his way in minutes. Once used, a new ID was issued and any record of his presence here deleted.

But there were cameras and watchful eyes beyond the reach of Air Command's heavy-handed oversight. Seth's face was known in many places as belonging to a rebel sympathizer, perhaps even Arawaj. Like any of the special ops agents, he ran a risk when making himself known to local personnel and so Seth rarely used his credentials to do his work. Of course, working without Air Command muscle kept things interesting and was why he had agreed to deep-cover operations in the first place. The last time he had worn a uniform was back at the flight academy.

He left the ship and walked through the short umbilical to submit to the mandatory decon scan looking for unacceptable pathogens, weapons, explosives and whatever contraband was disallowed here today. At the exit, he winked into a lens probing the deep violet of his iris for further clues of his identity. As a visitor without official business here on Pelion Station, he had left his weapons on the *Dutchman* and he felt strangely nude when he stepped into the docking port. He let his eyes roam over the open concourse, crammed with shops vying for commuter coin, to satisfy Khoe's voracious curiosity.

"Are those Aramese?" she asked when he walked toward an information column. Some travelers stood there, working their way through maps of the station and helpful tips about how to behave here. Among them, two bipeds, clearly of a Prime species but covered in hair so thick as to resemble fur, carried a third in a sling between them. Both wore vests and belts designed to keep them cool in the fluctuating drafts wafting through the hall. "Is that one sick?"

Maybe, Seth replied silently. He scanned the hall for signs of Air Command. *There's a clinic here specializing in exobiology. They've been doing some very fine work with that.* He watched three soldiers prowl along the gates, no doubt looking for evildoers in the crowd. Other uniforms here seemed to belong to

Azon's own cadre of security personnel.

"So crowded here," she said. "Oh, look! That's a baby Caspian! They're so cute!"

Seth grinned, never having considered Caspians to be especially adorable. Their yellow raptor eyes always made him a little uneasy. Had he ever seen one blink? The infant on a passing adult's shoulder looked like a scrawny little bird to him.

He approached the information panel and placed his hand on it. Khoe disappeared from his vision as she focused all of her attention on the station's systems. Seth watched the soldiers stroll back toward him. Different ones, he realized, looking a little menacing in their gray Air Command uniforms. Sensors of every kind studded the multi-storied parking rings to guard the safety of the station and yet patrols seemed doubled here now.

Khoe, let's not go poking too far for now. This doesn't smell right.

"I smell *churry* samosas," she said. "I found something."

What?

"The fake orders apparently made by Azon Corp. They wanted the Outrider to survey some minerals in the Tor Ag sub-sector. Which just sounds boring."

And?

"I'm walking my way back. The order came from within this station. Service sector. You can let go now. I'm linked through your data sleeve and encoded."

Seth strolled away from the info pillars and toward the row of shops. Each inhabited an equally-sized module but made inventive use of the small space by seeming to fill every last bit of it with their merchandize. For the most part, these vendors sold supplies to departing travelers but some offered hot food, trinkets from foreign places, and currency for trade. His supply of the triangular coins used on Aikhor was a little low and so he stopped to check the exchange rates.

"Definitely originating from the Service level," Khoe said. "Looks like they just used a com system down there to infiltrate Azon Corp."

Risky. Or talented. Can you tell who created that order? A name would be good.

"You think he would have put his name on that?"

No need for sarcasm. Seth passed on the absurd price of the currency and walked away from yet another patrol heading his way.

"Left a trail, though. Sort of. I'm going to see if it turns up anywhere else."

What sort of trail? The Alpha resonance?

"No. A pattern to the code he's using. It's unique. I can follow it like a scent."

Besides the *churry*, the only scent Seth picked up was that of air that had been scrubbed too many times and the Aramese standing next to him. He was used to this; the actual scent of fresh air blowing over a planet's surface was more of a novelty to him than this canned gas. *I'll trust you to know what you're talking about.*

"I think I see something. It's like flashes. I can see him moving through the system. Kind of like tiny comets. The tail fades quickly after it passes. As he erases what he's looked at."

Can you get a physical location?

"Yes. Over near the transporter loading docks. Below here."

Seth headed for the end of the concourse, taking care to walk purposefully but unhurried. The rail system linked this port to other parts of the orbiter, including the lower ring and the mostly restricted administrative on the top tier. He passed a bank of lifts and entered a drafty tunnel leading to the rails. Segmented trains stopped at regular intervals to pick up and unload personnel. He stepped into one pointed out by Khoe.

Can you tell how he did it?

"He just did it. I could launch an expedition to Centauri from here if I wanted to. You just need the right access codes."

He watched her pretend to view the colossal city-station

rush past the window, sitting upright on a bench like any of the other passengers. She noticed his eyes on her and let her wild tangle of braids float on the breeze although the car was fully enclosed by a transparent dome. *You know, that whole idea is just very scary and probably why nobody wants us here in Trans-Targon.*

"Fun, though. Of course, not everyone is as smart as we are. You just happen to have an awful lot of information on your ship for me to learn. This Dyad must have, too. The information he has doesn't just lie around somewhere." She pointed out of the window to keep his eyes on the wonders to be seen out there. "He's been in Air Command's drawers, too. They should have noticed that."

Seth muttered an oath under his breath. Search and destroy, such were his orders. He began to understand that a little better now. That doing so meant destroying a Dyad, a species to which he now belonged, didn't really bother him. He had double-crossed, arrested, and killed many of his fellow Centauri in the name of Air Command as well as his personal little war against the corrupted and malevolent, no matter on whose side they worked. He felt no more attached to Dyads than his own people. But it wasn't until the subspace entities joined to form a Dyad that they inherited their host's disposition. They were the main victim here, he thought, driven only by instinct until they touched a sentient mind. Khoe was right; they did not belong here.

This didn't stop her from enjoying herself as she pointed out whatever she found remarkable in this mega-capsule floating in space. He smiled when the train momentarily left the interior to round a new sector under construction and she exclaimed over the massive scaffolding shaping a new addition to the orbiter.

But when the rail shuttle dove back into the station's innards she turned to him with a pensive look on her face. "Are you going to kill him? The Dyad?"

"What? No," he replied, startled by her question. As far as he knew, Dyads shared only tactile sensations and the sort of verbal communication made possible by their host's neural interface. And yet she seemed to have arrived at the same dark thoughts as he had. "I don't even have a gun with me."

"You don't need a gun. I've seen you dispose of people. It's frightening."

"We need to talk to him. He might not be the one who sent that ship to Chitta Moor. Maybe he can tell us how many other Dyads are out here."

"None on this station. You'll arrest him?"

He sighed. "Dyads are dangerous. You know that."

"We're a Dyad. We're not dangerous."

"Depends on whose side you're on, doesn't it?" He closed his eyes and tipped his head back against his seat, knowing that he was also robbing her of vision. There was nothing to see down here, anyway, except for her own, inquisitive face.

Was he really so sure about these strange entities? Khoe learned with everything she saw and touched. She assimilated more information in an hour than he could learn in a lifetime. Perhaps her own intellect did not exceed his, but her memory was as flawless as Ciela's. Was she truly a reflection of himself or had she become her own person, as different from him now as she appeared to be? If so, could her allegiance change?

He was dangerous, in that she was correct. His undefined commitment to Air Command often meant that he willingly strayed into other territory, sometimes even thwarting military operations that didn't sit quite right with him. He even shared the Arawaj ideological opposition to Commonwealth expansion even though his own people, foreigners in this sector, were leading the expansion. Invasion, as some called it. How was Khoe to distinguish foe from friend if even he didn't know where to draw the line? She had the means to launch battleships and destroy entire cities if she wished, whether or not he agreed. The only thing she needed from him was his touch on a button.

And wasn't this happening in Chitta Moor, with that new keyhole? Everything he knew about manipulating the fissures leading into subspace involved more energy than any planet, no matter how desolate, would withstand. Even a crew working for Azon Corp, whose primary objective was the accumulation of wealth, would not risk the lives of everyone living there, voluntarily or not. So were the entities, desperate for survival, forcing their hosts to do their bidding?

He opened his eyes to study Khoe. She looked up to return his gaze although she was merely seeing herself through him. Would she, someday, force his hand if they were not in agreement? Was his personal mission in these wars really clear to her? He doubted that it was clear even to him.

"We need to find him," he said. "We need to know more about the Dyads or we'll never get out from under this threat. Killing them isn't the answer. We'll try asking nicely. How's that?"

She smiled at him and returned her gaze to the window.

The train slowed and stopped at a few more stations before reaching the one Khoe wanted. Seth stepped outside and looked around. This part of the ring seemed to house residential blocks, perhaps for dock workers and repair crews, far less luxurious than the visitors' rentals on the outside section of the ring. No greenhouses and recreational areas broke up the narrow channels between apartment modules and dorms. He stepped aside to let a few sleds pass by and from somewhere they heard voices. At some point, attempts had been made to infuse these halls with a little cheer by painting the wall panels, doors and floors in exuberant shades of blue and green. Then the paint had peeled and the pipes above leaked and patches of fresher color showed where someone had covered the inevitable graffiti.

Khoe had returned her attention to the information and security systems as he walked down along a hallway she pointed out. She floated along beside him in that odd, not-touching-the ground way she had of appearing to walk. The faint strains of a Magran flute wafted through the maze of corridors. A child shouted something and another answered.

"Oh," she said. "Dear."

"What?"

"We're being followed."

He turned to see no one behind them. A quick look at his proximity scanner showed a few people behind these walls, some others in the distance ahead. No one seemed in a hurry. "Where?"

"In here," she said, meaning the orbiter's communications network. "Station Security. I think they noticed me. Things are closing off. They've taken some major file systems offline. They must think we're a threat."

"Get out of there. Quick."

"I can stay ahead of them. I found him! The Dyad. He noticed us, too."

"How do you know?"

"The pattern of his movements. It seems deliberate now." She smiled. "He's matching my pattern. Maybe he's recognizing us as Dyad."

"What is he signaling?"

"Can't tell without an interface with him." She gestured at his data sleeve. "I'm tracing his trail onto the physical layout of this place. You should be able to follow."

Seth squinted at the map and overlay that appeared on his forearm. They were close to the exterior wall of a receiving dock. Beyond a set of doors up ahead his scanner detected people but few weapons signatures.

"They're sending guards now. You need to go down one more level. Hurry."

Seth raced down a set of moving stairs and slammed through a double-door, suddenly wishing he'd found a reason to carry a gun onto the station. Then again, shooting security personnel on a station guarded by Air Command was probably not a career move he ought to consider. He found himself at the foot of some colossal piece of machinery rising to the roof of the chamber.

"What is this?" He followed some conduits with his eyes to where they disappeared through the roof. The hall reverberated with an unpleasant thrum and the whole space was only dimly lit, as if no one ever came down here except to pray to whatever gods were represented here.

"Air recycling," Khoe said, ruining the mystery. "The engineering for this is over that way. I think that's where the Dyad was last accessing."

A glance at his scanner now showed two teams of three, heavily armed and heading this way. "How are they tracking us?"

"They're not," she said. "I'm not that clumsy. They're going for the Dyad. He's not dropping his signals."

Indeed, the two teams had broken up and headed into other directions, around this hall. Seth hurried past the eerie mechanism ruling this chamber, feeling a bit like an insect bustling among all this. He paused near an exit to the engineering sub-station to check his scanner again.

"Think this might be him?" He tapped the interface to take a closer look. "Damn," he added when he saw the lone figure suddenly turn into four. "Looks like they got there, first."

"I'm sorry," she gasped. "I didn't see that shortcut."

Seth stepped back to where he had seen some of the conduits lead from the room and followed them around a bend and out of the hall. From there he gripped an overhead pipe, wincing when he found it hot, and swung up into the ceiling of the corridor. The smaller conduits up there seemed agreeable to holding his weight as he moved toward the four people near yet another large chamber. The sound of voices led him the rest of the way.

"There!" Khoe whispered. "That man on the floor. That must be him."

Seth shifted to peer through the racks of pipes to get a better look. A gallery of sorts overlooked a deserted mechanical room, stuffy and hot and sounding like something drumming a long distance underground. Two men and a woman in Security uniforms stood with their backs to Seth, their attention on the Dyad they had managed to bring down. Seth shifted again to see his lower legs dangling over the edge of the gallery and the heavy boot of a guard pressing each of his arms to the floor.

"You can just ask Denton Tague if you don't believe me," they heard him say, sounding utterly terrified of the men holding him captive. "I've got to get that calibration done. Let me up. That hurts."

"The file copies." A box-shaped Mraki guard, who looked like he might have long ago seen some action as a front line grunt, leaned forward to add more pressure.

Their victim cried out in pain. "Stop, please! I don't have any files."

The woman among them crouched down, a scanner in her hand. "I'm not getting anything," she said. "No hardware on him at all." She rose again and worked with her sensors. "Just some weird interference. These damn machines are making a mess of these readings."

"Why doesn't he just let them have it?" Khoe said.

Seth shrugged, wondering the same thing. It would take very little for the Dyad to eliminate these guards. Not only were they touching him directly, they also stood on solid metal plates. *Maybe he doesn't even know how.*

He crept forward a little more. The Dyad was clearly a Human elder, looking frail in rumpled shirt and trousers emblazoned with the Azon Corp logo. Although most Humans resembled each other via fairly uniform, lightly bronzed skin and dark hair, occasionally some of them stood out as genetic throwbacks to their ancient tribes. Seth had met Humans with yellow or red hair, some with Delphian-pale skin, others with eyes of green and blue. This one was rare among the people of Trans-Targon, having skin of the deepest brown he had yet seen on a Human. The tightly curled hair was cut close to his scalp and peppered with gray.

The Dyad moaned again when something else hurt. "I

don't have anything for you. Why are you saying this?"

The Mraki bent to grasp the man's collar to jerk him to his feet, giving him a good shake as he did so. "We've been looking for you for weeks. Kind of tired of being played a fool here. You better come up with some good reasons for hacking the entire system. Targon itself wants answers."

"Targon?" the Dyad stammered. "Why Targon? I've just... Uh."

Gods, shut up, Seth said to himself.

"I can feel them," Khoe said. "I think his entity noticed me, too."

The guards moved back to the main corridor, shoving the man ahead of them. Something seemed to startle the Dyad into looking up to where Seth crouched among the vents. "By the gods," he whispered.

The others looked up, too.

Seth let himself drop from the ceiling. He swept the legs out from under the Mraki, letting him fall against the female guard. When she stumbled, he reached for her gun, twisting it until she let it go. He shot the third man, hoping that the gun was set to something less than deadly, before he turned back to the woman.

"Khoe!" he called and grasped the guard's arm. Something surged through his body when Khoe converted existing energy into a pulse that immediately dropped the woman to the ground. Seth bent and also stunned the Mraki he had dropped.

A silence followed, interrupted only by Seth's gasps for air. He shook his arm, numbed by Khoe's electric pulse. When they had first discovered this useful trick, it had left him tired and sore. Eventually, her little boosts had become an exhilarating rush of pure energy.

When the Dyad turned as if to escape, he grasped him with his other hand. The wrist felt brittle, as if a simple twist might break it. "Don't. Nothing more to fear here."

"But..." the man stared at the fallen guards with a mix of fear and surprise. "How did you..." He turned his head to look past Seth. "No," he said to the empty space, "I don't know how he did that."

Seth released him to pull a second gun from the guard's belt. It always felt so much better to be armed. "Tell your friend we're here to help."

"We?" The dark-skinned man looked around. "Who's here?"

"You know well what I mean. They call us Dyads. But you can call me Seth." He gestured at the man's arm. "Are you injured? They stomped you pretty good."

"I think so. Bruised maybe. My name is Isaaron. Why are you here?"

"Later. Let's get somewhere safe."

"Seth, behind you!" Khoe yelled.

Seth whirled around to see the other set of guards, suddenly aware that he was holding guns while there were three uniforms on the ground by his feet. "Crap."

"Drop that weapon!" someone shouted.

He obeyed. "I can probably explain this," he said.

The last thing he saw was the barrel of a gun pointing his way.

TEN

It didn't take long for Seth to realize that he'd been shot. Nothing felt quite so horrifically painful while no particular body part hurt more than another. The exquisite pain in his head distracted only in some minor way from the feeling that every nerve in his body was suddenly too short for where it was going and vibrated like a badly tuned drum harp. Somehow, the memory of having been shot like this was never quite as bad as the reality.

They had dragged him, barely conscious, out of that sub-station to a waiting skimmer and tossed him aboard. Then they'd loaded up the dark man, too, whatever his name was, practically throwing him across his lap. He realized at that point that his hands were locked behind his back.

Khoe?

No answer. Seth blinked into the bright overhead lights, unable to move in the back of the skimmer, sure that someone was pointing a gun at him. He slumped back, declining to ask for another shot.

"He's all right," a woman's voice said when the guard in the front seat waved a scanner at Seth. "Damn Centauri don't break so easy."

"You didn't have to hit him twice," her companion said.

Seth tried to sit up to ease his aching body but barely

found the strength to turn his head. Isaaron, that was his name, sat stiffly beside him, fear and worry on his deeply grooved face. There was blood on his forehead that hadn't been there before, but it didn't look like they had shot him as well.

"I have no idea what this is," the guard with the scanner said. "Look at these readings. Ever seen anything like it?"

"Is he transmitting something? Might have accomplices here."

"He can't be. We've taken his gear. I can't even tell where it's coming from. But it's on both of them."

"Better have that deck checked for radiation. Who knows what he's been playing around with down there."

Khoe!

"I assure you, I was merely performing my duties," Isaaron said, holding up his identification tag. "If you contact my supervisor, this will all be explained. I have no idea who this man is."

Seth flexed his fingers, numb from the damage he'd taken and numb from the restraints around his wrists. His shoulders ached. The view outside of the skimmer's windows blurred and tilted and he closed his eyes, willing himself not to pass out.

They arrived somewhere and he was manhandled out of the vehicle, into a gated section that he recognized by smell and sound as soon as they entered. All jails smelled the same. He was pushed and pulled in several directions before he was dropped onto an unyielding cot and someone finally released his hands. A door slammed. He closed his eyes and remained motionless for a long time, unwilling to sleep, but unable to do much else. Time passed without meaning.

Finally, Khoe's voice: "Seth?"

He found himself sprawled on a cot, one foot still on the floor, in a drab box of a cell. When he turned his head he saw two other bunks. The far one featured a silent and motionless Isaaron sitting with his back against the wall and his arms crossed over his belly. No one had bothered to provide him with a bandage for the cut on his forehead. His dark eyes regarded Seth without expression.

Seth sat up in careful increments and ran his hands over his face and into his hair. He winced when he encountered a painful spot along his jaw. "Khoe?"

"Are you all right?" She replied at once, appearing beside him. "I've been trying to wake you. This really hurt! Where are we?"

"I'm all right. It wears off. You're not damaged?"

"No. I'm so sorry. I should have paid better attention to your scanner. Then I would have noticed those guards sooner."

"I should have, too." He looked over to Isaaron. "What happened?"

The Dyad shrugged. The movement seemed to pain him and he stopped mid-shrug. "We got caught, that's what happened. I've managed to keep hidden for weeks now and the moment you showed I get caught. Coincidence?"

Seth ran his hand over his jaw and then found a swollen lip. He checked his fingers for blood. "How'd I get that?"

"You accused one of the guards of having Rhuwac bed mates."

"Clearly they have no sense of humor. Why were you hiding down there?"

"Why are you here?" Isaaron asked, ignoring Seth's question. "You've got one of them in your head, too. We can tell."

Seth nodded. "Subspace entities. They've been here before. Are you able to talk with yours?"

"Yes. He's been helping me." Isaaron heaved himself from his cot and walked around the other one to sit down closer to Seth. He nodded toward the door to their cell. "They've contacted Targon and now Air Command is sending someone to come and get us."

Seth sighed. "Air Command knows about us. About our friends." A glance at the man's face convinced him to skip the part about the death sentence hanging over their heads.

"I know some people on Targon. I might be able to talk to them. I can't guarantee either of us will ever see the stars again. Welcome to the rest of your life as a lab rat."

"I understand the research opportunity, but I'm sure Targon's treatment of new species doesn't mean..." He looked around the featureless room. "...this."

"It does," Seth said. "Targon doesn't think of this as first contact and we won't like being researched. They'll do whatever they must to find out how we're affected." He glanced at Khoe who had sat down beside the other Dyad. "Unless we let them go."

Isaaron jerked back as if Seth had slapped him. "Out of the question!"

"Yeah." Seth smiled when he realized how good it felt to meet someone who understood what it meant to be a Dyad. "They grow on you, don't they?"

"Neryon can be a little unnerving. He's taken to look like a Shaddallama. We argue a lot."

Seth pictured this Human accompanied by the short, multi-jointed and mostly unclothed natives of the desert planet and had to smile. "You argue? About what?"

"A new low-impact thruster Azon is working on. It's completely impractical on anything but a shuttle in its current design." He looked to his left for a moment and then shook his head emphatically. "You'd never land that in anything more than point three G. Anyone can figure that out. I wouldn't even bother modelling that. I can work that out on paper."

"So you were spying on Azon?" Seth said.

"What else is there to do here? I tried to get out but they revoked my ID a few weeks ago. So far, every time I try to get on a ship I run into trouble." He rubbed his lips together, looking a little embarrassed. "Or it just looks too risky. I've never had to stow away before."

Seth stood up and walked to the door. When he placed his hand on it Khoe shook her head. "Manual lock. No intercom. They've even disconnected the camera." She pointed at a spot near the ceiling where only the smallest speck showed something hidden up there. "I think they know we're not to be trusted around any sort of network. I have no interface to work with."

Seth placed his ear to the door to listen to sounds outside. There was nothing.

Khoe put her hand on his arm. "They'll be questioning Ciela. What if they arrest her, too? We need to warn her."

"She's Delphian. I'm just her hired pilot who probably deserves being arrested for daring to use her as cover to infiltrate this station. By the time she's done lecturing them they'll send one of their own pilots to get her back home." This was one of many cover stories they had ready, each designed to avoid revealing their identities to rebels or Union members.

But despite his assurances, he worried. He had faith in Ciela's ability to hold her own among their enemies, and had placed his own life into her hands more than once. But somehow he trusted her sharp tongue more around rebels and outlaws than around Air Command. He returned to his cot and started to unfasten his shirt.

Isaaron raised an eyebrow. "Is it too warm in here for you?"

"Want to see my tattoo?" Seth said.

"Look, if you're bored you can explain the basic principles of propulsion to my… what did you call it?"

"We have no name for them. But out here you're a Dyad. Both of you together."

"They ought to have a name."

"I like him," Khoe said.

"You like everybody." Seth shrugged his shirt off his shoulder to reveal a tattoo on the inside of his bicep. He ran a fingernail over the image of an ancient ship under full sail to find the edge of the embedded chip beneath his skin. A short sequence of jabs at some of the sails activated the unit. "Can you boost that, Khoe?"

"Your friend's name is Khoe? That's pretty."

"Tell him I said thanks."

Seth sighed. "Transmit, please, Khoe." He initiated a brief code to let Ciela know that he was in trouble. Now it was up to her to wipe his access to the *Dutchman* via the data sleeve he no longer had and to either investigate what happened or contact the colonel for help. Seth left the transmission open for a little while before shutting it down again. With luck, the *Dutchman*'s system would have pinpointed his location. "Think anyone caught that?"

"I didn't notice anyone else listening in," she said. "Ask that man about his friend."

Seth covered the tattoo again and then sat back on his cot to study the Dyad. "So tell me about Chitta Moor," he said after a while.

Clearly, Isaaron had not expected the question. "Chitta… What about it?"

"I was there. So were your friends with the Outrider you stole."

The man's expression brightened. "They made it? Is it working? Tell me more."

"You first. Who are you?"

Isaaron seemed to blank out for a moment and Seth assumed some discussion between him and his invisible friend Neryon.

Can you communicate with that one? he sent to Khoe.

"The only telepath around here is Ciela. I can only talk to you."

The Dyad on the other cot returned his gaze to Seth. "I was aboard a B-CIT out of Feyd's trade fleet. Chief engineer there. We had a bit of a rough jump a few months ago. When we came out I had Neryon in my head. I don't have to tell you how unsettling that is."

Seth nodded.

"Anyway, eventually he told me about their troubles in subspace. They're dying. Did you know that?"

"Yes. Simply entropy."

"They will reverse it."

Seth raised both eyebrows and looked over to Khoe. She shrugged. "Reverse it? How?"

"Gravitons."

"Gravitons?"

"Maybe not so much reverse it as simply buy them more time. Couple of billion years maybe." Isaaron flashed a smile that erased the years from his careworn face. "By infusing their space with new energy."

"You'd need an awful lot!" Seth said, incredulous.

"Yes."

Khoe tilted her head, considering this. "Didn't you say they were using accelerators on Chitta Moor? From the ships they stole?"

Seth nodded. "Whatever they're building requires accelerators," he said to Isaaron. "We've seen four or five transmitters, packing a lot of power. We were told they were trying to open a new keyhole there."

"A new keyhole? And that doesn't strike you as peculiar? Even if we knew how, it'd be far safer to do it off-planet."

"Well. Yes. So what's going on?"

Isaaron stood up, still cradling his bruised elbows in his hands, and wandered around the small cell. "Neryon and I tried to find a way to help his people. Bringing them all out here is not an option, obviously. We came up with a plan but we needed more expertise. And hardware. So we sent another ship, the Azon Outrider, out to Chitta Moor."

"Did the crew know what you were doing? That you intended to have them turn into Dyads?"

After a moment, Isaaron shook his head.

"Why Chitta Moor? It doesn't have much to offer."

"In fact it's perfect," Isaaron said. "Remote enough to escape notice, decent atmosphere. But mostly because of kolterium."

"What about it?"

"One of the rare earths mined on Chitta Moor contains kolterium, even more rare. It's the main reason the operation was begun there fifty years or so ago. The original mine tapped out pretty quick but there'd still be some deposits. Kolterium, of course, is used to create gravitons for our own ships."

Seth stared at him, astounded by this revelation. "Is that possible? You think randomly firing bosons into subspace is going to fix the problem? Reset the clock?"

"As a force carrier, gravitons'll add energy; probably create a gravitational field sufficient to keep Neryon and his people from coming apart. It would have to be one hell of an accelerator. And insanely dangerous."

"How about a fully shielded vessel at the bottom of a very cold, deep lake?" Seth said, remembering the peculiar arrangement in the surface mine. He ran both of his hands over his face and rubbed his eyes. "By *Cazun*, this might actually work."

"Well, there is a problem," Isaaron said.

"What problem?"

"We can create a beam to carry the particles, but we haven't found a way to properly target the keyhole without losing too much along the way. There will also be scattering caused by the atmosphere. So I came here, to Pelion, and got myself hired down in that dungeon. It let me get at the information we need."

Seth grinned. "From Azon Corp?"

"Who better? They are developing technologies we haven't even dreamed of. And not just for Air Command. I found a lensing formula that might just let me focus the beam from the surface into the keyhole. We just need to add the correctly oscillating gravimetric pulse to the beam itself."

"How?"

"Dyad power," Isaaron said grandly. "We'll create the resonance ourselves."

"Does he know his Dyad power could have clobbered those guards?" Khoe said.

Seth winked at her. "So that's what the guards were after? The files you stole?"

Isaaron looked over to where Seth assumed his

Shaddalama-shaped partner to be. "Yes, although the formulas are just memorized. In my head. Or rather, Neryon's nervous system. Unfortunately, we were discovered. I've been hiding since, waiting for a chance to get into subspace and head out to Tor Ag. They were to signal their whereabouts to help me detour to Chitta Moor."

"That they have," Seth said. "And caught everyone else's attention, including Air Command."

"You saw the accelerator, then? Describe it to me. Did they get the shield grids worked out?" Isaaron's face was alight with curiosity. Seth could well imagine arguing for hours with this man over the smallest detail of some engine component. At least, he could imagine *someone* arguing – his own mechanical interests lay only in whether things worked, and who could make them work if they didn't. No doubt, Neryon had turned out equally fascinated by engineering, well-matched for the job of finding a solution to their problem. Was it, somehow, by design that the subspace inhabitants had found their way to Isaaron? He glanced at Khoe, wondering not for the first time what had brought her aboard his ship to begin with.

"We saw it but they would not talk about it," he said. "They are waiting for you."

Isaaron sighed and looked at the barred door. "That's the rub, isn't it?"

"Seth," Khoe said, shifting from Isaaron's bunk to sit beside him. "We can't wait here for your colonel to come and arrest you. This isn't right. We need to get out. My people are counting on this man."

He reached out to flip an errant braid from her face but, realizing that they were not alone, completed the gesture only in his thoughts. "I was just thinking that." He turned to Isaaron. "Do you have any idea where we are?"

"Yes, this is an administrative wing near the new arrivals port. Newcomers to the station debark here for health and security checks before they're allowed entry. After that they can get clearance to land at other docks."

"Good, that means we're close to where I left my ship."

"I guess they're holding us here until Air Command comes to collect us. This room is used to hold the more suspicious characters until they can be investigated."

"That'd be us. They'll send Vanguard. So far our existence is classified. They'll probably sedate us or something to take us away. But they won't harm us. It's not likely that even Air Command will execute suspects on a civilian orbiter." He looked to Khoe. "I'm guessing if they knock me out, you'll be out, too."

"Yes," she said, looking worried. "And it's not pleasant."

He tapped the chip embedded in his arm. "This isn't letting you get anywhere?"

"No. It carries only to the *Dutchman*. I tried to find some other access node but the signal just isn't designed for that. There are dampeners on it."

"By design. It's not easy to pick up on scanners."

"It's almost frightening, isn't it?" Isaaron said. "What these beings are capable of. Neryon took only hours inside my ship's system and then here in Azon's databanks to surpass my skills and find what I was looking for."

"It is frightening," Seth agreed. "Unfortunately, some Dyads are not especially concerned about others. Targon's exobiology lab foresees a time when we could be little more than their life support system. It worries them."

"Surely they don't all see us that way." Isaaron seemed to be addressing his partner.

"Their actions mirror what goes on here in real-space. They know only what they are shown."

"Like children," Isaaron smiled.

"Dangerous ones. There are Dyads among the Shri-Lan. There might be more out here."

Isaaron's eyes widened as he realized the implications of that. "I had no idea! Neryon just wants to save his people. I thought all of them would share that goal. There is nothing about him that makes me doubt that."

"That's another worry. That we might not actually know

what they do. To us, I mean. They may be influencing our own behaviors. How we feel about them. What we believe." Seth glanced at Khoe. "Our attachment to them."

Khoe frowned at that. "Is that what you think? That we're making you do things? You know that isn't true."

Seth looked at his hands to avoid her eyes. He didn't know. How could he? Everything about her fit into his head like it had always been there. Familiar, comforting, and undeniably useful. An extension of himself while seeming so very much her own person. How could any of this be real? "I know you mean well," he said.

"That doesn't answer my question."

Isaaron sighed. "It seems that your comment has upset Neryon. He wants you to know that he needs my help, nothing more. I'd rather not pass along some of his saltier reply."

"Don't bother," Seth said, regretting his words. "Khoe's not happy with me, either. I'm sorry, Khoe, I didn't put that right."

"There is no right way to put that," she said.

Sounds outside interrupted the awkward silence that followed. Seth came to his feet and once again put his ear to the door. Some voices nearby, but too muffled to discern. A door slammed. "Someone's coming, I think."

"What are we going to do?" Isaaron said, alarmed.

Seth looked to Khoe. "No zapping people until we know who's coming. These are not enemies."

"I wasn't going to zap them," she said sullenly.

"Zap them?" Isaaron said. "Zap them how?"

Seth put his finger to his lips, listening. Someone was definitely moving around out there. It sounded like something substantial being moved. He wondered if they'd arranged for stretchers to take them away, unconscious. He certainly wouldn't attempt to arrest a Dyad, not even one as mild-mannered as Isaaron seemed to be.

A heavy bolt clanked in the mechanical look. Seth moved aside to press his body against the wall beside the door, waiting for the guards to enter. Perhaps there was a chance to disarm them.

"They'll just shoot us again," Khoe said.

I'm quick. Stop pouting already. I said I was sorry. He got no further than that when a gun poked through the door, directly at his nose.

"You are so damn predictable, Kada," Ciela said when she stepped into the room, nudging him back with her pistol. Her eyes scanned the cell and then, seeing that he was safe, she flung herself into his arms. "You had me so worried! Are you all right?"

"Ciela's here!" Khoe exclaimed and stretched her arms around both of them.

Seth squeezed Ciela tightly. "Khoe's hugging us, too," he said. "Do you mind?"

She looked up. "That's all right. You're hurt!" She touched the bruise turning purple on the side of his face.

Isaaron had come to his feet and stood nearby, looking bewildered. He tried a wan smile. "I have to say, one doesn't often see a Delphian with a gun."

Seth released her. "My navigator and leading lady, Ciela," he introduced.

"Not in that order, I hope," Isaaron said and touched Ciela's hand in the way Humans greeted each other. "I am Isaaron Toise. And, yes, I'm a Dyad."

Ciela peered at him curiously. "Uh, hello. Are we arresting you?" She turned uncertainly to Seth. "When we're not getting ourselves arrested, I mean."

"No," Seth said and accepted the gun she handed him. "I'll explain later. How did you get here?" He went to the door and peered outside. "I see," he added when he saw two guards on the floor at the end of a short hallway.

"They're not dead," Ciela assured him. "I have a skimmer nearby. But I'm afraid we've lost the *Dutchman*."

Seth froze. "What?"

"I'm so sorry! They came just after I got your message. I couldn't very well pretend that was my ship at such short notice. They confiscated it and gave me a room to wait for someone to come and get me." She grinned. "They told me you were a wanted fugitive. I insisted they let me take my guns, seeing how you're so dangerous."

"Is the ship all right?"

"They just locked up the entrance to the umbilical. It's under guard until Air Command gets here." She motioned to Isaaron to leave the cell. "The man is married to his ship, I'm sure," she said to him.

Seth sighed and pushed the thought of the *Dutchman* in Air Command hands out of his mind. Just a ship, he thought, grinding his teeth. Some hardware, nothing more. One thing at a time, and moaning after his boat wasn't one of them. He stepped into the hall when Ciela's eyes caught his and he felt her hand on his arm to squeeze it gently. She knew quite well how much the *Dutchman*, his partner and his home for years, meant to him.

"This way," she said. They stepped around the unconscious guards. "There's an access panel to the com system by the exit. Let's get somewhere safe."

"I know a few places," Isaaron said. "I've been hiding for a while."

Seth placed his hand on the panel and nodded to Khoe. "We're getting off this station. Until we know what orders those Vanguard agents have, I don't want to run into them. We'll make a full report once we're away from here. That accelerator on Chitta Moor is the priority now. Let's find a plane and shake this place."

"What?" Isaaron said. "You can't just 'find a plane'. We're already in deep trouble."

"So what's a little more?"

Khoe's image wavered a little before his eyes. "The main file system is still on lock-down and they're concentrating on that. I made it look like someone's accessing from the lower ring so they've sent a detail down there to look for more intruders."

"Are any ships cleared for leaving the station?" Seth

asked.

"None without big security, but there is a pier with small craft called Ten-Ninety. Mostly stuff for sale, but not guarded all that much. They'll be unmanned, I'm guessing."

Ciela opened the door and peered outside before waving them onward.

"Oh, dear," Isaaron said when they encountered another downed guard. "That man is bleeding."

"Gave me a hard time," Ciela said. She glanced at her scanner to look for upright people. Someone wearing an Azon staff suit stood by the transparent entrance door, looking out onto the arrivals concourse. Both Seth and Ciela hid their weapons before crossing the lobby. She pointed to a metal door to their left. "Too many people using the lifts. Stairs through here. Hurry."

They rushed into a service stairwell and then took the steps two at a time. Seth looked back, a little worried about Isaaron but the Human elder kept up well. Only three flights up another door led onto an elevated platform.

"Easy, everyone," Seth said as they walked out into a small crowd of Azon staff and visitors.

Before them stretched the primary tunnel leading around the great wheel of the station. Here the business and residential components of this city gave way to a central system of rails and open traffic lanes designed to move people and freight around the circle. It also allowed air to flow into all areas of the ring far more efficiently than the individual conduits common on smaller stations. Except that this tunnel curved downward in either direction, this felt like they were standing on a terrace of a high-rise building among many. Small air cars of varied designs, some of them quite fashionable, made their way among the buildings like insects visiting a hive.

This platform, located near the docks, was crowded with people waiting here for transport. Rentals came and went, and some larger shuttles stopped to drop off passengers to find their ships. Seth wondered if there was anyone here more outstanding in a crowd than the dark-skinned man and the Delphian in his company. He was glad when they piled into the waiting skimmer Ciela had rented somewhere and lowered its dome.

Seth took the controls and then frowned at the display on the screen before him. "Is this right?" He pointed at the speedometer.

Isaaron, in the rear compartment, looked over Seth's shoulder. "Yes, all skimmers are throttled here for safety. They're just meant to move between buildings, not win races."

Ciela drew her gun and ejected a thin blade from its handle. With it, she began to pry the cover from the control panel to access the car's maintenance system.

"They found the guards!" Khoe said, just as an alarm rang from somewhere. It stopped almost immediately, leaving some of the commuters up here looking around themselves in puzzlement. "I'll keep cutting that off, but I can't keep the doors closed."

"They're on to us," Seth translated for the others. "Isaaron, which way to Ten-Ninety?"

"You can take the speed rail to the Tenth block. Well, it's a wedge, really. I don't know why they call—"

"Which rail!" Seth said, pointing at a confusion of traffic above them where several rail lines sorted vehicles into orderly rows. Like cables through a conduit, they streamed rail cars and private vehicles through the orbiter's main ring.

"The upper one. Orange beacons. It'll skip most of the sub-stations."

Seth hovered away from the platform and threaded his way into the lanes approaching the rails. Attaching themselves to a fixed line rather than making their own way through the vast halls was an unattractive option. Ciela would soon override the car's maximum speed setting, but racing past security scanners would surely raise some flags to guards now on alert. And so he followed a commuter shuttle as it entered the collector lane to the rail. At last it was their turn to nudge their vehicle below the clamps and felt the soft thud as the skimmer was secured. They all instinctively gripped their armrests as the car was moved sideways and immediately shot forward, accelerating along the vast curve of the ring.

"Look down," Khoe said. "I want to see."

Seth glanced over to Ciela who kept her eyes firmly on the skimmer's dash. He put his hand on her knee but obliged Khoe by looking through the dome to watch the city go by below. And a city it was, even if fully enclosed. The Azon Corporation ventures occupied different color-coded levels, each with their own rail links to shuttle workers and materials throughout the station.

"I wish they'd slow down," Khoe said. "Look at that greenhouse. So many flowers."

"Those'll be saltbean pods," Seth said. "Delicious."

"Have I had those?"

The rail above them came to such a sudden stop that all of them lurched forward. Isaaron let out a pained groan when he braced his arms against Seth's seat.

"Attention passengers, please prepare for a brief security check," a cheerful voice emitted from the skimmer's com system.

Seth cursed. "Cut us loose, someone," he said, meaning Khoe or Neryon.

"That seems hardly advisable," Isaaron said, anxiously peering down at the vehicles moving on the ground.

"Neryon," Seth said. "Want to see your people again?"

A brief silence followed. Ciela turned to look behind them. Seth, too, saw angry blue lights flickering back there, likely attached to an emergency vehicle. At last Isaaron rose and pressed his hand to a plate set into the ceiling of the skimmer. After a moment or two Ciela cried out in panic when the skimmer disengaged from the rail clamps and plummeted toward the orbiter's gravitational center.

Khoe laughed.

Seth resumed control of the skimmer, letting it dive

toward the ground before leveling out. Obediently, it sped up to the velocity at which it was designed to travel, leaving more law-abiding traffic behind. "Which way, Isaaron," he snapped.

The Human had turned an interesting shade of gray. "Straight for a while." He turned. "They're after us. Look!"

"Ciela?"

She worked with the skimmer's mapping system. "Ten-Ninety?" He nodded when an overlay appeared on the car's navigational system. "It's a small dock at the end of the water depot."

Seth slid the map over to his side of the car's dash and tapped in his course. A warning message flashed in the air above the display, which he ignored. Ciela waved it away like an insect.

"You better hope this thing has the buffers to handle that or it'll be short trip," she said and turned to Isaaron. "Hang on to something."

He just stared at her, already with a grip on his armrests that had turned his fingers bloodless.

The car followed Seth's directions and cut across the skimmer lane, dodging traffic in ways that were surely illegal here. It located the entrance of a tunnel meant mostly for pedestrians who either walked here or used a conveyor to get to their work and homes. Some of them scattered when the skimmer raced over their heads. The buffer sensors lining the hull did their job and kept them away from the walls and obstacles. Unfortunately, it also pushed a few of the pedestrians off their feet.

"Sorry!" Khoe yelled cheerfully, waving at them.

"We lost the guards," Ciela said, kneeling on her seat to look back the way they had come. She wrapped her arms around the backrest when their vehicle rattled past a series of columns, confusing the sensors. "Cowards. There's plenty of room in here."

Seth slowed the car when they approached an intersection and then swung the car into a gap between what looked like water silos. He let it settle to the ground and exhaled audibly.

"Nice." Ciela smiled at him.

"Out." Seth opened the dome and turned to help Isaaron climb out. "You all right?"

The man nodded but was clearly unfamiliar with Seth's driving habits. "That tunnel is not meant for cars," was all he managed.

Seth nodded to Ciela to lead the way, following the map on her data sleeve. "I suppose they'll revoke my vehicle privileges now. Khoe, check security on that dock."

They walked past a few people working on some piece of the station below the floor, tugging Isaaron along when he stopped to inspect the project. A lift took them to a passage offering a spectacular view of the planet below and this time Seth had to keep Khoe from the distraction by averting his eyes. By now someone would surely have noticed the skimmer parked where parking wasn't allowed.

"Through there," Khoe said. "I've disabled the doors. There is no one beyond that point. All security is electronic."

"See how handy we are?" Seth said to Isaaron before realizing that the man would not have heard her report.

"They've found us," Ciela said with her eyes on her proximity scanner. "Four on foot, behind us. Armed in a big way. Vehicles below, heading to the pier from there. They might try to cut us off through that entrance."

"Go!" Seth said when the doors to the pier opened. "Ciela, ID those ships and find a cruiser that's ready to go. Something that hasn't been here for very long. Khoe, I think we need a diversion." They ran out onto the concourse lined by five umbilicals on either side. Six ships were moored here and Ciela scanned each as they passed, looking for a likely escape.

"This one," she said. "Fleetfoot. It'll do." She started tapping on the pressure door's key plate to gain access to the umbilical leading to the ship itself.

Silent streaks of tracers raced along the walls and floor of the pier. One strafed across Isaaron's chest and Seth shoved him behind a support brace before the more deadly beam followed. A man's voice shouted at them to stop and drop but the damage to the walls belied their intent. Who had given the order for live fire?

Seth shot back at their pursuers to force them to take cover. "Khoe! Come on!"

"Yes, I got it. Things are complicated up here. They don't trust anybody."

The overhead lights turned orange, casting an otherworldly glow on thus-far invisible emergency markings along the walls. A recorded voice began to transmit instructions for evacuating this sector of the station.

"Now what have you done?" Isaaron exclaimed.

"Nice work, Khoe." Seth saw one of the guards at the door fall to his aim. The other three had halted their attack as if unsure of their duty now.

Ciela pushed Isaaron into the airlock leading to the cruiser and then drew her gun. "Go. Your turn," she said to Seth and took over his sporadic shots at the concourse doors.

Seth turned to place his hand on the cruiser's access panel. His hand tingled as Khoe penetrated the ship's system to override the securities that kept others from operating it. "Your *Dutchman* is much tougher to break into," she said.

"I hope so," he said when the door slid aside. "Ciela! Let's go."

She raced past him into the small ship and he let the door close behind him. They were both familiar with the Fleetfoot cruiser, a small class designed, like the *Dutchman*, for a minimal crew but capable of carrying more cargo or passengers. He dropped the two steps into the cockpit, leaving Isaaron standing, bewildered, in the narrow corridor.

"Secure yourself," Seth called back to him. "There's a cabin to your right. Should have restraints in there."

Ciela was already engaging with the ship's pre-flight protocols via her neural interface. "Give us a hand, Khoe?" she said and reached to touch Seth's temple. It took only a moment to initiate the khamal. "Could use a boost to get that coolant stirred. It's been sitting."

Seth checked the overhead screens and then raised a holographic model of their ship, looking for anything that might keep them from launching safely. "Ship's in good shape. I wonder what it's selling for."

"Kind of low on coolant," Ciela said, taking the navigator's bench by the forward console.

"We're green for go," Seth said, focused on feeling his way through the ship's systems to remind himself which of the *Dutchman's* familiar modifications were unavailable now. "How are things with the tower?"

Ciela switched the com system to show the station's grid as well as several real-vid angles. Voices over the com system made it clear that the evacuation was proceeding as had no doubt been rehearsed in the past. Azon Corp knew how to protect its valuables. They watched as ships and escape shuttles streamed away from the orbiter, following precise instructions.

Seth launched the cruiser, rising through the station's gravity well until he could engage its own. Looking as unhurried as possible, he mingled with the fleet of ships heading toward the planet. "We'll go down and around Pelion and then head to the keyhole. They'll start looking for us as soon as things settle down. I want to be long gone by then."

Ciela looked around for Khoe. "What did you do back there?"

"Catastrophic failure of the Level Two generators, caused by the construction on the lower deck," Khoe said. "And some guy pulling a manual alarm by the main concourse. Confirmed by two independent failsafe systems."

"Not really?" she said.

"No, but the evacuation order is given automatically."

"Clever," Seth said. "They wouldn't reverse that until they're damn sure there's no problem with the generators."

"Which won't be long." Ciela plotted their course for the

keyhole. "Can you disable the transponder, Khoe? We're leaving a trail." She tilted her head. "Not a bad little ship, actually. Nothing like the *Dutchman*, but it'll get us out of here."

"Don't remind me," Seth said.

Once beyond Pelion and the confusion of the sudden evacuation, they shut down the com system, not really caring if anyone hailed them out here. They were just one ship among many in this busy sector and, without the ship's ID transmissions, nameless and unaccountable. Seth rather liked that feeling. They renamed the ship *Sidara*, after the heroine of a book Khoe had found in Seth's database.

He followed Ciela into the cabin where Isaaron had spread out a datasheet on a table. He barely looked up when they entered but kept mumbling to himself and possibly to Neryon as he calculated something.

Ciela dropped onto the opposite bench with a loud exhalation of air. "I don't think we'll be invited back there any time soon."

Seth flopped onto the lower of two bunks along the wall, not bothering to remove his boots. "Something tells me there isn't a thing to eat on this bucket."

Isaaron observed Ciela, perhaps still amazed to find a Delphian engaged in these pursuits. "Stealing a ship is no small offense."

Seth shrugged. "They stole mine. And let's not forget about that Outrider you borrowed."

"Well, I suppose that is true. In a way."

Ciela leaned forward to look at Isaaron's calculations. "We'll be at the keyhole in a few hours," she said. "Where are we going, other than where they won't find us?"

"Back to Chitta Moor," Seth said.

"What? Why?"

"He's the Dyad they're waiting for." Seth pointed to Isaaron. "To finish their project. They're trying to build a delivery system to push gravitons into subspace. That should provide the energy they need. He came out here to get some formula for that."

"Lensing formula," Isaaron said. "I can't pretend to understand it all, but Neryon says it will work."

"Neryon, eh?" Ciela said, amused by the Shaddalama name. "That's your Dyad-pal?"

Isaaron nodded.

"Gravitons. We should have thought of that. Most of our kolterium used to come from Chitta Moor. That stuff is hard to find now."

Seth grinned. "We probably had our hands on it when Lieutenant Zire had us make that delivery out to the accelerator. For a short while, we were rather wealthy."

"It doesn't take much, fortunately," Isaaron said. "My biggest worry was finding enough thorium to power the accelerator. If they managed to build the transmitter according to specs, I should be able to adjust the beam correctly."

"If all you need are these particles, why would your people go through all this trouble on Chitta Moor? Steal ships to get raw materials. People died on the way there. Some may not survive much longer. That woman we brought back with us might lose her baby as well as her mind. We could have helped. Could we not just deliver gravitons into subspace using our own ships? Torpedos?"

"Probably not in the quantity, as a single event, as the Dyads have determined," Seth said. "And we don't have the know-how to create such an event." He gestured to encompass the room and the ship that contained it. "We barely produce enough gravitons for our ships and stations, never mind enough to hold together an entire universe."

Isaaron blinked and turned briefly to Seth. "What woman? Who died?"

Ciela frowned. "You don't know? Dyads don't form easily. A lot of attempts to… to merge end up badly."

"I had no idea!" He paused for a moment. "Neither did Neryon. What happened?"

"People die, that's what happens," Ciela said. "Or they go

mad. The pairing simply fails."

Seth sat up on his bunk and propped his elbows onto his knees. "We don't know enough about Dyads to understand the process. But from what I've seen only one in ten or so actually makes it. Maybe less."

The Human's shoulders slumped as he leaned back in his seat. "This is terrible," he murmured. "Nobody was supposed to die. People should not have to pay for this."

"You should have informed Targon," Ciela said. "With stakes like these, they would have helped."

"I'm surprised to hear you say that," Seth said.

"We have learned to fear you," Khoe said before Ciela could reply. "Our imperative is to avoid your space, after what happened before. We were hunted by your people. Exploited. Air Command wanted to destroy us and that is still their mission. How can we turn to them for help?"

The furrows in Isaaron's forehead deepened once Ciela translated Khoe's words for him. He gazed at the space where, presumably, Neryon appeared in his vision. "I don't like the implications of this. The choice not to tell Targon was mine." He turned back to Ciela. "Was it not?"

She shrugged, but her shrug was meant for Seth.

"Do they affect what we think of as our own free will, you mean?" he said, pondering this. "Control our thoughts and actions? Honestly, I don't know. They are part of us. We assume that they copy our innate personality when they merge with us. But who's to say it's not also the other way around? We could well be echoing their fears. I've also picked up a good aversion to telling Carras what I've become. And I trust him more than I trust most officers."

"With good reason," Ciela said. "But it's not too late. Now that we know what they're doing at Queta Station, we need to get Targon on this. Astrophysics needs to know about the graviton theory. Air Command needs to get to Queta Station to clean up the rebel situation and let that team work in peace. Skoth threatened to destroy the transmitter if they won't open the keyhole."

"He mustn't!" Isaaron exclaimed. "That subspace trap has nothing to do with my transmitter. I suppose it's the entities still in subspace that are manipulating the exits in that span."

"He doesn't know that." Ciela touched Seth's neural node to sever their mental link. She went to the door. She seemed to want to say something more but then just smiled. "So who else is hungry?"

"She's upset," Khoe said after the door slid shut.

"How would you know?" Seth said.

"Doesn't take a genius."

"She's not upset. You read too much."

"Go after her. I'll stay out of it."

Seth looked to Isaaron. "Did she seem upset to you?"

The Human nodded.

Sighing, Seth got up from the bunk and went into the corridor transecting the ship. It was barely wide enough for one person, making him once again question the forethought of the designers of this class. The *Dutchman*, like the Eagle class, featured an open design for maximum functionality. And less claustrophobia, he thought.

The small galley near another crew cabin was empty but when he turned back Ciela came in from the corridor.

"I found a datasheet for you," she said. "Fairly standard but better than nothing. You can copy my programs over."

He took the sleeve from her and put it on a counter. She smiled when he pulled her into his arms and bent to kiss her. "I was worried about you, back on Pelion," he said, biting his tongue before revealing that Khoe had sent him after her. He had known many women in his life and never understood even one of them. But bringing up Khoe at this point was probably not recommended. "When Isaaron said Station Security went to question you."

"Bah, easy."

He kissed her again, adding a little heat, and let his hand stray experimentally to her backside. She wrapped her arms around his neck and pressed closer, responding to his touch as ardently as always. Relieved, Seth wondered if Isaaron would mind if they disappeared for a half hour or so.

But then she drew away with a small gasp. "Is Khoe here?"

"What?" he said, groaning inwardly. "No."

She looked into the corridor as if not quite believing him.

"She's tucked away." He smiled and stroked a blue strand of hair from her face. "There is just us here."

She sighed. It had that trembling quality that called for caution.

He pulled back a little but kept his arms around her. "Are you all right? Too much excitement today?"

She shrugged, then nodded. "Maybe." She looked up. "They will hunt you, Seth. They will kill you if they can. Even the colonel will. You know too much. You're not allied to anyone. They won't want you on the loose out here."

"I've managed to evade someone or another for as long as I can remember."

"And luck runs out, Seth! You have no idea how scared I was when I got your message. They said you were arrested and Vanguard was coming for you. That means they know you're a Dyad. Why else send them? And when I got down to where you were the guard said they shot you. I was so mad I almost lost my mind."

"Is that why you beat him up?"

She pressed her lips together. "He laughed when he told me they'd hurt you. So I kicked him when he went down. He wasn't laughing then." Her dark eyes gleamed with tears when she looked up at him.

"We've been through tougher scrapes, Arawaj. Don't worry so."

"I... I talked to Caelyn a bit about the Dyads. What they can do. You're wielding Khoe like a weapon. It scares me." She raised her hand when he started to reassure her. "I know you'd never hurt me, Seth. I'm afraid that you'll hurt yourself. That you'll lose yourself in this change."

"I haven't changed a bit," he said and again felt that

sickening feeling in the pit of his stomach, dreading what she might say next. "I just grew an extra head. It's nothing to fear."

She took a long and shaky breath. "Right. So maybe you don't need me anymore."

"What? Of course I need you!"

She lifted her shoulders. "You need a navigator."

An uncomfortable thought wormed its way into his mind. "Is this about Khoe? About having her around?"

"She'd be a six-legged *churry*, if she thought that's what we wanted. Don't make this about her." She looked away. "I just don't know if I can keep up with all this."

This time the room seemed to lurch in some weird way and he gripped her shoulders, maybe to keep himself upright. "Why are you talking like this? You can keep up with anything. Are you saying you don't want to?"

"Do I want to see you hunted down and killed by our own people? Locked up in a cage, maybe, so they can take Khoe apart? Probably not!"

He resisted some insane urge to shake her out of this bizarre mood. "Let's not do this. Not now. This is too new for both of us and this is not the time to figure this out."

They both heard a door further down the silent corridor. "Sethran?"

Seth briefly closed his eyes, annoyed by the interruption. Ciela rarely voiced doubts about anything they did, trusting her skills and his experience to see things through, even in the bleakest moments. Where did this despair come from?

She looked out into the hallway. "What is it? Is someone hailing?"

Seth followed her back to the cabin where Isaaron stood before his datasheet. He regarded it warily, as if it would leap up and attack him. The display currently showed a jumble of drawings and calculations, along with what looked like the coordinates of major keyholes. Khoe appeared as soon as Seth tried to decipher it.

"This is some information Neryon and I... err, found on

the Azon orbiter. It was sent here by Targon Astrophysics, looking for help with our subspace problem. Top secret, of course. It includes readings taken at points throughout Trans-Targon, or rather during subspace trips from one place to another. We've been working on it for a while. At first we weren't in agreement but I think we can—"

"Isaaron," Seth interrupted. "What is it?"

"A timeline, of sorts. Showing the subspace spans that have already dissipated, and where. This sector of Trans-Targon will be cut off within days. We'll not be traveling anywhere." He waved a hand at the sheet. "Targon days. That is not a lot."

Ciela's face had turned ashen. "Air Command is not going to get to Chitta Moor any time soon."

Seth's eyes raked over the formulas, ignoring what he could not understand and adding up what he could. "No. But we will."

ELEVEN

At worst, Seth had expected a challenge from those on the ground on Chitta Moor, but only silence greeted them as they approached the planet. The com satellites in orbit still functioned, as did the single transmitter designed to send message packets through the keyhole to distant destinations.

"You'd think nobody cares," Seth mumbled as he scanned through a selection of ground frequencies used by the station and some of the outlying mines.

Ciela, standing behind his bench with her elbows propped on its headrest, looked up at the monitors. "What time is it there?"

Seth grinned. "You think they're all sleeping?"

"Too much to ask for, I guess."

"Will you hail them?" Isaaron said, looking anxious. Since emerging from the keyhole they had coached him to act the captain of this ship for their landing at Queta Station. Seth expected no suspicion of yet another lost ship having been forced to Chitta Moor on its way elsewhere, but after his run-in with Skoth's lackey, showing his face on the stations' monitors was probably asking for trouble. And so the cockpit's com camera was focused on the Human instead. Isaaron had paid close attention to their instructions and memorized responses to what he might be asked. Seth suspected that he was actually disappointed when no one hailed them.

"Let's knock on the transporter's door," Seth said, looking for the hulk in synchronous orbit above Queta Station. He entered a code that would hopefully be understood by a senior officer aboard the ship. Belatedly, he realized that he had neither the *Dutchman*'s resources nor his own data sleeve to back up his claims of who he was. They waited in tense silence until a garbled reply arrived. Seth switched the com to the secure frequency created by someone aboard the transporter, audio only.

"This is Captain Wodja aboard the *Griffin* out of Callas. We see you, Pilot," a man's voice, rich with a Northern Callas inflection, reached them. "Transmit ID."

"Negative, Captain. Protocol Brishan Four, Targon Nine."

The reply was guarded. "State your intent, Pilot."

"I'm looking for Captain Bryn. We last saw him on the surface."

Pause. "Captain Bryn is dead, sir. Some... unpleasantries down there."

"What happened?"

"Unclear. He insisted on transporting survivors back up here. Perhaps aware that he would not hold his position much longer. He stayed with a handful of troops in the surface. We got the news this morning. Not heard from any of them since."

"I'm sorry to hear that, Captain."

"I'm afraid we may be forced to the surface. We're past capacity and the air scrubbers are barely keeping up. Food only for a few more days. Daily casualties of this weird plague that's affecting a number of people here. We've moved the bodies onto one of the shuttles but we'll soon have to jettison what we can't accommodate."

Khoe sighed a tremulous exhalation. Seth watched as Ciela shifted closer to where Khoe hovered and put an arm around the smaller woman's shoulders, heedless of how odd that must look to Isaaron.

"Please hold your position as long as you can, Captain," Seth said. "Air Command is aware of the situation."

"If you say so." The officer's voice made clear that hope was no longer something he had in abundance.

"*Sidara* out," Seth said, unable to find words that could possibly bolster the man's confidence. He looked up at Isaaron standing by the cockpit door before turning his attention to their approach to the planet. "Let's hope you have your formulas memorized correctly, Neryon."

No one hailed the cruiser plunging through the thin atmosphere to approach Queta Station without announcement. Seth tried another com frequency, still pretending to be a new castaway looking for a welcome. He overflew the jagged canyon, focusing cameras on the floor of the abyss. Some people still moved down there but there was no sign of ships where they had left them. The airways remained silent.

"What's all this?" Ciela pointed to a series of energy readings to the east that the *Sidara's* sensors found suspicious.

Isaaron squinted at the displays. "Energy spikes," he said. "Photons. I suppose they are trying random configurations in the absence of the actual calculations."

Seth nodded. "Not detecting any gravitons."

"There'd be no point to that until they've found a way to focus the beam."

"Let's head out to the site," Seth said. "If Queta Station is asleep, let's keep it that way. The quicker we can get you to calibrate those cannons, the better."

It took only a few minutes to cross the distance that Seth and Ciela had traversed on their last visit out there. From up here, the canyons of Queta Station were mere jagged lines splitting the wind-smoothed surface in the distance. Seth compensated when a few warnings appeared on the screens. "I can't get through that interference at all. We'll land nearby and walk the rest of the way."

"Seems wise," Ciela said. "We've got gamma. You would not want to drop shields with all that going on down there."

"Gamma radiation is probably a by-product." Isaaron seemed to be conferring with Neryon. "That accelerator is makeshift at best. They'd be leaking synchrotron radiation."

The *Sidara* swooped low over what by now seemed familiar landscape. They overflew some washouts and heavily eroded vehicle tracks connecting pockmarks left behind by surface mining. Nothing moved down there except for a few swirls of dust chased by the ceaseless winds. The science vessel still stood near the rim of the flooded cauldron, and the hulls of the dismantled ships lay like broken toys in the landscape. "I hope they're still standing," Seth said. "That radiation is at nasty level."

"Dyad, remember?" Khoe said. "It's just electromagnetic."

"Oh. Right. I'd forgotten."

"You've forgotten what?" Isaaron wanted to know.

"Given enough notice, our friends can divert energy to shield us from certain radiation," Seth said. "Pretty much like the ship's shields work. For a while, anyway."

Ciela raised both eyebrows as she looked to Khoe. "Laser guns, too?"

Khoe nodded. "Any EMR. If I know it's happening. It's not an easy trick."

Ciela whistled under her breath. "Wonder no longer why Air Command wants to get rid of you," she said to Isaaron.

An alarm sounded to Seth's left when the *Sidara*'s shields powered up. For a confused moment, Seth thought Khoe, firmly linked into the ship's systems, had triggered something at the mentioning of shields. But then tactical came online to inform them of ground-based targeting.

Isaaron groped for a handrail affixed to the frame of the cockpit door when Seth evaded a shot from the ground. Another sliced into the starboard shield seam, raising another alarm. He shifted more power to the shields and re-engaged the gravity spinners that were already shut down in preparation for landing. Within seconds, he had twisted the *Sidara* through several evasive movements designed to thwart the gunner's ability to target them.

"Damn, they're quick," he said and turned the ship away. This was not the *Dutchman* and whoever was shooting at them knew well what they were doing. Evading another shot that seemed more as a warning against further intrusion than meant to kill, he steered back to the canyons of Queta Station. "What, by Cazun's moldy beard, was that?"

"Nothing on the com," Ciela said. "They're not interested in talking."

"Those shots came from the accelerator site," Khoe reported.

"We'll try to contact them from a distance," Seth said. "I have the feeling that Lieutenant Zire has a way of catching their attention."

They flew over the broad end of the canyon, toward the designated landing site for new arrivals at Queta Station. But, when scanning the area using real-vid, they saw few people out in the open and none along the rebel camp by the creek. Smoke rose from one of the airfield buildings and more wafted through the mining town, obscuring any sign of life down there.

Ciela examined the images on their screens, looking for uniforms. "I'm not so sure that there's any Air Command left down there. Something ugly must have happened."

"What if those rebels have made good on their threat?" Isaaron voiced everyone's thoughts when the camera picked up a rash of laser scars marking the outside of a water tanker abandoned on one of the bridges. "What if they've taken over the accelerator? My team wouldn't be shooting at us."

Seth lifted the *Sidara* out of the canyon again and then brought it down not far from where they had borrowed the skimmer during their previous stay here, above the mine's administrative level.

Ciela was out of her seat before the ship had shifted into its standby mode. Muttering checklists to herself, she left to sort through the pile of gear they had found aboard the ship. Along with the *Dutchman* itself, they had lost their collection of weather gear, disguises, and clothing designed to blend into crowds on several planets.

Seth also got up. "Stay on the ship," he advised Isaaron. "Try to hail your people at the accelerator. Just don't say anything about why you're here, in case someone's listening. I'm assuming they know your name?"

"Yes, of course. What are you going to do?"

"Just taking a look around. Don't open the gate for anyone." Seth left the cockpit to join Ciela in the next cabin. She had found a thick wrap to disguise her face and to ward off the cold. The snug two-piece body suit she wore beneath it drew on a small power pack to provide a short period of shielding against most hand-held weapons.

"Will this fit you?" She held up another suit.

Seth grimaced. Although cleverly designed to fit under regular clothes, these suits tended to pinch in all the wrong places. He fingered the band of instructions inside the collar. "Made for Humans. I'll pass. Far too short in the legs." He demonstrated its deficiencies by holding up a sleeve against his arm, clearly not long enough.

She sighed, aware of his dislike of body armor, and handed him a long jacket instead. "I thought you'd say that. This one's got a graphene layer. Better than nothing."

"Nice!" He held it up for inspection before slipping into it. Also a little short in the sleeve, its well-worn exterior suited his taste far better than the tighties. He accepted a hooded scarf and gloves without demur and then holstered his guns.

"You think they're going to shoot at us?" Khoe said. "Maybe you really should put on that suit."

"Don't worry so much," Seth said, testing his visor. "I'll be fine."

"You keep forgetting that I'm inside that head you're risking, too."

"We'll try not to annoy anyone."

No welcoming committee greeted them when they stepped out of the ship and walked toward the edge of the canyon. They passed the array of ventilation shafts leading to some subterranean installation and found them operational. Seth put his hand on one of them to feel the slight vibration of distant machinery.

"Some people below us," Ciela said. She adjusted her scanners. "Population to the south, where the hangar is. More people on the canyon floor here. I can't see into the mine shafts."

They walked to the eroded edge and found the way barred by a pile of stone rubble and twisted metal that used to be the steep stairs leading down into the canyon. Seth leaned forward to see the ledge to the administrative level. Some furtive movement caught his eye but disappeared at once.

He shifted his visor over his eyes to scan south along the canyon for another way down. "Now we know why it was so easy to get a parking spot up here," he said. "Guess we'll have to try—"

Both dove backwards and rolled into the shelter of some boulders when projectile weapons stuck the rock near their feet. Someone shouted in the distance and more shots rang out. Ciela turned to see the tracers of lasers creep along the rock and scrawl over the low cloud cover above them.

She checked the scanners. "That's coming from the other side. The bridge is down, too."

"Back to the ship. Stay low."

A metallic squeal drew their attention to the ventilation stacks. The lid of a triangular metal box, partially inundated by the drifting surface grit, rose to reveal a black interior. Seth aimed his gun, too aware that the only cover from that direction lay on the canyon side of their rocks.

A hand extended from the opening, waving at them with some urgency.

Seth glanced at Ciela, who shrugged.

The lid rose a little more and now they saw the face of

Lieutenant Zire above the rim.

"Go," Seth said and waited for Ciela to scramble ahead of him to the opening. They crossed the open space and slipped into the hatch.

A dim light strip showed them the way down some metal rungs into a passage carved into the rock. Seth climbed down after Ciela, soon finding solid ground under his feet. A look around revealed a tunnel leading into blackness to their right and a source of stronger light to the left. Lieutenant Zire waited while Ciela slapped the dust from her clothes.

"You look familiar," the lieutenant said, with a tired trace of a smile. Her stained uniform was torn at the knee and lapel and she had carelessly tucked her hair under a black cap. "We feared you lost when no one heard from you again. By your presence here I'm guessing that you tried to get out and failed."

"Yeah, we liked it here so much that we wanted to make a holiday of it," Seth said. "What's going on? Why did they shoot at us?"

"The prisoners started a riot last night," she said and turned to lead them along the shaft. "They're afraid. They don't know what's going on." She shook her head. "Hell, *I* don't know what's going on, either. Many of the guards are dead. We've got a handful of them left up here, but the only Air Command is Lieutenant Ash and me. The rebels took the remaining ships and left. We think they're holed up at the north sub-station. We're trapped here unless we want to try to get out across the plains. But there is no place to go. At least here we have water and shelter. We took the bridge down ourselves."

"She's a Dyad!" Khoe gasped.

I know. I wonder if she's sensed you yet.

They entered a room carved out of the rock. The side facing the rift was fronted by one of the building modules that lined the platform up here, its windows protected by metal bars. Along the wall, some equipment still worked and monitors showed the displays of whatever cameras and sensors had not yet been found and destroyed. A Centauri lieutenant sat listlessly before them and barely looked up when they entered. Seth nodded at the burly Human standing by one of the windows with his eyes on the opposite canyon wall and a rifle by his side.

"What about the others?" Ciela said, skipping the introductions.

"The captain got most of the civilians out," Zire replied. "At least the ones that wanted to go. I don't know why he thought they'd be safer on the transport. There are some civilians still in the camp but they'll be out of food by now. The prisoners don't seem interested in harming them, but they're not sharing the supplies they've taken over."

"She meant the others out at the accelerator," Seth said. "Your science team."

"I don't know what you're..." Zire began, but then her words trailed away. She closed her eyes. "We're failing," she started anew. "Running out of power packs. Unable to calibrate the stream. Skoth and his group tried to get at the project. So now we have to use up even more energy to keep them out." She sat heavily on the edge of a table as if whatever was holding her up had finally collapsed. "It's all for nothing," she whispered. "The end of us. Is no one coming to help?"

Ciela moved first in the dead silence that followed the woman's hopeless words. She touched Zire's shoulder. "Not the end," she said. "Hang on a little longer."

The lieutenant looked up without lifting her head. Her eyes moved to Seth. "You're one of us," she said to him. "I can feel that." She touched her head. "Such marvelous possibility. Imagine a cadre of Union soldiers joined by these entities. What a force we could be. But that's not going to happen now."

Seth glanced at Ciela and shook his head. This was not the time to bring Zire and her partner up to date on Air Command's view of Dyads. "We've brought Isaaron," he said. "The man who sent the Outrider to begin the project.

But we can't land at the pit, the way they have it shielded now. They fired on us when we tried."

"Isaaron? Here?" Zire smiled tiredly. "You're too late. There is precious little thorium left out there. The accelerator isn't going to be much use."

"There's none left here?"

"The rebels got all we had when they took the Air Command cruisers. They killed the pilots. It's just a matter of time before Skoth sends his gang for your ship. I'd recommend that you leave at once, but there is no place to go."

"Khoe, how much thorium is aboard the *Sidara*?"

"Just the cubes in the drives," she replied. "But I think there is some here."

"How do you know?"

"I've been looking around," she said with a wave of her hand at the monitors. "I'm seeing the blanks left by the shielding. Of the cubes."

Seth stepped up to the monitors. "Show me."

A schematic of the opposite canyon wall appeared on a screen. The image showed the walkways and elevators fixed to the cliff along with the rails used to ferry ore from the mines. Khoe shifted the sensors to show the interior, now little more than a wireframe. "What is that?" He indicated a few connected cavities halfway up the rock face.

"Storage depot, as I recall," Zire said. She did not ask how he was able to access their system. "Taken over by the prisoners now. They've hoarded supplies there." She pointed to the catwalks around the opening. "That is the only way into those tunnels now. They won't let you get near that. It's all they've been fighting over."

Ciela looked closer to find the white blanks on the screen, indicating something invisible to the scanners. "What would they have here at Queta Station, other than fissile thorium, that requires shielding?"

Zire peered at the screen. "I have no idea. What kolterium is still found is kept elsewhere."

"Who else is up here that might know?" Seth said. "Where is the mine boss?"

"They tossed him off the bridge days ago."

"That can't be anything but thorium cubes," Ciela said. "The prisoners might not even know it's there."

Seth nodded. "Guess we'll find out. Infrared, Khoe."

The display changed again to show the thermal signatures of moving bodies near the entrance and on the scaffolding outside. "Can't really see far into the cave with this," she said.

He tapped Zire's arm. "They have no need for thorium without ship. Will they negotiate? Do you have anything to trade?"

"Bullets. They're shooting at anything in uniform. Fear, revenge for past treatment, no real reason for any of this. There is no way out unless that keyhole starts working again."

"Those are just prisoners on that side? No hostages? Guards?"

"Not that I know."

Seth stared at the screens for a moment longer. "Contact your people out by the accelerator. Tell them that we have Isaaron and to expect us."

"What do you have in mind, Kada," Ciela said when he turned to the tunnel exit. "I can see the gears turning."

"I think today's the day you're going to get over your fear of heights, darling."

She looked at Khoe, who was equally puzzled. "I don't like the sound of this," she said, hurrying after Seth to the ladder leading outside. "Not one bit."

They made their way outside and dashed to the waiting *Sidara* without drawing more fire from below. Isaaron met them at the door when the seal released. "I'd started to worry," he greeted them. "What have you found?"

"Trouble," Seth said. "Khoe, would you learn to fly this ship, please?"

She disappeared at once.

"Wait a minute now…" Ciela said.

He walked along the central corridor of the ship, looking for the hatch to the lower hold. "She can fly the *Dutchman*. She'll fly this tub just fine. Though I think I might slip into that set of tighties, after all."

She sighed. "You're going to go after the power packs, aren't you? This ship isn't going to fit into the canyon, if you're thinking of flying down to that entrance. Not even with you piloting. It's just too narrow up here."

"True." He lifted a handle from the floor to hoist the hatch. Lying down, he peered into the space below and then came up grinning. "Do I know my ships, or what? We've got a sling."

"You can't be serious," Ciela said, following him into the cabin where they had piled the ship's spare gear. "It's a shooting gallery out there."

He dropped his coat and then took off shirt and trousers to squeeze his long limbs into the shielded body armor. "I know. But we won't make it down there on the open stairs. Are you with me?"

She glanced at Isaaron, still hand-wringing in the doorway. Taking a deep breath, she reached up to help Seth stretch the armor over his shoulders. "Where else would I be?"

They suited up as best as they could, adding graphene-reinforced hoods and additional weapons. They had none of the additional armor that was usually worn over the tighties and so Seth put his trousers back over the suit. The snug gear just didn't seem right on a man, he thought, even if Ciela smirked at his vanity.

"How are things going, Khoe," Seth said when they entered the cockpit. Ciela dropped into the bench beside him.

Khoe was already running through pre-flight. "The starboard thrusters are balky," she said. "Misaligned."

"I noticed. But the canyon edges are solid rock, so we'll be fairly stable." He took Ciela's hand and pressed it to his lips. "Get ready."

She nodded and slumped back to call up the innate talent of her ancestors to seek a khamal that allowed her to block distraction and achieve a level of serenity that was not easily disturbed. Seth watched her close her eyes, wishing he shared her gift.

"Take us up, Khoe," he said.

The *Sidara* rose from the ground and hovered for a moment. A maelstrom of dust swirled around them and into the canyon.

"Are you sure about this?" Ciela said. "You're going to be flying this ship remotely. With your head. That never ends well, even without people shooting at you."

"Yeah, but we have Khoe," he said, his mind on manipulating the sling mechanism in the lower hold. "My attention will be on too many things. You're leading this expedition. Take no prisoners."

"You're not even funny, Kada."

The *Sidara* edged over the canyon, already reaching for the opposite ledge to allow its thrusters to support it above the chasm. Seth engaged the real-vid cameras and found people guarding the scaffolding around the storehouse, looking up at them. He rolled his eyes when someone aimed and shot at the ship. "No hyperspectral sensors on this thing," he said, again feeling the pain of not having the *Dutchman* under his feet. "Still can't tell how many are inside." He linked to the ship's tactical controls. "Let's make a little room."

Without warning, he opened fire, using projectile weapons to blast into the cliff's superstructure. The relentless barrage continued until the rails came apart, tearing the catwalks and stairs from the rock. Isaaron's hands flew to his lips when several people tumbled into the canyon along with the twisted pieces of metal. Soon there was nothing left below and above the entrance except for the support beams driven into the rock. A prisoner appeared at the opening and fell to Seth's aim. No one else emerged.

"Oops," Seth said when the metal platform outside the storage chambers slowly bent and then also tore loose from its supports. They watched it crash to the valley floor. "Didn't mean for that to go."

Ciela exhaled sharply. "Well, better now than when I'm standing on it."

Seth directed Khoe to shift the *Sidara* until they hovered above the entrance and then anchored the anti-grav beams to either side of the canyon. The lock was uneven and the wind above and through the canyon created worrisome turbulence but it would have to do. "Just hold it here," he said. "How's your aim?"

"Only as good as yours," she replied tersely.

He grinned at Isaaron. "I taught her everything she knows."

The man made an unclear sound that might have been an invocation to some deity. "You're leaving me here?" he said when both Ciela and Seth got up to leave the cockpit. "Are you telling me that you're going to hold the ship here, hovering over this abyss, while you're not actually aboard?"

"We'll want tea when we get back," Ciela said.

Seth tapped his neural node. "Khoe is linked to the ship through my com band. Between us we'll be in full neural link with it, don't worry." He hesitated. Perhaps Isaaron needed something a little more diverting than making tea. "Stay in the cockpit and monitor the proximity sensors. We'll need to know if they find something more destructive than pistols. Somewhere I'm sure they have laser cannons or explosives in this mine."

They went into the corridor where Seth lowered Ciela into the hold before dropping down, too. The sling hoist stood ready above the cargo hatch in the floor. Ships of this class were often used for transporting materials into rough terrain inaccessible by larger vessels. In places where landing was impossible, a sling hoisted goods and passengers to and from the ground. Made of graphene netting, it had a flat bottom platform wide enough for both of them.

Seth took a deep breath when he felt Ciela's gentle touch in his mind, soothing his sudden apprehension when he reached for the hatch controls. He smiled, allowing her to calm his frayed nerves, grateful for her presence. "Ready to lose that fear of heights?"

"Not really."

"Khoe?"

"We're holding fine. Sensors are picking up people below and to the right of the mine. Armed. I've been taking a few shots."

"Switch to lasers," he said. "Not as spectacular, but we don't want to weaken the rock face more than we already have." Seth motioned for Ciela to climb aboard the unsteady platform, where she knelt and gripped the webbing. A blast of cold air rushed into the hold from below when he opened the hatch. After an experimental glance into the canyon, she fastened her eyes him. Once Seth was also aboard, both activated a thin aura of shielding tied to the power supply at their belts. She wobbled slightly when her shield made contact with Seth's armor. "This'll only last a few minutes," he reminded her.

Ciela gripped the netting tighter with one hand when the platform descended, her gun ready. She gasped when it dropped faster than expected toward the mine entrance. Almost at once, someone below opened fire. Most of it went wide but both Seth and Ciela ducked reflexively when a bullet slammed into the netting and the basket began to swing.

"Compensate," Seth said to Khoe. She had withdrawn from his vision to keep focused on her task, but a camera below the *Sidara* showed her what she needed. The ship rocked by increments until the basket hung more or less stable. Ciela's fears were well-founded. Remotely controlling any ship was of course routine for both Air Command and civilian operators. But doing so using only a neural implant, inside a turbulent planetary atmosphere, was actually forbidden in most populated areas. He himself might trust a

Delphian with it. Today, given no other choice, he trusted the subspace entity in his head.

He leaned forward as they came to the level of the entrance. A projectile hit the wall over their heads. Ciela cursed and returned the fire, dropping someone from the ledge below. She did not watch his trip into the gorge. Some tracers streaked across the rock face and Seth grinned when he realized that, behind them, Lieutenant Zire and the other soldier stood at the ruined ledge and assisted Khoe's carefully aimed volleys at the prisoners to force them back into the shafts. "All right, go."

Ciela looked like she'd much prefer to continue dangling in mid-air like a prize in a shooting gallery than make the leap from the unstable platform to the gaping hole in the cliff wall.

Seth gripped her arm. "Nothing to it. Don't look down."

A projectile whistled past them and he whipped around to fire back at the Feydan woman in ragged prison garb that had stepped out of the cave. Once again, the platform twisted, and then finally made contact with the rock. "Now!"

Ciela threw herself onto the ledge and immediately rolled aside to fire into the open entrance to cover Seth's leap. Both scuttled forward, out of range of the gunfire from the outside. She grinned and tapped a fist just below her neck, an Arawaj signal for 'all's well'.

"We're in, Khoe," Seth said and switched his visor to night vision. That, and an overlay of the thermal sensor, showed them the way deeper into the shaft. "Ask Isaaron how much he thinks we need." Seth closed his eyes for a moment to perceive the ship's sensors. They came to his mind, as images and sound via his neural interface, as clearly as if he sat before them. The *Sidara* held her position with barely a wobble, oblivious to the angry fire from below.

"As much as you can carry," Khoe replied after relaying his request via the cabin speakers. "We may need to make more than one attempt with the graviton pulse, he says. Oh, look. There are some people below. I think they're from the camp."

"Try not to shoot any of those. We'll—" He ducked behind a column of rock when Ciela fired into the dark. Someone cried out in pain. He nodded to her and they stormed forward, blasting at the orange shapes that appeared on their visors. Soon they found the way blocked by a metal sheet set into the wall.

Ciela stepped over a body and ran her hand over the door, finding no interface. "Manual." She moved back again to give him room to shoot the lock out.

The door sprang open after just a few shots. Two man-sized shapes launched themselves out of the gloom at the intruders, guns ready.

Ciela cried out, leaping aside as if stung. "I'm hit!"

Seth reached for one of the prisoners and did not have to prod Khoe to feel her surge of heart-stopping energy slice into the dense body. The convict's body shook in a violent spasm and crashed to the ground. Seth's gun took down the other.

"Is she hurt?" Khoe exclaimed. "Seth! Is she all right?"

Seth crouched beside Ciela, looking for blood. He breathed harshly, feeling the painfully exhilarating aftermath of the power that Khoe had momentarily whipped through his body.

"Hit the top of my foot." Ciela cursed her assailant's parentage.

"Yes, she's all right, by the sounds of it. Don't shout in my head. Keep your mind on the ship." Seth peered back into the shaft leading into absolute black before taking a closer look at Ciela's foot.

"Didn't go through," she said through clenched teeth. "Gods, that hurts. I think it's broken."

"Watch for any others," he said and ducked into the storage room. He scanned the open shelves to look for the cubes Khoe had detected among the meager supplies. Finally, he spotted some crates in a corner and kicked them aside to reveal a careless stack of power packs. "Found them," he called to Ciela. He pulled a tarp from another crate and threw it on the ground. Grabbing as much as he thought he could carry, he stacked cubes onto the sheet and then dragged the whole thing out into the shaft. "Can you get up?"

She was already pulling herself to her feet. "Go. I'll cover you."

He leaned into the task, cursing the uneven ground and the rubble their assault on the entrance had flung into the shaft. The combined sensations of Ciela's pain, Khoe's fear, and his own worry about a bullet from behind weighed upon him far heavier than the load he dragged out into the murky daylight. "We're out, Khoe," he snapped. "Pay attention now."

Ciela shoved him aside and for a moment he thought she had groped him for support but then he realized that she was shooting back into the dark. A projectile whined against the rock near his head. He dropped the tarp and fired back until nothing more came at them.

"There's probably another exit to this tunnel." Ciela peered up at the ship hovering above them. "I'm thinking it might be safer if we went that way."

He steadied her when she hopped sideways to keep her balance. "So are you going to carry all that, then?" He yanked the tarp to the ledge. "Khoe, bring that sling in as tight as you can."

Ciela leaned against the rock wall, waiting for more of the inmates to emerge from the depths of the mine, while he moved the shielded thorium onto the platform. The seal tabs on the cubes showed no leak but Seth wondered how they'd been handled before ending up in this depot. He worked quickly, expecting the alarm on his sleeve to alert him of radiation at any moment. "Now you," he said at last, turning to Ciela.

She reached for him and hobbled to the ledge. "Uh, I think I'll take the next one," she said, looking down.

He grinned and held her arm tightly until she perched on

their cargo. Her face remained immobile, a clear sign that her foot bothered her as much as the precipice below them. The sling sagged noticeably. "How's the weight, Khoe?"

"Maybe *you* should take the next one," she replied. "Or dump some of the cubes."

Someone shouted from the opposite side of the canyon. He saw Lieutenant Zire wave to them but her words were torn from her lips by the ceaseless wind. She pointed up along the canyon.

"Ship heading this way," Khoe said, turning her attention to the *Sidara*'s mid-range scanners. "One Trident. From the north."

Seth gripped the webbing and stepped onto the edge of the platform. The hoist above them creaked alarmingly. He reached the ship's navigational controls, again using Khoe as the interface, to gain altitude and take the ship out of the canyon rather than wait for the sling to winch back into the hold.

Ciela squeezed her eyes shut when the sling began rise, far more slowly than it had let them descend. Seth leaned inward as much as he could when the platform began to swing below the ship. It wobbled dangerously when he reduced the ship's thrusters on the opposite canyon wall.

"I can't watch this," Khoe said.

"You're not supposed to! Stay on navigation." Seth closed his eyes once they rose above the canyon, putting all of his faith into his link to Khoe and the ship to move the *Sidara* horizontally. He exhaled sharply when the dusty ground appeared beneath them.

"We're clear!" Khoe cried.

Seth looked up to the hatch of the *Sidara*'s hold. At last, the winch began to reel them in. A dark face appeared in the opening, beckoning toward him as if that would hurry the process. When they finally entered the ship, Isaaron reached out to guide the sling and then shut the hatch. "Thank the gods you're safe!" he exclaimed when he saw Ciela and the trove of thorium cubes.

Seth stepped off the platform but Ciela, with a grin on her ashen face, waved him away when he reached to help her up. "Go. Get us out of here," she said.

"You're hurt? I'll help," he heard Isaaron say when he heaved himself onto the main deck of the *Sidara* and raced for the cockpit.

"I've got the course to the accelerator laid in," Khoe said when the ship gained altitude.

"Wait," he said and swung the ship around. "I want to get the lieutenant out." He crossed the canyon, adjusting the external cameras to look for the officer and her people. Indeed, she had been watching and signaled that she saw his maneuver before disappearing inside the bunker. They hovered anxiously near the exhaust vents above the control rooms and only moments later the hatch was flung aside and the officers emerged, followed by two others in company uniform.

"Look out!" Khoe shouted.

A shadow swooped past them, tearing into the ground with projectile weapons. The shots glanced harmlessly off the *Sidara*'s hull but did not miss their intended target. Zire was flung back under the assault and the others racing after her also fell.

Seth cursed and set off in pursuit of the rebel Trident. It swooped along the gorge and then below its rim as if mocking Seth's less agile Fleetwood. He tipped the *Sidara* on its side, used to far more delicate maneuvers, and followed. Not in the mood to play games with the enemy pilot, he targeted and unloaded on it, mostly out of anger, and watched it jerk sideways and then career into the rock face, sending shrapnel to the valley floor. Seth shot out of the canyon and headed for the accelerator.

Khoe said nothing while they left Queta Station behind and headed out into the flats. He kept his eyes on the sensor readings that told them the energy emissions there had stopped. They overflew the area before landing not far from the lip of the cauldron. Plumes of dust rose up to obscure the sun before the winds took them away again.

"Guess they got Zire's message, seeing how no one's shooting at us," Ciela said when Seth found her and Isaaron in the galley, which apparently also served as a med-station here. He had strewn supplies all over the floor and the counter on which Ciela now sat, her foot elevated on a folded blanket. "That was a rough ride, captain."

Seth nodded. "You all right?"

"Yes, it's not broken." She winced when Isaaron's stabilizing gel tightened to the contours of her ankle. "What's wrong?"

"Zire and her crew are dead," Seth said. "For no damn reason." He turned when Khoe called for his attention and studied his data sleeve when she relayed an image. "Someone's coming from the pit. Good, they brought a skimmer."

Ciela swiveled on the counter and gripped Isaaron's arm when he steadied her.

"Stay here, please," Seth said. "You can't walk around with that out there. And we're likely to get irradiated again."

"What? I don't want to miss this!"

Isaaron chuckled. "There won't be much to see. A little firework, that's all. Once the beam is steady it'll do all the work itself."

"Please, Ciela," Seth said, still seeing visions of Zire torn apart by the rebel guns. "You're in pain. I can see that."

She tilted her head and, after a moment of observing him with those keen blue eyes, nodded. "She held her ground well, Seth."

He shrugged, feeling a little sheepish that she had seen through his show of concern. "You can use the monitors to watch. I'd also feel better if someone kept an eye out for more rebels. I'm pretty damn sure Skoth is on his way here."

"They'll take the thorium," Isaaron fretted. "We have to hurry. Please!"

"The skimmer's here, Seth," Khoe said.

Ciela hobbled into the cockpit while he dropped into the

hatch to the lower deck and then helped Isaaron find the ladder to make his way down. Once more, they opened the cargo doors, this time to see solid ground below it. Seth jumped down and waved to the approaching skimmer while Isaaron also exited.

"Um," Isaaron squinted against the sun nearing the horizon to identify the three men and a woman when the car's dome retracted. "Those aren't my people."

TWELVE

The skimmer slowed and it seemed that it was studded with guns pointing their way. Seth stepped away from under the *Sidara* and waited for the vehicle to settle on the ground. The woman in the rear seat stood up and lowered the scarf covering her face.

"Sethran!"

"Doctor Hedvig!" he replied, happy to see smiles on the faces of the other three as well. "Didn't think we'd see you again."

She stepped out of the vehicle and hurried toward him. "I'm so glad to see a friendly face! And you brought power packs! We were worried that Lieutenant Zire's message was yet another ruse. I'm sorry about shooting at you earlier. We didn't know it was you." Her companions went to the hatch of his ship and one of them climbed into the hold to start shifting the heavy cubes to the opening.

Hedvig looked past Seth to Isaaron who was now coming out of the *Sidara*'s shadow to approach the skimmer. "Mr. Toise? Isaaron Toise?"

He nodded and wiped his hands on his trousers before shaking hers. "I'm afraid I don't remember you," he said.

"I arrived later. But I've learned so much since I got there! Your design is correct. The transmitters work." She turned to point into the pit below them as if the four improvised emitters didn't stand out in the dusty crater like something from another world. "It's not all good news, I'm sorry to say. Skoth turned on us. I thought he was here to help. But they came this morning and wanted our ship, our supplies. The power packs, too."

"What happened?" Seth said, only now spotting mounds in the distance that looked uncomfortably like gravel piled upon a corpse.

"We told them what we were trying to do. They didn't listen. They didn't believe us. They wanted our navigator and then force us to restore the keyhole."

"They don't have a spanner?" Seth said.

"No. Even if the keyhole is restored, they can't leave here without one. Things went very badly. Some people got killed. They fired on us before we got the shield up." She put her hand on Isaaron's arm. "I'm sorry; some of your people are... There are too few of us now."

"Who else is left?" Isaaron said.

"Soji can operate," she said. "The other two are... I don't know. Hurt somehow. They don't seem to remember things."

Isaaron stared at her without comprehension. "We need those people! The Dyads. We need them to activate the transmitters."

Seth gripped Isaaron's arm when it seemed that the man was about to hurl himself down the rocky slope to see to his people. "What do you mean? Can't you run this?"

The engineer sunk down to sit heavily on a boulder, his voice breaking in despair. "You don't just throw a switch on this," he said. "There isn't a processor made that can work this out. We need the entities for this. The ones that have been working with this crew."

"How many do you need for this?"

Isaaron licked his dust-caked lips and then rubbed his face with both hands, leaving pale streaks on his dark brown skin. Seth had to remind himself that, although the Human seemed fit, he was an elder among his species and probably more frail than he appeared. He looked around. "Do you have any water?"

One of the men loading the power cubes into the skimmer handed him a bottle. Isaaron sipped like he didn't really care. "I need four Dyads that can handle the processors. That have experience. That can work with the algorithms. It's dangerous work."

Seth looked around. "These men won't do?"

Doctor Hedvig shook her head. "They're not joined. They came here to help us build the emitters. We lost some of them, too, in the attack."

A crackle at his wrist alerted him to Ciela in the ship above them. "Seth, they're coming. Three cruisers. They'll be here in under an hour at current speed."

Seth gripped Isaaron's shoulders to help him to his feet. "Let's do this before Skoth gets here. We've got the doctor, you, this Soji she mentioned, and me. That's four. You know Khoe is pretty sharp. Will this work?" He nodded to the doctor when she looked at him in surprise. "Yes, I've picked up a houseguest, too."

"Are you out of your blockheaded mind?" Ciela's voice interrupted. "Do you have any idea how much power these things are packing?"

"We have no choice," he replied. "Get the guns ready. Lock down the ship. They'll probably want a navigator more than the cubes."

Isaaron scratched his head, looking around with a mix of hope and trepidation. "Might be enough." He addressed Hedvig. "Is the Outrider able to get into orbit? We'll need to open the keyhole from there and survey the trajectory. We can't do that from down here."

She raised her com band. "Mister Goran, please launch when ready. We're going ahead."

Isaaron fussed over the distribution of the thorium cubes in the skimmer. "Make sure that each station has six of these, and keep some extras. Replace any that are tapped even a little. We'll need a full charge. The transmitters will need to run for several hours. Careful!" He watched them start to make their way into the cauldron. "I need to get down to the main control shed to calibrate the beam."

"This way," Hedvig said.

Seth waited until the hatch above him slammed shut before hurrying after the others into the pit. Most of the way down followed an old track made by machinery, but then the doctor turned toward the edge of the water where loose rubble and larger boulders made things treacherous.

Isaaron took no notice of this as he kept up, stepping almost heedlessly over the debris. Scraggly growth offered a few handholds along the way until they reached the flatter shore. A few massive boulders sheltered a geodesic dome just large enough for a small team of scientists as they went about their work. Conduits extended from there into the water and along both sides of the shore. All of them looked skyward when the Azon Corp's pretty Outrider launched and headed for the clouds.

A young Magran in coveralls awaited them. "Mister Toise!" he called to Isaaron. "We've done it. Wait till you see the response rate we're getting. Come see."

Seth left them to their discoveries and looked out over the lake, still not able to shake the feeling that something sinister brooded in its depths. Something did, of course – he felt the peculiar vibration in the air as the accelerator did whatever accelerators do except that this one was little more than a cobbled-together assembly of units designed for small cruisers but operating with power far beyond their specifications. Something down there glowed; possibly a glimpse of the sunken ship's cabin lights.

He spoke into his com band. "Ciela?"

"Yes! What's going on? I've lost visual of you down there."

He looked around. The team with the skimmers was hurrying from one of the four transmitters to the next, ensuring that each had the correct power supply. "Wish I knew. Keep an eye on the Outrider. If anything gets in its way, take it down."

"Do you think this is going to work?"

He nudged one of the conduits with his foot, wishing them both back aboard the Delphian orbiter above Magra, enjoying their tea. "No."

"Seth…"

"I meant yes," he said. He should have tried to find a pilot to get Ciela out with as many people as they could fit on a ship, he thought to himself. At least that would have meant safety for some of them. But where would she take them? By now, how many exits remained for her to choose? "I love you," he said. "Did I mention that?"

"Don't be talking like that, Kada!" Ciela said, trying to sound flippant and failing when her voice cracked. "Get busy down there so we can ditch this rock."

He felt a hand on his arm and turned to see Khoe looking up at him, worried. "It can work," she said. "You'll see."

Seth smiled at her and then pulled her close to kiss her forehead. "Yeah, 'course it will."

A panel on all four emitters turned orange at the same time. The vibrations from below increased until the ground itself seemed to tremble. The resonance took on a rhythmic pulse that modulated for a moment and then settled into a steady beat.

He turned when Isaaron and his team emerged from the cramped shelter. His eyes were fixed on a datasheet but Seth thought he exuded a confidence that he had not seen on the man before now. He stood straight, feet firmly splayed on the ground, and pointed to the emitters. "It's time," he said. "Soji, you take that one. Seth and Lara, you go to those. I'll run the one here. Just interface with the access panel and let the entities do their job. They'll also be able to shield you against most of the radiation."

Seth jogged along the shore, passing the first transmitter, and then reached the one Isaaron had pointed out for him. "Now what?"

"The panel at the side," Khoe said. "Activate it."

He placed his hand on the dark interface which came alive at once. Khoe faded from view as she concentrated on the circuitry. "Keep your hand on that. I don't want to do this remotely."

He looked up at the emitter rising above him like some piece of forgotten machinery in a salvage depot. It, too, vibrated and soon the orange panel turned blue. Looking across the lake, he saw Isaaron near his transmitter, looking impossibly small compared to the size of what they were about to try.

"Keyhole is opening," she said. "Close your eyes. There'll be some arcs."

At some unheard signal, he felt a painful tingle begin in his palm and then spread through his body. "Gods, Khoe!" he groaned.

She did not reply and he reminded himself that the impulses from his pain receptors was also something they shared. A brilliant flash burned through the lids of his eyes when the emitters combined their output to create the photon beam needed to carry the gravitons into space. He ground his teeth as he fought against the impulse to pull away. Years ago, he had gotten stuck in one of Zera's endless electrical storms. The air had smelled like this there, too, and felt like every bit of moisture had been sucked out of it. The moments ticked by like hours. Something cracked through the air and he felt the beam falter momentarily before stabilizing.

"Yesss," Khoe hissed. "Let go."

He recoiled and stumbled over a rock to land heavily on his backside. Something dug into his tailbone and he was almost glad for this far more reasonable pain.

"The beam is stable."

He got up, checking his fingers for blisters. "What does that mean?"

"I have no idea. But it's what Isaaron wanted. We've got gravitons heading into subspace."

"Enough?"

She shrugged.

He saw some of the ground crew scramble toward one of the other transmitters. Its repurposed laser cannon tilted at an odd angle and the side of its casing was blackened. Soji lay on the ground nearby, but he moved his arms in a weak gesture to show that he was not badly hurt. Seth hurried back to the control hut, hampered by the wobble in his knees. The doctor and Isaaron seemed uninjured although both looked like something had just touched them with a live wire.

Seth activated his com band to reach Ciela when he saw the smile on Isaaron's face. "We're still standing," he reported. "Mostly."

"Neryon is very pleased with himself," Isaaron said. "We've got amazing output."

"Party later," Ciela's voice reached them, crackling through the radiation. "Skoth is on approach. Looks like they're circling the beam coming up from the lake. They've got guns on you."

"Talk to them!" Isaaron said. "Or shoot them down, whatever. They can't interfere with this! Get them to understand."

Seth nodded. "Hail them for me and see if you can boost the signal a bit, Ciela."

A few moments later another static crackle came from his com band. "Skoth," he said. "Nice of you to drop by. Careful where you step, this place is a bit of a mess."

"Kada."

"Yep, that's me. Look, the only thing that's getting us out of here is this generator. So be a good soul and stand down, will you?"

"You crossed me, Arawaj. Took out my runner. I don't know what you're up to but I'm damn sure I won't take your word for anything." He seemed to reconsider this for lack of anyone else to ask. "What does this thing do, other than shoot photons into the sky?"

"Trade secret. But it's not going to open a new keyhole to

elsewhere. It's going to let us get home by dinner time." Seth winked at Isaaron and held up his crossed fingers. "If you ask politely I'll let you come with us, seeing how you're short by a navigator and I'm not giving you mine."

There was a brief silence. Seth felt a buzz on his wrist and looked down to read Ciela's message. *Please stop pissing the rebel off.*

"That thing is going to restore the keyhole to Mrak?" Skoth said, sounding half convinced.

"Aye."

"That's going to open the door for Air Command to come down here."

"Yes."

Some moments passed, filled only by some hissing conversation aboard the Feydan's ship. "You have about thirty seconds to get airborne before I change my mind and help myself to your navigator, Arawaj. I don't need you for that." Skoth broke his com link without another word.

"Rebels, eh?" Seth said to the others. "You just have to know how to talk to them." He looked around. "So let's go. Gather your crew."

Isaaron shook his head. "I need to stay. We can't leave the accelerator. It's not clear how well the transmitters will keep up with the planet's rotation. And, once we're sure we've been successful, we will need to dismantle the control mechanism so that it can't be used again. It's a dangerous weapon in the wrong hands, potentially."

Seth frowned. "Are you sure? Air Command will get here, at some point. They will know you're a Dyad."

"We'll deal with that when we have to," Doctor Hedvik said. "We've got the Outrider."

"You're needed in Trans-Targon, Doctor," Seth said to her.

"How can she return?" Ciela said from aboard the *Sidara*. "She's a Dyad."

Seth looked to Khoe who, after a moment, nodded.

"It's possible to... separate while in subspace," Seth said.

"During the jump. The entity can pick up the Alpha resonance in subspace and follow it." He sighed, remembering. "It's a bit painful."

Doctor Hedvig gasped and looked to Isaaron. "Seth has more knowledge of this than any of us, dear," he said.

She looked out over the lake, lost in her communication with her visitor. Her lips tightened and she closed her eyes for a brief moment. "So it'll be," she said, barely audible, but firmly. "We'll be hunted here forever. I don't have your talents for survival, Sethran. My place is on Targon."

"What about Soji?" Seth said. "He's hurt."

Isaaron looked to the youth who leaned heavily on two of his crewmates. Both of his hands were badly burned but he seemed oblivious to the pain. "He's needed here," Isaaron said, a question in his voice.

Soji nodded. "We're not done here. We don't even know if this is going to work. Please just take those rebels away from here. We'll track you. By the time you get to the keyhole we should have funneled enough gravitons to interrupt the beam for you to get out." He shrugged. "And I'm not sure... I don't know if I want to *not* be a Dyad. It's..." He seemed at a loss for words and looked to Seth. "You know."

"I do," Seth said.

Another hail from Seth's wrist squawked at them. "You're out of time, Kada," they heard Skoth's voice.

"That we are," Seth said. "Ciela, can you start pre-flight, please? I'd like to get out before we lose any more exits, no matter where they are."

"What are you talking about, losing exits?" Skoth said.

"You weren't supposed to hear that. We're taking off shortly. We're going to pick up the transport on the way out."

"Why?"

"It's a nice ship." Seth closed the com link again. "There are a lot of Dyads aboard," he said to Isaaron. "Failed merges, injured people. Ciela will jump us to Targon, if she can, so we can alert the clinic about them before Air Command gets involved."

"That'll also bring the rebels to Targon," Soji pointed out.

"You don't say," Seth grinned.

* * *

Stepping aboard the *Griffin* felt like wading into the aftermath of some horrific disaster or perhaps a battle where civilians had borne the brunt. And, like so often in times like that, the survivors had little interest in who won the battle.

Seth had locked the *Sidara* onto the transport and they had cautiously entered the loading area. Unlike some of the long-range commuters and explorers, this ship was designed to transport a maximum number of people with the greatest efficiency. Every bit of space was used for accommodations or supplies, without luxury or wasted expense. And now it was crammed beyond specifications. Both Seth and Ciela gasped when the overused air assaulted their senses.

This deck was intended to temporarily store shipments of goods and offered a larger space than the narrow corridors beyond. Now people crowded this area, obviously instructed to move as little as possible, looking tired and utterly disinterested in the new arrivals.

A Callas native met them by the airlock. He had stripped off his gray Air Command jacket but the insignia identified him as Captain Wodja. "Hello," he said. "Welcome aboard our disaster zone." He waved them along a zig-zagging path through the mostly silent civilians. "I'm still not quite sure what to make of your message. This way, please."

"Captain," Doctor Hedvig said. "I won't be needed for navigation. I am somewhat trained for medical intervention. Can I be of help?"

"Yes, please!" he said and waved to one of his aides.

Seth winced when he saw a woman with two very small children on the floor, huddled under a single blanket. "There is a little more space and a few supplies on our ship," he said. "It might help, too."

Chris Reher

"Thank you, every bit helps. Let's head up to the bridge."

Once behind the closed door of the ship's control room, Ciela exhaled a shuddering breath. "This is terrible. How long have you lived in these conditions?"

"A few weeks. Things were tolerable until Captain Bryn sent everyone up here," Wodja said.

Ciela went to the navigator's station. "May I?" she said to the Centauri woman seated there. "I'll need command access."

The officer nodded to a Magran woman, the actual captain of the private vessel. "She'll be taking us through," he said. He turned to Seth. "We've got the juice to get to the keyhole. But up until now none of the ships that tried to get through have made it. And I really don't know what we're supposed to do about that graviton discharge we're seeing." He indicated a bank of monitors. "Those three other ships out there are not responding to our hail. Will they be boarding as well?"

Seth shook his head. "Hitchhikers." He placed his hand on the com console beside him to let Khoe take a look around. This vessel had little need for elaborate security and she slipped into the system without notice. "Let's get under way. It'll offer some hope for your passengers."

"Go help the others," Ciela said without looking up from the helm. "I'll find you later."

He grinned at the captain. "I've got my orders. What can I do?"

For the next few hours, Seth worked beside Doctor Hedvig to help with the casualties. There was only one medical doctor aboard but some of the civilians had training. Seth suspected a Caspian female working alongside the volunteers to be an Arawaj rebel but she said little and worked as hard as the others. Ciela joined them after exploring the ship's controls to lend her soothing mental touch to the worst of the cases.

Khoe identified a disturbing number of Dyads among the passengers, many in a confused state, some outright catatonic. Two had to be restrained when the ship picked up speed toward the keyhole although it was unclear what excited them. Two uninjured Air Command soldiers also hosted subspace guests but seemed unwilling to share their experience.

They were not far out from their destination when Seth asked the ship's captain for the use of his cabin and pulled Ciela from her duties.

"Don't tire yourself out," he said after closing the door on the sound of the unhappy travelers outside. "You have a tough jump ahead of you. Rest a bit."

"I'm all right," she said. "Are you worried?"

"Me? Nah." He sat on a narrow bunk along the wall. The captain's quarters were no more luxurious than the rest of the ship, but at least it was quiet. He indicated his neural node to request a khamal. Khoe shimmered into existence as soon as their mental link was made.

"Come sit." Seth pulled Ciela down to sit beside him. "I have an idea."

She raised an eyebrow. "Oh?"

He tapped her data sleeve. "You still have the Alpha frequency on that? The artificial one?"

"Yes," she said, puzzled.

He looked up at Khoe. "They're averse to it. We're going to use it during the jump. I'm hoping it'll incite the Dyads here to separate. From what we've seen, some of them don't even know what's going on. With luck, they'll naturally gravitate back into their space."

"Some won't want to," Khoe said.

"It will save their lives. And those who aren't already suffering certainly will when Air Command catches up with us."

"What about Khoe?" Ciela said. "Won't it drive her away?"

"It didn't before, I guess because she knew what it meant," Seth said. He reached out to take Khoe's hand. "But I need you for this. I need you to help them get home. And then to make sure they don't return. If that's even possible."

Khoe looked down at his hand. "You want me to leave you?"

"No. But I think you have to. The Dyads' future here will be ugly. Do you really want that? We can't hide. Maybe there is some other part of this galaxy where you can find people who won't be afraid of you. It's not here."

She nodded, reluctantly. "Maybe. I'm scared here. It's cold and loud. And you keep getting shot at." She lifted Seth's hand to let his fingers stroke lightly over her cheek. "And then it feels so wonderful." She looked at Ciela although Seth's eyes were still focused on her unhappy face. "But I will lose this, sooner or later. Your Air Command will not stop hunting us. I need to go."

"Seth, are you sure?" Ciela said. "Is this what you want?"

He nodded. "Khoe's right. We can't be a Dyad." He turned to her. "And you were right, too. I need to be me. I want Khoe to live the way she's supposed to, not become a weapon for me."

Ciela looked up into Khoe's unhappy face. She took Seth's hand squeezed it. "What do you feel when we do this?"

"I feel what he does," Khoe said. "I feel you holding my hand."

Ciela reached up to touch Seth's face and then pulled him closer to brush his lips with hers. He saw the surprised smile on Khoe's face and took Ciela into his arms to return her kiss, taking his time to allow Khoe to experience every touch and every moment that passed. He let his hand slip beneath Ciela's shirt and heard Khoe gasp when he touched the sensitive ridge along Ciela's spine. And although this gift was for Khoe, Ciela, too, held nothing back and it was only with reluctance that they finally drew apart.

"That was so fabulous!" Khoe chortled, startling them. "Do that again."

Seth read the fathomless blue of Ciela's eyes and smiled. "We've got work to do."

* * *

The Centauri at the helm of the *Griffin* looked up when Seth and Ciela entered the darkened bridge. "Approaching the keyhole," she said. "There's a lot of debris ahead but the graviton pulse has stopped for now." She looked over her console in wonder. "I'm able to see the terminus at Ud Mrak. Barely stable, but it's there."

"Nice work, Isaaron!" Seth said to the absent engineer.

The ship's captain waved to them without comment, busy with instructions for the rest of the crew to prepare their passengers for the jump.

"Are those other cruisers still with us?" Seth said.

"Aye." The com officer switched one of the overhead screens to show Skoth's small fleet still flanking the transporter.

"Guess we didn't need them," Seth said. *Khoe, can you get into those ships and see if you can take them out? Do what you like. Use your imagination.*

She winced. "You want me to kill them?"

No, we'll leave them for Air Command. I just don't want them to enter subspace with us. It's going to be a tough jump for Ciela, and they'll add interference. She doesn't need the extra baggage.

"What did you mean when you said you don't need them?" Ciela asked.

He shrugged. "Insurance in case we run into—"

"Keyhole is opening, Captain," the helmsman said.

Ciela rushed to the navigator's bench. "I'm not ready. Give me some time."

"I'm not doing that," he said. "Someone's coming through."

"On screen," the captain said.

They watched the deep nothing of space where only the blinking overlay on the screen showed activity at the keyhole coordinates. Indeed, the energy readings spiked and suddenly a battlecruiser appeared in the distance. The *Griffin*'s sensors alerted them to guns and defensive systems activated.

"What are they doing?" the captain said. "Hail them!"

A harsh voice already cut into the open com. "Stand down your engines, *Griffin*."

The captain tapped the com console beside her. "Air Command, we have a ship full of casualties. Requesting assistance. Why are you targeting us?"

"They're scanning us, sir."

"Captain Wodja to the bridge, please," the captain broadcasted throughout the ship.

Looking for Dyads. Seth projected. *And finding lots of them.* He tapped his own com band. "How about giving us a hand, Skoth?" he said. "Show us how tough you are."

"This is a trap, Kada. You knew this was going to happen."

"He sounds angry," Khoe observed.

Seth tapped the pilot's shoulder. "Mind if I play?"

The pilot looked at his captain, unwilling to relinquish the helm.

"Get off my damn bridge," she snapped and gestured to the pilot who drew his gun and moved toward Seth.

Seth's hand snapped to the man's pistol and a surge of energy thrummed through his body, through the gun, and into the Human. The man convulsed briefly and fell to the floor.

Seth pointed at the captain. "You don't need that gun."

She blinked, bewildered, but lowered the pistol she had pulled from her console. It suddenly showed a spent power pack. "You killed him?"

"No. Sit, please."

The entire ship shuddered when a warning shot from the battlecruiser glanced over the *Griffin*'s nose.

"Shields up," Seth said to Khoe.

"What are you doing?" the captain said, seeing the transporter's meager tactical station come to life. "That's Air Command and this tub is barely holding together."

"They're not here to help us," Seth said, sending a mental command to seal the cockpit door against the Air Command officers likely on their way to the bridge.

"Skoth's engaging," Ciela said. They watched the three rebel ships head toward the battlecruiser, powerful enough to keep it busy for a while.

"You're in," Khoe said just as Seth felt his neural interface link to the ship's controls. He followed Skoth toward the approaching Air Command ship, accelerating steadily.

"You'll get us all killed!" the captain shouted. "Have you lost your mind?"

"Shh…" he said, pleased by how effective a simple wave of his hand was to convince the woman to shut up. "Let the Delphian concentrate."

Ciela murmured to herself as she settled into a khamal, her concentration on the keyhole ahead of them.

Khoe, link her sleeve to the com system. Broadcast the Alpha resonance only inside the ship as soon as we jump.

"It's probably going to hurt," she said.

Ciela's jumping straight for Targon. We'll be fine. You'll be fine, too.

"Good. I love you. I'll miss you both."

You won't even remember us.

"True. Live happy, Seth."

Seth evaded the Air Command ship, putting the *Griffin* outside the intense skirmish now taking place around the battle cruiser. A few hits slammed into their shields but Skoth's gang harried them with well-placed volleys. Seth winced when one of the smaller ships disintegrated, victim to the disciplined fire placed by Air Command's tactical staff.

"Going negative," he said and began to feed the keyhole, expanding the tiny rift into something wide enough to accommodate the Griffin.

"Do not enter that span, *Griffin*," someone shouted at them. "I am ordering you to remain in this sector."

"Listen to him!" the captain said, staring in disbelief at a control room entirely out of control. When both Ciela and Seth ignored her she slapped the internal com. "Prepare for jump!"

It was the last thing Seth heard that day.

EPILOGUE

What Seth would remember, later, was mostly the pain. The odd thing about pain was that one never quite remembers how bad it had been. Perhaps some neat trick of evolution prevented an actual memory of pain. One only remembers the fact that there was pain. Of course, encountering that same pain again later was one hell of a reminder.

The fog surrounding these strange musings eventually lifted when Khoe's physical presence dissolved from Seth's brain, helped along by one of Targon's resident Shantirs.

He did not remember coming out of subspace. There was some vague awareness of people arriving aboard the *Griffin*, of shouting, of people in white coats arguing with people in gray uniforms, of being moved around from one room to another, of Ciela's voice. Then nothing except the empty spot in his head that used to be Khoe.

Seth opened his eyes, becoming aware of something lying on his chest. An arm, he realized, belonging to Ciela stretched out beside him on this bed. She was dressed in a long blouse and tights, unarmed, and apparently asleep. He reached over to stroke her hair and felt the arm tighten across him.

"Do I still have most of my brain cells?" he tried his voice.

"So we hope," she mumbled. "How do you feel?"

He pondered this. Someone had looked after his body well; he felt neither in pain now nor dehydrated. "Never better."

"Liar." She raised her head to gaze into his face. "You've been out for two days," she said. "We're on Targon. They... the Dyads are gone. Two people died on the way through. A lot of them are still feeling the after-effects. But none of the entities came out. At least that's what the colonel told me."

"Is he pissed?"

"Yeah." She ran her fingers over his forehead. "The Shantir told me Khoe is gone, too. I'm sorry, Seth. I kind of liked her. She was a big part of you."

He smiled. "You're a big part of me. You're all I need in my head." He let his eyes roam around the room before things got too maudlin. A clinic of some sort. Windowless. Stark. "Jail?"

"Sort of. This is the secure wing in Exobiology. There are still guards outside. I'm being watched, I'm sure." She sat up when the door opened. A medic entered and fussed over the monitor beside Seth's bed. Behind her came Colonel Carras.

The two men regarded each other warily for a long moment.

"Am I in trouble?" Seth said when the medic left and they were alone again.

The elder Centauri pursed his lips. "Something tells me you should be, but I can't actually accuse you of anything. Again."

"And Queta Station?"

"The town was destroyed in the riot, which saved us the trouble. The conditions there were barbaric, and not just for the prisoners. We're transferring the remaining inmates to a facility on Magra." He nodded to Ciela. "Shan Ciela gave a report about the accelerator. The graviton transfer worked, it seems. Most of the keyholes have stabilized, although we're having to rebuild a number of jumpsite gates. Astrophysics is reviewing the entire process. It changes a lot about what we know about subspace."

"What about the Dyads?"

"We found no Dyads," Carras said without changing his expression. "It seems they all returned to subspace when you took them through."

Seth and Ciela exchanged a worried glance. "Sir, none left on Chitta Moor?"

Carras looked from one to the other for a moment before turning to the door. "I'll have you out of here by the end of the day. Your visit to the Azon Corp orbiter has been deleted." He looked back for a moment and Seth thought he saw a glint of humor in the Centauri's eyes. "I've arranged for payment for returning Doctor Hedvig as per your assignment. Good job."

Ciela raised both eyebrows when the door closed behind the colonel. "I thought he'd yell."

"About what? He wanted us to track down the Dyad on Pelion and that's what we did. Not our fault if they lost him again."

"You believe him? That they found no Dyads on Chitta Moor?"

"Not really. But Isaaron had the Outrider. Chitta Moor has many moons, crammed with irradiated equipment. Let's just hope he's all right."

"Oh, I have a message for you from Caelyn!" She folded her legs and tapped her data sleeve. A vague hologram of the Delphian's face floated into view.

"Centauri! I hear you made it back. In one piece instead of two." Caelyn grinned like a man with a delicious secret. "I thought you might want to know that someone dropped the *Dutchman* off for you on Magra Torley."

Seth gasped. "What?"

"Seems like no one at Azon had any right to keep it, so a certain red-headed Vanguard officer brought it out here. She said for you to clean your damn cabin, and that's a direct quote. But seeing that she's the only person other than you two cleared to access the *Dutchman*, she had to sacrifice."

Seth grinned at Ciela as the message ended. "I'm sure she did."

Ciela slid off the bed and into her boots.

"Where are you going?"

"Did we get new orders from the colonel? No. So we're either fired or he knows I'm desperate for a vacation. Some place with fresh air and sunshine." She kissed his stubbled cheek. "Going to book us a flight to Magra."

* * *
*
*

ABOUT THE AUTHOR

Chris Reher is a first generation Canadian currently and out of necessity residing on planet Earth (which, in the general and interplanetary scheme of things, could *really* use a catchier name. Imagine heading past Proxima Centauri and someone asks you whence you came and you tell them "dirt". All theological implications aside, that just won't do.)

When not finding ways to defy the laws of physics or torture her subjects or entice them with inter-species hanky-panky, she designs web sites or writes about designing web sites. She enjoys long walks on the beach or, given the local beach shortage, writes about beaches far beyond Proxima Centauri.

www.chrisreher.com

Also by Chris Reher

Quantum Tangle

Terminus Shift

Sky Hunter

The Catalyst

Only Human

Rebel Alliances

Delphi Promised